# Table of

Cosmic Pizza Buffet Book Production Crew (CPB BPC)
present:

*Burdens*

Written by:
Peter Trinidad

Edited by:
Brian Bethel

Chapter Illuminating and Cartography:
Gregg Lewis

Full Color Book Cover:
Maarta Laiho

Dedicated to the memory of Wayne Parker

# *Writer's Note*

Pollution plays an important role in defining post-apocalyptic story telling. By including it, the image adds an extra layer of existential guilt. It exposes the horror of our own sin and hubris. The corruption displayed need not be integral to the plot either. Just merely dash it in. Voila! Your speculative fiction story became post-apocalyptic ... somehow. Sardonic thoughts boil to the top and stagnate into a filmy membrane of despair, covering the good stuff underneath and cooking them a little extra.

I have to admit, the whole environmentalist craze ran a bit before my time in the States. When I emerged from my larval haze of incogniscience, the cultural malign to pollution had soaked into the pavement. Tim Curry gave voice to my nightmares, and a silver-skinned hippy in a green mullet taught me all the valuable ways I can keep the good earth verdant – sans fertilizer. The term became confusing, and adjusted.

Like all useful words, "Pollution" began to mean more. The pejorative edge it had gained over the years made an effective weapon for people of the speaking and writing profession. They could brandish it and slice at any form of excess deemed undesirable.

We gained "Noise Pollution" as a term for making too much disruptive sound, upsetting the delicate mating patterns of manatees and foam mascots. Today, I can shake my bony fist at the hip jammers, with their obtuse sub-woofers, blaring something akin to mechanical failure as a style of music. I can say, "You are creating noise pollution," and hand them a scientific article (which failed peer review) on how their decibel level is starving Canadian alligators.

You can see pollution in the Internet now, sometimes describing pop-up windows and spam. We're polluting the airways now by running radio devices on all wavelengths of transmission. We're polluting even when we dispose of garbage correctly, raising the ph of small ponds.

In these cases, it is possible to argue a misuse of the term. The micro-organisms in the pond will set the pond right eventually. The sun emits much more electromagnetic radiation than my wi-fi enabled appliances. I can delete my electronic inbox without littering the ground with paper, and I can't blast my baritone-intensive remix of The BeeGees all day long. When I am done, the 'Pollution' evaporates in these cases. We still claim it is there, however.

I think I can break down how the naming works.

- All living creatures create byproducts as a result of being alive.
- Successful creatures produce more, and higher concentrations, of byproduct
- It is possible for disposal of byproduct to slow or be defeated, causing piles of excess to form
- We are successful creatures
- We make and tend to many piles
- We should be ashamed of ourselves

Excess is key in describing pollution, an excess we cannot or will not allow to dissolve naturally and do not intend to consume. If I am right in my assumption on the newly-emerged version of pollution, this can open new avenues into the post-apocalyptic genre of fiction – or at least beef it up.

Enough speculation. Let's start the freak show!

## *The Ugliness Becomes You*

Webs of rusted steel girders tumbled down to the accumulating wreckage filling the streets. A flurry of sparks flung into the red sky. The rising cinders danced and congregated in the air until a cloud of dust created by the crash rose above them and snuffed them out. The city burned, and the buildings which could not burn shattered under the colossal horror creeping through the sky. Crawling about the darkening sky, buffeted by the upward drafts of fire, a rolling black cloud of tumorous protrusions tore at the ground. The thing appeared to struggle with itself. It formed moaning faces, hands, claws, pulsing organs, segmented eyes, tendrils. Growths erupted from itself. The faces swallowed roof tops. The tendrils tore open streets. Occasional screams and gun fire rang out from the raized city to be quickly drowned out by the disharmonious chorus of moans from the creature followed by the rumble of crumbling structures.

Miles away from the Asmodial Cloud bodies were stacked and burned. The Abberants made quick work burying their old masters. Their silhouettes, vaguely human, coursed about the ruins pulling corpses from the rubble. The larger creatures hauled sleds and wagons through the shattered streets. Their taxis gradually filled with the dead.

At one of the larger bonfires sat what must soon be the last two people left in the world. Both men wore jumpsuits bearing the symbols of the Chimera Group, a pair of white, open hands.

"We're almost done Travis," one of them spoke. He turned from the burning pyre to address his friend. "No time for second thoughts. Even so, if you care to change the plan it would only be a variation on what is happening now. Wouldn't it?"

Travis, a young man with long brown hair pulled behind his head, eyed his friend pleadingly. No reply escaped his mouth.

The older man with dark, receding hair shrugged in defiance. His eyes flared with amusement more than anger. "The mono culture of humanity is over. I mean, Travis, if you and this angel friend of yours you keep talking about want the old ways back and swear it'll work out – that's great. That's super, but that won't change what we've done."

"We've made a mistake," Travis spoke.

"The whole plan was to make a gigantic mistake if I remember correctly."

Travis covered his face and sighed. "No Leonard. I'm saying we were wrong all along. I can't. I can't explain what the angel showed me, but we're going about it all wrong."

Leonard rubbed his temples with one hand. "Sorry, your experiences are strictly your own. They appear in your head and stay there." His face darkened. "And mine are strictly mine. What are you suggesting? What happens now?"

"I don't know"

"Then the plan doesn't change," Leonard blurted

curtly. An aberration approached the funeral pyre from downwind. The bull-headed creature towed the bed of a pickup truck it had snapped from the cab. Its head cowered low in an attempt to avoid the stench rolling off the flames. Lifeless bodies filled the makeshift wagon, stacked lengthwise. Slowly, the courier pulled out of the smoke to catch sight of the two humans. The creature's upturned face showed traces of surprise and fear.

"Gather wood for all the fires," Travis shouted to the Abberant. "A few others as well."

The shaggy figure sent several confused looks to both Travis and Leonard. It had the horns and nose of a bull, but the rest of the face was disturbingly human.

"As he said," Leonard reinforced Travis's command. He didn't need to look at the half human face to feel the fear and panic. The bonds forged him to the Abberants and allowed him to manifest the terrible cloud in the sky. Leonard saw into every single one of the beasts' minds. The fear of his betrayal spread about the various packs of creatures. If he turned so easily on his own kind what would prevent him from killing them next, wipe out everything? Worst of all was the fear of losing the presence of his mind. If Leonard Wainwright died, would their consciousness expire as well? They had seen how the Asmodial Cloud collapses at his whim. "It's nearly over," Leonard tried to reassure his follower, but he felt the immediate doubt from his connection.

The aberration continued his duties. Leonard did his best not to pick the creature's mind.

Travis stood up to grab Leonard's shoulder. "There was nothing wrong with the world before we started. I understand that now.

"Hunger, poverty, civil wars, every government trending toward totalitarian. We agreed on the problems endemic to civilization, and evolution without strife is pointless.

"Every life we ended chipped apart the workings of

something greater, thousands of years in the making. Every human life is precious."

Leonard brushed away the hand on his shoulder. "This is one hell of a time to say that," a wave of anger broke out from him causing the streets to erupt with roars and howls of rage. Surprised, Leonard reigned in his emotions. "There is no going back now."

From inside his jumpsuit Travis pulled out a slender piece of glass. The object fit tightly in his hand at a pistol grip. His pointing finger rested near the trigger which could spin and fire six chambers. The glass revolver needed no bullets. Instead the device discharged the light trapped within the pitch black stones inside the gun's innards. Five minutes of sunlight at the single pull of a trigger, or so the hypothesis went. Travis scratched his head with the refracting barrel.

"We could stop here," Travis told himself pacing. "Let me think," he trailed off into muttering. "The way it works is, it stacks onto itself without collapsing and quickly folds into itself to be not stacked. To make one again, but this time two. Rogue, rebellious elements arise to make two when one is too big of a number. Even so, the enriching continues sometimes leaving the curve. The curve is an observation, not a rule. Right. Okay. Resources. Hostile elements both real and imagined. Culture and learning. Always three prongs it seems. Need to shape the end. A spear that is too long points downward – never straight."

Leonard let Travis keep going. His colleague was the greatest mind ever produced, but when he thought out loud one could wonder the opposite.

The beast controller raised a hand and willfully pushed the Asmodial Cloud further away to the city's waterfront. He wanted to see it, but he didn't care to watch it. A speech came to mind, and he opened the bonds to communicate with the hundreds of Abberants wandering the streets

"*Life is unable to flourish in the absence of death.*

*Soon you will claim a grand birth right. Freedom with no one to answer to except your peers. Bountiful stretches of land springing abundant life and unending quantities of food. The world will be yours to take and use as you see fit.*"

The old human stopped broadcasting through his bond. "They ain't buying it. Christ, I've become one of the things I hate." He spun around to Travis. The younger still scratched his head with a lethal weapon. "You might as well shoot me Doctor Plainer. This whole chore was insufferable four months ago."

Travis conceded an agreeing nod at Leonard, pointing his gun like a wagging finger. "That would," his eyes drifted off Leonard's face into the sky blacked with the ash of burning bodies "I don't think that works."

"Sure the hell works for me! Didn't you just tell me you want to roll this business up?"

"If we did, the correct end result wouldn't happen," Travis touched the barrel of the revolver to his lips. He began to nervously chew on the end as if it were an end of a ball point pen.

Doctor Wainwright knit his brows in frustration.

"Leonard!" Travis exclaimed suddenly. "I think I got it!"

In an instant came a click of what sounded like a cigarette lighter. Doctor Plainer's brilliant mind lit up in fire as if were a match stick. The glass revolver fell from his limping hands hitting the pavement with a dull crack. Amazingly, Travis managed to stand on his feet for half a minute as his melon burned. He even let out a few shrill screams while skin rolled away from his flaming head. However all good things must come to an end, the skull collapsed into itself, and the body collapsed on the pavement.

Leonard watched the entire spectacle, blinking a few times, but not looking away. His four-month death march let him see a few slaughters up close, and several more impressive ones from far off. In his mind he graded the suicide with 'C' for effort but an 'A' for presentation. The screams really did it for him – so dramatic.

"Like I said Travis," Leonard let out a tired grunt. "This world doesn't need heroes because monsters slay themselves."

A wet, splashing groan broke his train of thought. The Abberant stacking the burning pyre knelt on the ground. A steady dribble of puke and saliva dripped from its muzzle. The dribble connected to a current coursing through the cracked pavement.

"If you watch horrible things the ugliness eventually becomes a part of you," Leonard shouted at the creature. "When we're done, I want you to find some place far away from here. Go somewhere green with fresh water and wild flowers. Make a huge litter of kids, and be damn sure they never see anything like what we are doing! This horror, everything we've done, dies with us so they can be happy! You get me?!"

The shaggy figure did not stir. Its wet eyes caught the light of the burning pile of corpses reflecting off Leonard's eyes. The two burning motes in Doctor Wainwright's face pinned the creature in place. Even though the Abberant stood head and shoulders above the puny human and possessed the strength to lob a single body several yards, fear is the slayer of the mind and no defense could stop it once fear takes its hold.

"I know every last one of you furry creeps think I'm the devil," Leonard advanced rapidly on the sickly half-bull. He pulled the face up to look at him using one of the short horns growing from its head. "You know what? You're right. I want you and the rest of you out. You run as far away from here as you can before I kill all of you like I wiped out this city. And when I find you, you better be so damned fat and happy ..."

He noticed the Abberant quivering uncontrollably. Leonard swore to himself he'd achieved his doctorate by learning how to do everything the wrong way. He softened his voice. "Just stop what you're doing and get out of here. Follow Modestine. She'll take care of things from here."

The Abberant's hooves clattered over the ground as it scrambled hurriedly away.

"We don't need heroes because monsters slay themselves." Doctor Wainwright shambled to Travis's smoldering head. He kicked a few skull fragments from the ashes. "We left one hell of a fossil record. Chances are these fuzzies will forget what happened here, dig us up in a thousand years, and write college papers on us."

He booted his partner in the side to better get at the glass revolver. "And they'd all be wrong!" A cackling laugh came over him as he picked up the weapon with its rubber grip. "Oh man. Science. Right? They'd get their doctorates on the thesis too. They'd be doctors like, ha! Oh wait a minute."

As Leonard pulled the gun free, the barrel separated from the body of the weapon. The tube hit the ground and rang a high tremoring pitch as it bounced off both ends faster and faster. Then it stopped entirely. It wasn't a perfect cylinder and couldn't roll away. With the barrel gone, the revolving tumbler lurched out. The tight fitting pushed out from the springs of the trigger mechanism. When enough play let out to the machine, the entire gadget fell to pieces. The trigger went limp. Flywheels and springs spilled onto the pavement. Something inside seemed to be burning as well.

"Shame," Leonard Wainwright let the ruined weapon down. "I was about to show how to do it right. Right in the cerebellum." He pulled out a small pocket knife and folded open the largest blade. To end this tragedy he had to burn. He knew the workings he set in motion. He knew intimately the thing he'd become. Every last ounce of synthetic cholesterol, dendron bridger, adapter set, and chemical motor must be destroyed one hundred percent. No evidence. Absolutely no chance of reconstruction.

13

"Always broken when you really want it," Leonard lamented. He absentmindedly ran the pocket knife blade up and down his arm, brushing the hairs. The edge wasn't sharp enough to cut a single strand free. Slowly he trudged to the bonfire. He looked over the pile for maybe a place to climb on top or an opening to jump in. He stood so close the heat felt like it was tanning his face.

Then something dawned on him. He never had seen it before even though he'd been watching fires like this for four months. He saw the curled up hands and feet reaching over the coals. The people underneath burned under the wood of their own houses. Skulls with empty eyes sockets stared in every direction. Grease hissed, dribbled, and popped from the rupturing organs of the fresh bodies the bull Abberant threw on earlier. This was the fate of every innocent person surviving the Tilt only for the Asmodial Cloud to arrive and rob them of all hope.

"Not that I ever believed in fairness, but this had best hurt."

"*We are afraid.*"

"You stay back," Leonard shouted. He spun around. The shadowy figures of human beings circled the surrounding area where the fire's light could barely reach them. As they advanced, cautiously, their outlined twisted and stretched away from the proportions of normal people.

"*We don't want to die. We are afraid.*"

They entered the light of the fire. All of the creatures held out their hands leaning forward, ready to leap out and grasp him. They exchanged worried looks with one another. They shuffled about to let the faster Abberants get a better vantage for a sprint.

"Stand still all of you!" Leonard ran his knife over both of his eyes and stumbled backward. He fell yards away from the fire writhing and cursing. Animal shrieks erupted in every direction for many miles. Leonard covered both hands to his face as blood wet every corner of his face, running up his nose and down his mouth. Currents rushed

14

down his cheeks and chin. The feedback from his connection to the creatures was overwhelming; torrents of fear, sadness, and pain.

"*We are blind!*"

Leonard kicked his feet wildly, pushing himself closer and closer to the fire. Their vision would return. His would not. He could already see himself in their eyes as the darkness unclouded.

"*No more. We beg. No more.*"

A handful made a desperate sprint for their master. Leonard jabbed his thighs. The knife sank in several times just above the knee. He stabbed and twisted the pointed tip of the pen knife over and over again. They all hit the ground in unison.

"I'm sorry," Leonard sobbed. At last his hands plunged into hot coals. "I'm sorry."

The Abberants around howled themselves hoarse.

Just as he finished digging out a pit of coals for his final tomb, a shadow drifted over the visions of himself. A tall figure knelt over Leonard's ruined legs and dragged him out of the fire.

"No Modestine. No. No. No."

He felt a loving embrace. "My fool girl. No."

The Story of The Ugliness Men

# Burdens

When men sin they pray to gods for forgiveness
They receive the cleansing
When gods sin, there is not forgiveness
There is only downward decay

Today,
you are a winner!
    —Peter Trinidad

pT #26

400 years later

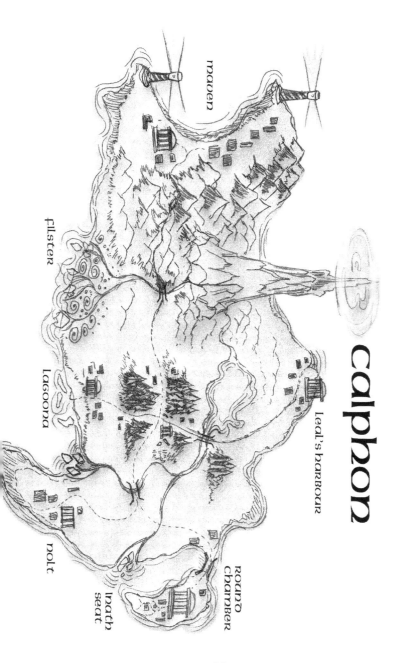

calphon

maoen

fílster

lagoora

Leal's harbour

rolt

round
chamber

hrath
seat

19

## *There is No You in Teamwork*

The earth gave a dull, faint rumble. Roots pulled free around the fresh stump. The stubborn root system of the fallen tree bent, but did not relent its firm grip on the soil. A few smaller trails pulled free opposite of the pull team. The flat ringed top bent forward as if giving a garish bow to those assembled, and the stump once again budged no more.

"Stop," The foreman told his work team. "That's everything we got. We burn this one."

The laborers muttered, milling about the truncated hub of a once tall tree. They unhooked their ropes and chains then led their various beasts of burden to other parts of the clearing in progress.

"This whole island was a barren sweep of dead kelp and rock when it heaved up four hundred years ago." The foreman bent down to examine the tree stump. He counted the rings and guessed them to number sixty or so. Many of the years were good as indicated by greater than average thickness.

"Are you sure your men can't uproot this Mister Graves? My father wants this soil to be as soft as possible in the event his grandchildren want to farm the land."

The foreman looked up and regarded the skinny young man, well-dressed and hardly soiled despite all the sod flying over the past week. The lad was the son of some rich family from The Stretch. His job, if it could be called a job, included walking about the construction site and looking busy enough to not help. The slender fop carried around a pen and book. All week he walked about the site, staring in the supply tent, and looking over people's shoulders.

"If I remember right, the house goes in back there," Foreman Graves pointed to a place nearly eighty yards away. "This stump would need to get out if we wanted to pour the house foundation on it. Not necessary you see. So we make it charcoal."

The pale skinned fellow wrote down a note in his little book. His mouth ran silently as his pen scribbled on the empty pages. In the distance someone shouted "Eyes up" and soon after came the crash of a falling tree.

"Would you like to do the honors?" Mister Graves offered.

"What?"

The rugged foreman jabbed his thumb toward the stump. "Would you like to set it on fire?"

"What, now?"

"Yes now. This stubborn knot is going to burn for days. Maybe even after we're done putting up the house."

"Is, um." the young fellow looked around for another person to pin the job on.

Graves nearly grinned. "You get to do the fun part Mister Walsh." He pointed at the supply tent in the far corner of the plot "Get a bottle of kerosene from the red crate. Soak down the stump. Let it set for ten minutes or so. Touch it off with some matches. Feel up to that?"

Surprisingly, the lad gave an anxious nod. He put down his little booklet on the stump and hurried away.

Saws began chewing at the fallen tree near the edge of the forest. The sound was not unlike a quartet of cellos all strung too loosely. The men looked nervously over their shoulders towards the wood. Earlier somebody spotted animal tracks in some freshly upturned soil. By the looks of things, word had gotten around, and every hand had walked over to see it once or twice. The print wasn't quite right. The toes spread too far apart for a dog or wolf they said, and an indent near it must've been a heel. Graves saw the mark himself, and could not quite make out all the things his workmen were pointing at. The supposed heel mark could've been anything as far as he was concerned.

On any other job, on any other island in the fourteen baronies of the Union, Foreman Graves would have rounded his team up to set the record straight. However the way the men behaved at the moment seemed reasonable. Workers grouped together in teams of two or three. They all fell the same tree, sawed the logs, and pulled the lumber away in tight groups. Often they combed the brush before setting to the next job. It was teamwork the likes of which Graves never saw before, and likely would never see again. He couldn't remember number of times he had to discipline a team, to make them watch each other and follow strict procedure to avoid accidents. If it took the scare of a pack of hunting Abberants, so be it.

Graves shared the eerie feeling though. An unnatural mist clung to the plot every day up till midmorning. Rustling and snapping noises periodically came from places no one was working. The surrounding farming community kept guarded postures and were generally unfriendly. The neighbors gave curt replies and brushing away any attempts at continued conversation. Also the ground proved absurdly fertile. On the first day Graves unearthed a wild onion well larger than a leek. The oak saplings in the ground often times made tap roots several feet in length with only an exposed length of a few inches on the surface. It seemed as if the plot, the farthest one out from the village of Lagoona was somehow transported from the cursed western continent.

23

The vine mound compounded with the scene. An entire hill covered from top to bottom with tangled stretches of all manner of melon vines rose up nearby. The mass grew taller than a sizable building. The leaves averaged the width of a shovel and most times stretched wider, much wider. The transfigured landscape loomed not even a mile away. Nobody ever saw anything like it, the way it shifted and stirred against the wind, the sweet smell of it whenever the plot happened to be down wind, the way lumps would rise and fall in its shape. Was rich old Mister Walsh building a house out here to be near it?

"The whole bottle foreman?"

"Eh what?"

The young lad waggled an open bottle over the stump.

"Oh yes. Soak it down. It's still green. So go slow."

Nodding, the well-dressed young man pocketed the book he left on the stump and began pouring out the kerosene like pancake syrup. After a few good circles he pointed at the green mass in the distance. "I did some asking around about the big mound over there."

"Did you?" The foreman realized he'd been caught staring at it. "Hardly a soul around here wants to talk about it."

"I had to go all the way down the road to Lagoona for anybody to talk. Turns out it's the home of the legendary war hero Andreas Viklund. He retired out here, about twenty five years back, went crazy, and grew that thing. Nobody has seen him since. People say he discovered some kind of secret to mastering Abberant magic. They made lots of wild stories, that he's a plant creature now. The leaves are a defense from some horrible monster lurking in the woods he's fighting, and they're blessed or poison or some nonsense. What they all agree on is the pumpkins and cantaloupe from it are enormous. The gourds get to the size of a burly man's torso. The watermelon are nearly unmovable."

"Hold on. Hold on. You mean to say he's selling his crops, but nobody has seen him in years"

The young master Walsh stirred a half empty bottle of fuel. "He does some kind of trade ritual with one of the local farm families, and they take care of all the shopping in town for him. Portram family. Very popular, as you can imagine. Town merchants mob them every time their wagons roll into Lagoona. The produce gets sold all over the island, most of it in Maven. On their honor they won't tell a soul about what happened to Sargent Viklund."

Graves rubbed his chin with his calloused hand. Despite all the odd things growing wild, the surrounding farms grew plants in typical proportions – tomatoes the size of a fist, orchards of plums and apples all normal sized, potatoes. "And what's your take on Sargent Vick?" the foreman asked.

"I plan to see for myself. As luck may have it, the Portrams enter the vineyard tomorrow."

The foreman belted out a laugh. "You want invite yourself into the home of the man who emptied the entire town of Jasper? The man who killed a black blood with a gas gun and a knife. The guy who falls asleep in battle and wakes up after napping on his enemy's corpses. For your sake, you'd better hope he's long dead."

"By my math, he would be seventy three right now."

"And in good enough shape to raise water melons the size of a baron's sedan. Something is in there."

Carefully, the young fop put the empty fuel bottle on the ground and picked up a book of matches. "An improbable, half man, plant creature? I imagine there perfectly rational method behind all this. I hear he was quite a brilliant man. He invented a wide variety of traps still used by the army today."

"Retired to a trap by the look of it."

"Certainly looks that way," the young Walsh ran his fingers together and suddenly produced a puff of smoke and a small mote of fire. He flicked the lit match onto the wet stump. In the distance another tree creaked and the workmen gave the traditional cry to look upward.

"You wanted that to soak in. The bark is the only thing burning off now" the foreman spoke flatly. A loud crash shook the entire site. The newly fallen tree was of good size.

Grabbing his temples, the rich youngster swore. "Flies and maggots."

"Stump was green anyway. You can set it on fire again in a few weeks if it dries out." Slowly the flames spread from the match. The shape almost made a perfect circle, dark all inside with bright yellow flames on the very edge. Graves changed the subject "Your father sure knows how to pick his neighbors. What you do tomorrow is none of my business, but it don't take an academy education to figure whoever lives in that mound there doesn't care for visitors. What am I to do when your dear dad shows at the end of the month with you dead or missing?"

"I'm sure he would understand my curiosity had gotten the better of me."

"Some men," Graves paused. "Some men when they come back from the continent, the things they see make them different. Something over there crushes a strong man's mind; takes away people's voices, or gives fits of terror. They blow their pensions the day they get them, and live out the rest of their lives on the fringes of towns shouting frightening blasphemies at whoever care to listen – or worse. By the look of things, Vick had ten times the amount of madness coming for a long time, and he has all of it."

"Interesting."

"No. Terrifying. I were you, I wouldn't pay him a visit and beg God he never pays you one."

Young Walsh sighed. "You and your work crew are getting too worked up over nothing. He's just an old man with interesting hobbies, and there are certainly no

Abberant curses raining down on this place. Did they show you the hand print yet? The hand someone found another earlier."

"I don't give a baron's bill hole," Graves spoke with no emotion and a dead expression. "Normal wolves is all. Regis Project made this wood. You can tell by rabbits and deer."

"All the same, they are frightened."

Graves nodded. "Good. It's better than letting them think everything is going to be all right."

The stump, fully engulfed in flames, crackled and hissed. It burned well into the evening when the work crew traveled down the town road to Lagoona. Curls of smoke still rose from a black knot in the ground when work resumed in the morning. Then at last it became a varicose ebony mark in the ground for years on end.

## The Good Things in Life

Joseph Portram was blessed with a pretty son and a handsome daughter. Despite his repeated attempts at encouraging hard labor, Carver Portram somehow grew to manhood fair skinned with shining locks of hair. His son had the posture of a gentleman, and a meticulous eye for looking his best in whatever clothes he wore. Lana Portram, on the other hand, had somehow inherited from her father. She worked best with her hands. She wouldn't rest until all jobs are done, and often times took up the slack of her brother. Appearance didn't much matter to Lana. Usually after a day she'd come into the house caked in mud and dusted in dirt while Carver glided into the living area like some kind of ballroom dancer, not a spot on him.

For years Joseph considered himself cursed, but lived with it. He loved his family regardless. They were good kids, hardly got into trouble, and made many friends. At least, Carver made many friends. Lana kept acquaintances to a minimum, and only kept one close friend over the years.

The fate of his children floated in the air. Soon they would both get to choose their Lot. Lana would go first as she was born eldest and Carver the next year.

Lana stepped out from the open doors of the barn leading a buckboard cart pulled by two mules. "Ready to drive out Carver? We're cinched up and ready."

"Yes indeed," Carver leapt off the fence he'd been sitting on. The floral pattern of his shirt shone crisp and bright. Light glinted off his shined boots as well as the shaded goggles he wore. His pants were cleaned and pressed in preparation of this day. Deep down he knew he looked spectacular, which was the root of the problem.

Lana, who wore overalls and a simple shirt, held up the reins. "Well. Your chariot awaits." Her head rocked about.

"Thank you." Carver vaulted onto the driver's bench. Lana handed him the mule team, climbed onto the bench with him and they set off. "Dad said he'd be along for the second wagonload," he said as they turned left onto the main road to Lagoona heading out into the country.

Early morning dew still clung to the ground. Not a living soul stood in the fields, but the smell and sounds of the harvest abided. Dark brown leaves spun and skittered over the roadway. An occasional ear of corn or overripe plum could be seen on the side of the road, discarded from the other wagons rolling through. The food rotting on the ground reeked, but the overall smell of harvest time was sweet.

"Your heart still set on the farmer's lot Lana?" Carver leaned in slightly.

Lana leaned in as well. The clatter of the buckboard was louder than usual. "If the baron allows it. There's a chance he could put me in artifice. Heard they're hurting for all sorts of artifice in Leal's Harbor and bunches of folk got moved there. Both the Naylor twins shipped out. Construction."

"Really?"

"Yeah, and lucky they didn't get split. The last group who got their lot here in Lagoona shipped out to five separate baronies. Baron sat them on the dock and their boats came one at a time."

"Shoot," Carver grimaced. "Anyone we know?"

"Can't remember their names. I don't think so."

A few moments rolled by before Carver spoke up again. "What are the odds someone will shove a gas gun in my hands and make me walk a wall next year?"

"That the baron will ship you to the Western Continent? If I were him, I'd hand you the merchant stipend. Spin you around and slap you on the back until you were out the door."

"Awww... no chance at artifice or farming?"

"Probably not and certainly not."

A hurt expression curled Carver's eyebrows outward. "I would do nicely in a factory, as long as the job is easy and repetitive. Civic works. I could fix streets. Straighten signs and light posts. Running the mail would be nice."

"Who knows what you'll get. Baron Asher is lousy with the lottery. It could be me walking a wall in a few months and you digging ditches in Acosta next year just because those were his latest envelopes dropped on his desk."

"There's got to be some reason to it."

Lana threw up a theatrical shrug. "Asher put Tiffany Lambert, little Tiffany Lambert, to military service."

"Good eye. Tiffany was vicious."

"Tiffany is the sweetest girl I ever knew!" Lana protested, clearly taken aback.

"Just to you, Sis. As for everybody else, you were either for her or against her."

"What do you mean?"

"Three years ago I turned her down for the Strawman Festival Dance for Beth Cuthbert. Next day Beth comes to me saying she can't go. So I ask Katie Murray. Next day she can't come either. Then Lorreta Holmes does the same. So I just walk in the night of the dance, no date, and who asks me for a dance?"

"I wasn't asked to that dance if I remember," Lana had only been invited to the most recent one, but once was enough. "Tiffany."

"Exactly," Carver's eyes glared over his shaded goggles. "She asked me to dance. I said I just came to see my friends and that I was off to help you with the other parts of the fair. That night soon became the single most frightening day in my life. She called in a bunch of her lackeys and – the hell is he doing?"

Standing in the dead center of the road, another well-dressed fellow waved a friendly greeting. His black pants and jacket were made of finely woven linen. The white shirt he wore flared a straight collar around his neck. His short black hair was trimmed back neatly.

"The rich guy I've been hearing about." Lana muttered

Carver whispered. "Who?"

"Son of a rich merchant. He's out building some kind of mansion near Burroughs."

"Abby Mother bite me! Why am I always the last to know?"

"News is only a week old, and you spend too much time in town."

"Hello!" The stranger blocking the road cupped both of his hands to his face. "Fancy giving me a ride?"

"Fancy moving out of the way?" Lana grumbled lowly. Carver didn't seem to hear.

"Lagoona is behind us. We're not going that way." Carver shouted back.

A smile spread across the stranger's face. He put down his hands and began trotting toward the moving cart. Carver stopped the mule team immediately.

Lana muttered some more. "Are all people from the Strand like this?" Carver caught her comment that time his brow popped above his goggles and quickly sank back down.

Stumbling on his last few steps, the business dressed fellow stopped directly in front of the two gray mules. He blurted out "Tracy. My name is Tracy Walsh. I'm new here."

"Hello Tracy, um. My name is Carver Portram. This is my sister Lana. Nice to, um, meet you." Carver gave Tracy a fake smile. Every aspiring gentleman learns how to wear a false smile. "As I was saying Lagoona is back there.

We are going there eventually, but I'm afraid we won't have room for riders when we do. We're sorry. We really are. Could you please maybe just-"

"That's perfectly all right because I was hoping to go the other direction."

Carver's lips shrank to a thin line on his face. He sat unmoving and expressionless.

Lana spoke up. "And where are you headed?"

"Well," Tracy sauntered around to Lana's side of the wagon. "I want to stop and visit the famous Andreas Viklund. You see we're neighbors now, and I have itched to meet him ever since I laid eyes on his miraculous vineyard. You've seen it?"

Lana nodded slowly. In the corner of her eye she saw Carver chewing his lip.

"Why it's a large mire of creeping vines, an ingenious fortification. Never seen the like. Sargent Vick certainly lives up to his reputation as a military mastermind even into his later years. Mind scattering. Absolute brilliance. I must meet him."

"Mister Viklund doesn't care for visitors. He wishes to be left alone in his twilight years."

"Was he not a close friend of your father Joseph? I was hoping to arrange a meeting or perhaps an invitation."

All subtlety aside, Lana rolled her eyes. "Get in. But first understand nobody gets to see Vick. Not you. Not anyone. Not ever. We know it's rude. We're sorry."

"Then how abou-"

"We can pass a message for you. If he's feeling generous, you can even get a bit of his crop as a gift."

"It will have to do." Tracy climbed into the back of the buckboard.

The three rode on in silence for several minutes. Carver drove the cart sitting more erect then typical. His face peered off into the landscape as if trying to read the tiny print of several signs far away. Beside him glowered Lana, forehead wrinkled and her arms folded.

Carver tossed his head back to address the hitcher. "The Strand, huh? Quite a bit different than Caiphon."

"Yes, the Strand is mostly trade centers and hardly any farm land. You have no idea how it feels to see a mountain after living in such a flat place for most of your life.

Lana and her brother simultaneously peeked northwest toward the snowcapped peak of Mount Mortimer. The red rock leered well above the distant tree line. A blue haze discolored the mountain, making the mountain stand out more than the other objects in the immediate area. All rivers and streams on Caiphon originated from the mountains. Spring time saw the water swell and rise as the snow pack melted and ran. Many other islands in the Union had mountains of differing sorts, but none as steep and treacherous as the Caiphon cascade; Mortimer being the worst of them all.

Few people climbed to the top of Mortimer, and most who claimed doing so were accused of lying. At only four hundred years old, the entire island of Caiphon still had not settled as a land mass. News of beaches sliding into the ocean, cracks opening in the ground, or a hill mysteriously appearing over night were not unfamiliar. Most chaotic of all were the mountains. Avalanches and and rock slides happened so frequently it made all attempts at carving a path through them a futile proposition – though people certainly tried. Rich veins of iron, silver, and occasional gemstones appeared in the mountains, causing a riot of fools willing to stake their lives for riches. Within weeks, their mountain paths were blocked. The tunnels they burrowed collapsed on their heads, and the very caves of riches they coveted disappeared.

The very journey to the base of Mortimer amounted to suicide, let alone actually attempting to scale his clefts. Mortimer's base reached no wider than the surrounding mountains of the cascade yet the height rocketed higher than all others by far. In places the climb was so steep it was almost straight upwards. To make matters worse the apex of the rock accumulated snow all year round due to the sheer altitude. If a keen enough eye watched Mortimer, it would see avalanches of snow tumbling down the spire; sometimes three or four times a day.

No. Not a soul climbed Mortimer or dared venture far into the cascades. Only Thomas Ludar dared and came back alive with photographic evidence. The picture quickly became the single most copied photograph in the Union, as popular as the castle of Wellborn, the Leviathan sighting from the Strand, or the news clip of New York City during the Tilt.

"Yeah, we got mountains, forests, beaches, a swamp west of here. Caiphon Lake is out by Leal's Harbor, fresh water, big attraction. There's Maven too, of course. To be honest, most of the exciting places are elsewhere on the island."

"It's true. It's a wonder why my father decided to retire out here. Not that this place doesn't have its own charm," Tracy craned his head between the Portram siblings. "By the way, are there any weird animals happening around?"

Carver's mouth hung open for a good few moments. Lana's eyes flared up. The hitcher swiveled his head back and forth, seeming confused.

Lana spoke up. "No. Nothing."

"Well, the workmen are finding prints and hearing things at the site near the forest."

"Deer? Somebody's cow got out maybe?"

"Wild dogs by the look of it."

"Oh right. Yes. You're seeing the red wolves. They hunt the deer and rabbits. Since you're right on the edge of the wood, not hard to imagine seeing wolves."

"There is talk of aberration."

"Nonsense. Red wolves can't birth Abby pups."

Carver chipped in: "No odd creature story around here. Head west to Filster, and they'll talk about Bog

34

Skipper, big mosquito that pulls people under the water. Crossroads talks about Leaping Louie, a dog with legs bending like a frog. It steals children from their beds at night and puts them back in the wrong order."

"The giant pike in Lake Caiphon, too," Lana added.

"I bet that one's true, but no. No Mister Walsh. No peculiar creatures in Lagoona."

Tracy lifted a brow and said in a wry tone, "With the exception of Mister Viklund."

"Nonsense. All of it." Carver flustered. "Sargent Vick is just a spry old man. His hobbies are a little weird, and he values his privacy. He values his privacy very much."

The vineyard mound appeared in the distance. A creeping yellow tinge colored the enormous leaves of the tangled conglomeration. As fall continued into winter, all of the leaves would yellow then fall away. The resulting pile would be a knotted mesh of brown wooded growth. In the spring the mound would quickly green back to life. It was one of the miracles of the mound, the vines behaved more like trees.

"Vick leave any kin? Sons. Daughters. Wife?"

"Nope."

"He's getting pretty old by what I hear. As his closest family friend, has he told you his last wishes?" Tracy look over the side of the wagon toward his destination.

"Are all folks from the Strand this morbid?" Lana asked Carver as if the rider wasn't there.

Carver shrugged.

"Curious that is all. Because to me, the situation your family has is convenient as long as Vick is alive. While old Vick is alive you get to sell his produce each year and keep a tidy sum for yourselves afterward."

"You accusing us of something?"

Walsh became defensive. "No. no. I just see your family is doing quite well. This buckboard wagon sits on

35

leaf springs, has two greased axles, and painted sides. Wagons such as this are a rare sight, even in New Kansas. The clothes both of you wear are machine-stitched. And the fabric of your shirt, Carver? I've seen it sold in the Strand; it's not cheap. So an inquiring mind would ask how someone comes by so much money if all their neighbors are not nearly as successful but in the same profession."

Lana tapped her brother on the shoulder. "Carver. Stop the wagon."

Caver pulled the reins and the procession halted.

"I get exactly what you are hinting at city boy, and what you're getting at is insulting. You think we run a racket here? Me, Carver, and my Dad? Think we're fleecing Sargent Vick because he's old and don't know better. Or worse, he's dead and we're deciding to use his farm for a tidy profit by pretending he's still alive – treading on his corpse?" Lana ran red with anger. Her neck seemed to double in girth from her strenuous, teeth clenching grimace. "I don't know what sick men slither out of the Strand to go around back biting, blood sucking, double dealing, and swindling but that ain't how business gets done here in Lagoona. And you've stretched all of our hospitality enough as it is before what you said. So I say you can walk."

Carver nodded and spoke with an oddly jovial tone, "Yup. Use the step off the back. You don't have to jump."

"Look. I'm sorry. I didn't mean-"

"It's quitin' time Tracy. Move yourself or get moved."

An awkward moment passed between all three passengers. Lana and Carver Portram glared insistently at Tracy Walsh who frantically stammered. The rude out-of-towner blabbered mixed apologies, timid laughs, and pleading gestures. He didn't step out of the wagon, however.

Lana nodded at her brother. "Do it Carver."

Carver reached under his seat. A short click came

from beneath the wagon. With that Lana hoisted up the closest end of the wagon bay, spilling Tracy onto the hard packed dirt. Carver started the mule team moving again. The wagon payload portion fit back into the flat position with a snug click. By the time the slick fellow recovered from his roll in the dirt the cart covered a fair bit of distance.

Lana's brows knit. "That's not the last of him. Think Burroughs could come up with something?"

"I don't know Sis. I don't know. If we pay him off, bribe him, what do you think?"

"Soon he'd want the whole vineyard to himself," Lana replied. "He's trouble. Big big trouble."

"How far back is he?"

Lana swung around. "Creep is just standing back there."

Carver turned around to get a look himself. He turned the pull team away from the road and through the grassy pasture leading to the vineyard. "Good. Blow the signal."

From her overalls, Lana produced a hook shaped flute. She held the bottom of the instrument on one hand while fingering the holes along the curve of the whistle's body with her other. She checked one last time on the outsider down the road before tweeting the melody; a short, rising tune in a somber minor key. After three repetitions of the signal a section of the vine wall rose up and split apart revealing a hidden path.

Carver drove the mules toward the opening. He took one look over his shoulder and whipped the wagon team to move faster. "Our friend is sprinting."

Lana blew a quick, undulating ring on the whistle – hitting both the highest and lowest notes. She checked on the pursuer "Look at him. He runs like an Acostan mailman in tax season."

Surely enough, Tracy gained ground at alarming speed. His mouth gaped open in an O-shape. The black hair on his head shifted about frantically. His arms pumped rhythmically at his sides, and his legs flailed furiously. He matched the speed of a horse and rider or perhaps a motorized vehicle. With buggy eyes and fishy expression, Tracy rocketed across the unkempt portion of the Viklund land.

Lana blew the warning again, but before she finished a green sphere launched from the vineyard. The object drew a long arc in the sky, then rapidly descended. A honeydew melon nearly the length of a bicycle wheel dropped onto Tracy before he realized he was under attack. A green blur passed in front of his eyes, and the next thing he saw was the dirt. The projectile clipped his legs, sending him tumbling into a heap.

"You think Vick taught him that?"

"Fifteen years of practice."

A long dialogue of curses and swears rose out of the failed runner as he rolled fitfully along the ground. The siblings exchanged surprised looks with each other every time they heard particularly inventive curses. Tracy's monologue continued until the wagon rolled into the vineyard and the tangled mess swallowed the path behind them.

# Tunnel Vision

Incessant rustling and knocking noises hovered above the Portram cart as it rolled along the hidden road. A wooden gating mechanism rattled underneath the vine masses, lowering and closing the path just as it raised and pulled back the growths. The going was slow as more of the defenses needed to be cycled before Carver and Lana could reach the center. In all the shaking, rattling, and clacking both of the riders could faintly hear Burroughs plodding about from one switch to the next.

Sargent Viklund passed away, fifteen years gone. The old man left behind no surviving heirs and never explicitly named a benefactor. His legacy was something peculiar. Twenty three years ago Andreas Viklund petitioned for his retirement stipend and left the armed services on the exact day he aged fifty years old. He bought an aging mare from a horse breeder in New Kansas then set off to homestead in Lagoona all by himself. The retirement money built a modest farm house and barn on the southern shore of Caiphon. His new home next to the sleepy town of

Lagoona pleased him greatly.

Six months into settling in, a noticeable bulge formed underneath Vick's riding horse. Four months later the foal was born. A surprise struck the old Sargent as the young animal did not trot about on four hooves. Instead the foal stood on two. Sargent Viklund's horse, Valencia, birthed an Abberant child.

Such events happened from time to time on the Western Continent, with feral animals, but never in the Union. The Mandross Imperative bred the chance of aberration out of Union livestock hundreds of years ago. There was Burroughs, however, weaving about on his new legs and shivering in the cold world.

Andreas Viklund didn't kill the wholeborn Abberant immediately as was the law. Letting the baby live amounted to treason and certain death. Perhaps Vick looked death in the face enough times to not care. He was no stranger to putting Abberants down, even defenseless ones. Despite all reasons to kill Burroughs, Vick took the baby indoors and gave the Abberant a name.

Lana knew Burroughs from age five; Carver age four. The three of them played together, running about the vast vacant fields north of Lagoona back when the Portrams were Viklund's only neighbors. They caught frogs, picked flowers, got into trouble, ran races, sledded in the winter, tended both of their parent's gardens in the spring, built rickety forts in the northern woods, all together. They learned to read and write by lending their school primers. All three of them were there the day old master Andreas died in the accident. It was also the day their father Joseph discovered Burroughs.

Years afterward they were still friends, but new neighbors began appearing. Then Burroughs started the vineyard. The vines ran together and started covering everything, and before long they became everything. Burroughs had such a way with plants. No conscious effort on his part made the vines as they were, they simply grew their way because he was around. With secrets to keep and more and more prying eyes appearing over the years, the Portram siblings visited less and less frequently until they only showed twice a year.

"What is the story with the trespasser?" rumbled a low, soft voice from the nearby.

"He's the rich guy moving in north of here. He's poking us pretty hard, and more suspicious than anybody else we've had to tell off. Trouble. He's big trouble."

"I see," came a reply. "He's walking away as we speak."

The last vine trellis cycled open, revealing the long hidden farm house. The house itself was unremarkable, brick chimney, wooden walls, a few windows. A lumber lattice work covered the house like a second roof. Errant creepers hung from the openings in the green ceiling. Fruit hung heavily on the vines. A few melons rested on the roof of the cottage. Others managed to reach the ground. Slivers of light poured through the lush canopy, projecting bright shapes on the moist, weedless ground.

Suddenly, the outline of a bulky man emerged from the foliage. On approach, Burroughs' spade-shaped ears and longer face became evident. Though his knees functioned exactly as a person's, Burroughs walked stooped. The hooves ending his feet were wide with three distinct ridges running up them; appearing like three or five horse hooves fused together in a stretched circle. He stood tall, sinewy, and covered in coarse hair forming a blotched brown and white pattern on his arms, legs, and face. A dark brown mane ran his spine, like a horse, stopping a few inches into his shirt collar. The face he wore had many of the distinct features of a person with the exception of it being stretched outward into a square muzzle with two small nostrils on top.

Lana skipped off the rolling buckboard as Carver continued to roll up to the farm house. "His name is Tracy. The fellow is a snake, thinking we run sort of racket here on land we don't own."

Burroughs rubbed his chin with his three fingered hand. "You say he's from the plot clearing the forest north of here?"

"That's right. Rich merchant family from the Strand."

"And this Tracy has no idea ?"

Lana shook her head.

"Then you'll be fine."

Lana raised a brow and gestured a tossing motion with both hands. "What if he comes back? When he comes back."

"I have prepared."

"What do we do?"

Burroughs pointed toward Carver securing the wagon. "Same as always." He walked away, leaving Lana with her arms folded.

It was a typical Burroughs answer. Lana knew a time when he was not so closed, secretive. She felt silly for even thinking he would answer any other way.

"The new Twin book came out a month or so back," Carver spoke while sliding a case from the buckboard's foot rest. "Ussopolis. It's a big hit. Let's see, a few cheese wheels. A popular poster," He held out a rolled tube. Burroughs took it. "It's pretty. The art is called Depressionism, don't ask me what she was sad about, because I don't get it."

Burroughs unrolled the printed poster. A skinny cat chewing on a plunger made for a majority of the image, with a more abstracted bath house in the background. Despite the odd picture, the painting was truly well done. Every hair on the cat's face stood out in amazing detail. The colors were vivid and well blended while the dropped shadows cut sharp, decisive edges into the piece. It had to be the most beautiful act of stupidity the world would ever witness, to be cherished for generations.

Carver watched as Burroughs eyed the poster

skeptically then looking back. The long-faced fellow did so half a dozen times before rolling the poster back and nodding. Carver smiled. "It's unbelievable. Isn't it?"

"Yes."

"Well. Besides that, a few colored candles, Acostan soap, and five more yards of the thickest canvas. You got a list?"

Burroughs pulled a note from his hand-stitched breeches. "A few things."

Pulling up his tinted goggles, Carver read through the list and tucked the note into his shirt pocket. "Not a problem."

Lana rejoined the group. All walked around the secluded farm house. Opposite the building lay a sizable stack of pumpkins, gourds, cantaloupe, and watermelon. The watermelon had grown into the shape of giant cucumbers. All produce was hand-picked and the best for the year.

"Pretty soon, Burroughs, it's just going to be you and our dad." Carver spoke flatly. "Maybe. We'll be sure to keep you in the know."

"Many happy wishes on your lottery."

"Yes. Well. Lana will be first in two months."

Lana said nothing. She goaded a cantaloupe up from its resting place on the ground. The melon reached wide enough to plug the end of a large barrel. Gingerly, she hoisted the round object onto one shoulder and shuffled away.

Carver crouched by one of the pumpkins and waited. Burroughs took a hand hold on the opposite side. The smaller sibling let lose a theatrical grunt as the pumpkin lifted up. "Sis is set on staying if she can," Carver rasped out in an exhale.

The three piled the wagon up to capacity, yet much of the bounty remained unmoved from the pile behind the farm house. Before turning around the buckboard to leave, Carver flicked the shopping list out of his shirt pocket. He waggled the slip between two fingers, "Anything else?"

Burroughs shook his head and made his way to cycle out the gating mechanism. Before stepping over the first vine he froze. The triangular ears on his head darted about, facing forward, facing sideways, turning up a little. He paused completely for only a moment then disappeared into the jungle. Wood knocked against wood and the vines rose and split apart to reveal the way. The Portrams guided their buckboard through the narrow opening. The vineyard rose and fell all around until, at last, the final way swung out.

At the end of the green tunnel appeared a man on horseback. Joseph Portram regarded his daughter and his son with a smile and a nod. He then nudged his saddled steed into the vineyard entry. The older Portram wore a brown duster along with a simple red cotton shirt and work jeans. His dark hair thinned into noticeable peaks and streaks of gray ran through both his hair and his trimmed mustache.

The horse he rode had a pattern of light brown and white fur, a coat in much the same pattern as Burroughs – not surprising at all considering Grit and Burroughs were brothers from the same mother. As fate would have it, Grit was born a normal horse unlike his brother. Some families are peculiar indeed.

"Mister Portram," Burroughs announced in his low soft voice. The wooden trellis gate swung open once more.

Joseph cleared his throat and progressed into the overgrowth. "I would like to chat Mister Viklund."

"Of course."

Lana watched as much of her father's exchange as she could before Carver drove the cart too far away. Leaves rose and fell in a straight line toward the center of the mound, as if the vineyard swallowed her father like a large lump of bread.

Less than an hour later the Portrams drove their white buckboard amidst the limestone and wooden buildings of Lagoona. The market square at the very heart of the coastal town bustled at its regular rhythm.

A large purple coral formation stood out in the middle of the ramshackle clutter of merchant kiosks and open wagons. The lustrous conglomeration of petrified sea life stretched into many intriguing and alien shapes except for around the base which smoothed downward enough for market goers to sit in some places. It was the town jewel, a sort of statue treasured for generations.

Business proved lucrative. New merchants came visiting Lagoona and Carver struck some high prices on quite a few pieces of large produce. In particular, a pair of construction workers from the Strand sank several Gella notes into the largest watermelon.

There were also a good many things to buy. Lana remembered market square being the place for people of Lagoona to trade with one another, with a few outside merchants from time to time. In the past three years more and more interested merchants turned up in the small coastal town. They built homes and warehouses at the docks and set up more permanent kiosks. Likewise, the variety of wares increased.

Carver pulled out the shopping note after moving the last bit of the wagon's load to another produce vendor. He shared the note with Lana and together they found everything listed with enough money left over for lunch. They left town chewing on pressed sandwiches

Just before clearing the last picket fence, Lana managed to single out Tracy among the other pedestrians. She received a fiery glare as the dusted son of a rich merchant limped into town.

When Carver and Lana returned for the second load, they found their father had left. They asked about their father's meeting, and Burroughs told them it was mostly small talk and nothing to worry about.

The Portrams made two more rounds after the first, returning home with a large stack of Gella. Lana held the stack of bills. She sorted the money by number and counted out the total. The new seven Gella note featured a portrait of Judge Hamby. Lana pinched the pile in her fingers.

"Hey Carver."

"Yeah?"he watched the setting sun scrape the top of Mount Mortimer.

"Are we doing the right thing?"

The brother paused for a minute. He pulled the expensive tinted goggles off his head. It was just another thing bought using the money with their deal with Burroughs. "I don't know. I wish I knew."

Two months passed by. The season began to change.

# Imminent Domain

Standing on a improvised platform of lumber, Burroughs tipped up a leaf from the top of the canopy and looked out at the Walsh house. The stately ranch house reached two stories tall with steeled roof and white washed walls. A wrap-around veranda circled the building with shadows shifting around under its shade.

Outside on the Walsh grounds stood twelve armed men. Most of the men carried gas guns of various models with the propellant bottles fitted into the stocks. A few among them wore pistols and sabers. They milled about the yard, holding conversations, scratching their heads in mild confusion.

All of them were from the Inath Seat, no doubt about it. Every one of the dozen wore the dark green suit with a red belt running across the right shoulder and a yellow belt running across the left shoulder. The stripes crossed at the midsection. Every suit looked cleaned, pressed, and presentable. The Inath Seat wrote and kept the law for the entire Union, and when the local militias were not enough, the Marshals stepped in. Wholly separate from the Army, the Marshals answered only to the judges of the

Inath Seat; but it appeared they made an exception for the Walsh family.

A dark welling knot pulsed in the back of Burroughs' mind. The day of the accident fifteen years ago played in his mind over and over. He recalled the fearful scene of his mangled father. The screaming came back to him, and the taste of blood. He remembered the drained face of Andreas Viklund pleading to Joseph Portram saying it was not Burroughs' fault. The Abberant child was not to blame. He remembered his promise made at the death bed.

It was the day Burroughs lost his innocence. It was the day he understood he couldn't have what the other children could have.

The world is a cruel and unjust place. Those who wait for justice wait forever and those who seek it hardly find it. If you want to keep your head clear, give up any pretense of justice or fairness when planning your decisions.

So the day of Burroughs' undoing had arrived. He expected the day would come. Defeating the regiment would incite further armed aggression to his home. Exposing himself would provoke immediate use of lethal force, and even catching a glimpse of him would open the way for the Army to declare martial law in the area and purge all Lagoona. There was no winning. He knew it. There certainly was survival, but it meant sacrificing everything.

The marshals began walking to their horses grazing on the greener area of the Walsh plot. Burroughs lowered himself from the platform, gathered the gear he prepared, and waited. Within minutes a pounding of hooves approached the vineyard. Burroughs slung his pack over his back and waited.

A voice shouted. "By the exchequer of the Inath Seat, this land is to be reclaimed into the keeping of Baron Asher of Caiphon. We have attained a warrant for the requisition by judge's declaration of Andreas Viklund reaching legal death. Any squatters are hereby under arrest. Give yourselves up now, or we will force you out."

Burroughs stepped over a few vines as the Marshal gave his threat. With a snap, the horse Abberant freed a unripened cantaloupe from the vineyard and hurled it overhand. The projectile hit the backs of the leafy canopy creating a sound not unlike someone spitting. Almost a second later came a juicy splat followed by the shouts of men and the baying of steeds. Gunfire riddled the vineyard. Burroughs ducked down and shuffled away.

"Leave them," the commander's voice raised up. "Those of you with horses circle around and stop anybody who tries to run. The rest of you with me."

The ears on Burroughs' head searched around to hear how many men still rode on horseback. Seven it sounded, but he could not be sure. They made so much noise, and the hissing of the marshals climbing into the vineyard seemed to eat away at the northern edge.

An occasional curse belted the air as an invader stumbled onto a snare trap. The vines leapt skyward as the pent-up tension released. Marshals tumbled about, grunting and shouting in pain.

"Bottles broke off Captain."

"Then you'll just have to bludgeon the squatter when you find him. Keep pushing."

Burroughs kept his distance. The invading marshals' progress was slow, but it got angrier minute by minute. When he could, Burroughs tried demounting more of the marshals outside the vineyard. He threw the smaller, harder fruits from the vineyard with only his hearing to give direction. His attempts made limited success. Two men fell off their steeds and the five others moved back out of range.

A loud thwack sent the outline of a man flailing through the air twenty yards upward. The canopy caught his fall, but did not soften the landing by much. The unfortunate marshal moaned and coughed loudly.

"You better hope I don't find you!" his friend screamed.

In response Burroughs tugged a vine in the network and sent most of the fruit raining down.

"You having fun, huh? Is that it?" The angry marshal shot two rounds. He frantically ratcheted the injection mechanism. "You think you're funny?"

A vine the width of a log fell down over the rifle crushing weapon and stunning the invader.

"Captain. We should fall back."

"No. There is an opening up there. Everybody keep moving."

Battered and worn, the green-suited law men stumbled into the center of the vineyard. They eyed the farm house suspiciously, and one of the men whose gun still functioned aimed at the doorway. Not a soul appeared to be home, and not a sound came from the ruin; save for the knocking of the trellis roof overhead.

A gunman inspected the window of the house and waved his friends over. Inside was an unkempt bed, a pile of books and a table. Not much more caught their eye except for a burned pile of paper and garbage in the fireplace. They spilled into the single room. The captain sifted around the half burned pile, turning up a few bits of glass from a picture frame and some metal pins.

Suddenly a cacophony of hissing filled the room. Outside the small house vines began descending. The creeping plants blocked out the windows and door. One creeper ran down the chimney and slithered about the room. As suddenly as it began, it stopped. The marshals stood frozen. Moments later a loud crack collapsed the roof onto their heads.

The seven marshals outside the mound watched in awe as the hill sank down. A shock wave rippled through the entire tangled vineyard and a billowing fog of dust as thick as a pudding rolled out in every direction. The panicked horses reared back and whinnied as the approaching brown wall swiftly enveloped them, turning everything a musty brown for close to a minute.

By the time the mounted men could regain sight of the spectacle, Burroughs' shadow passed among them and reached the edge of the forest at a speed Abberants were loathed for.

Burroughs turned around for a last few glimpses of his home before plunging into the forest. Did somebody see him? He didn't know. He did his best to protect the Portram family for their kindness – even though he waited till the last minute.

> Ownership is an illusion most people love to buy into.
> It makes them happy to think a stretch of land, a cow,
> or something clever they invented can somehow tied to
> them by an invisible force; the Right, or Ownership.
> When in reality this magical bond is purely imaginary,
> and everything just comes and goes. That's life.

In a second Burroughs caught himself staring upward at the tops of the trees, standing dead still. An entry from Sargent Viklund's memoir gave him pause. He read through the whole journal before burning it. He regretted doing so, granted he could have evaded capture with it. He wasn't willing to take the chance, however. The journal named his friends and therefore became a threat to what he planned.

A quick adjustment to the straps of his pack and Burroughs bolted further into the forest. The dust was everywhere on him. Dust caked his clothes, scratched his throat and nose, and burned his eyes. He paused occasionally to cough and wheeze. Breathing deeply hurt and his draws became shorter. A few times he held his breath to listen for sounds of pursuit, but heard nothing. When his pace became leaden and this chest stabbed with pain, Burroughs finally stopped.

Pine trees stood all around. Their scaly bark trunks

reaching up, splintering into scattered branches many yards overhead. Cones and dead branches littered the floor of the forest.

Crunching and crackling followed Burroughs everywhere he stepped. No birds sang. No wind blew. No animals foraged along the floor. The lone creature stood completely undisturbed, a feeling he enjoyed.

He put down his pack and sat quietly. When his body stopped aching, he gathered his thoughts to plan the next move. Nothing came to mind. So he did nothing. He busied himself with reorganizing his pack, reading the map, picking apart pine cones, throwing rocks, and munching on dried provisions.

It would get cold soon, but the chill hardly mattered. The mildly frigid autumn nights barely bothered Burroughs, but it did make falling asleep difficult.

A road ran from Lagoona through the forest all the way to Leal's Harbor in the north. The reappearance of faster boat travel, however, made the dirt path obsolete. Hardly a soul walked the road any more. Disrepair made itself evident along the way. Over time the woods reclaimed pieces the road. Trees grew straight out of the packed dirt and rain washed away the edges. Still, Burroughs would not risk walking the road just in case somebody came down it. He entered the woods east of the road, and he deliberately trod down the rougher paths.

Wandering north, Burroughs found a small depression in the forest floor. A dried creek bed with tree roots running down the edges in the fashion of a mangrove. The bed was smooth and solid. Oaks provided the cover instead of the typical pine. In the pit, Burroughs lit a fire, unrolled his bed roll, and let his thoughts linger.

The angry marshal came to mind "Do you think this is funny?" he asked. Such an odd threat, almost an invitation. He didn't find anything humorous about the suffering he gave the marshals. Anger wasn't it either, or sadness. Did he really feel nothing, not even fear?

Burroughs sighed, running his right thumb over one finger of his hand. He pressed and rubbed on the reddish brown calluses. Two large knuckles made up his fist as he clenched down.

The Abberant muttered a single word, "Monster." He spoke his own damnation and weighed the evidence in his mind. Burroughs continued to ponder his position. Would he have instead been monstrous if he beat the threatening officer into the soil and broke his legs under a hoof. Would he laugh at the screaming? Perhaps do all the same angrily? And then he would be a monster who only knows fear and hate.

But no, everything which took place in the vineyard happened as plainly as action and reaction, with no emotion whatsoever.

The marshals, oh, they felt. They screamed in anger and jittered in fear. Burroughs smelled their sweat and heard their rapid breath. They were real people with real emotions. They kept families and friends. They contributed to a society which appreciated them. What was Burroughs compared to them? Some creature walking as a man but lacking the fullness of a human being.

In all this depressing, gloomy speculation Burroughs detached himself; feeling ... nothing, only thinking.

He slept comfortably in the tiny gorge. Acorns from the oaks satisfied his appetite. The dead silence of the forest never broke the entire night.

# *An Associate Will be with you Shortly*

Morning light crept into the woodlands. The hour was so early the light seemed to come from everywhere as if the forest began glowing. Burroughs rolled over in his large, hand-stitched bedroll coughing. Streams of mucus rolled out of both his nostrils. The dust from yesterday became a brown cake in his nose and along the edge of his eyes. Burroughs expelled the surplus mucus and coated most of his arm in it.

The unfortunate problem with owning a muzzle instead of a nose is the longer snout is capable of storing an alarming amount of fluid, about a handful. Burroughs' held at least as much. He flung what he could and got the rest matted in his fur. To his relief, the sound of a creek trickled nearby. He scrambled up the grade of the dried creek bed, holding his right hand out as far out as possible.

Sure as sun in summer, a small stream ran nearby. The creek ran oddly close by. Burroughs wondered why he had not heard it earlier. Regardless, he tipped his inflexible hoofs until he fell to his knees on the bank. He plunged both hands in at once into the slow current then immediately coiled back out with an animalistic yowl.

Something stung him, his left hand. The jolt ran up

54

his arm to the back of his neck. He checked the water. Nothing appeared to be swimming around, and the creek was clear enough to see to the bottom. He carefully sank his left hand in again, fingers first then the down to the wrist. The right hand went in soon after. No second after washing the slime off his right hand, a second shock rocketed through his other arm. He kicked away from the shore and checked his hands for cuts or burns. There were no noticeable marks on his palms, only six points of throbbing pain at the base of each of his fingers.

A minute later began the greater peculiarity.

"**Hello. Somebody here?**"

A buzzing voice rippled out of the moving surface of the creek. Something moved under the surface, but had no shape and no shadow. The apparition scooted a few yards up river then down, creating a small wake behind it.

"**I can't see you darling. So you'd best speak up.**" The voice was very out of place. It had the dulcet tones of a lady, perhaps middle-aged.

Burroughs froze absolutely still. Whatever stung him was blind. He shortened his breath until it was barely audible and watched the invisible creature search around the surface of the water. It seemed incapable of running onto the land, but frighteningly agile at cutting through the surface of the moving creek. Though the memoirs of Sargent Viklund covered many creatures in its pages, this one was not among them.

The long faced fellow wondered the benign nature of the blind ghost. "Hello?" Burroughs' word turned upward in pitch seeming to question the intention of the bizarre visitor as well as his judgment of the situation.

"**Right. There you are.**" The translucent spot surfed to the closest edge on the shore. "**Is there something I can help you with? I see you were trying to swim, but had a little trouble.**"

"No. I wanted to wash my hands."

"**I don't,**" The water creature paused. "**Then why did ... did you fall in and damage your head?**"

Burroughs crossed his arms. "I tried washing my hands and you shocked me."

"**Oh, good one. Now it's my fault. That's you isn't it Liz? Let me guess. You really stepped in it, and now somebody has to clean up.**"

"My name is not Elizabeth."

"**And what would your name be? Mine is Cherille Greaves.**"

"Burroughs. Burroughs Viklund."

The sprite muttered something. "**You said Viklund?**"

"I did."

"**I see. Well, not literally, but it's starting to make sense. Could you put your hands back in the water? I promise I won't bite.**"

Burroughs edged cautiously to the water. The voice sounded honest enough.

"**I will take care of everything. No worry burning your brain out.**"

No shocks harmed him as he sank both hands into the cool creek for the last time.

"**You seem to be missing a few fingers. No. That's not it. Just relax.**"

A warm sensation filled Burroughs' palms. Suddenly an irresistible outpour of tears filled his eyes, clouding his vision. He tried to wipe away the moisture, but his hands and head could not move. The lids of his eyes widened as far as possible. Streaks flooded his mind as his eyes rolled around in his sockets like marbles. Then at last he was set free. Cherille kept true to her word. The entire ordeal was painless, but very disturbing.

"**Never mind,**" The voice relented. "**I have no idea what is going on here. I hope that didn't hurt.**"

Burroughs pulled himself back up the bank, further confused. He wiped the tears from his eyes. "I'll be fine."

"Are you sure? Because the short time I got in there showed me your cranium is bent lengthwise. Your hands are scarred up so much both your bottom two digits are gone. You have some kind of skin condition I've never seen. Your feet are crammed into some odd shaped boxes, fused in there it seems. Why, you're an absolute mess."

The horse Abberant cocked a brow. "I was born this way."

"Oh. Bless your heart."

Burroughs let out an exasperated sigh. The thought of leaving crossed his mind, but since he was in no hurry he decided he had little to lose by entertaining the apparition a little longer. Before continuing he checked the forest for onlookers.

"I'm an Abberant, if you have heard of them. Both my mother and father were horses, but I was born able to walk and think like a human being." His speech slowed when he claimed to think like a human being. A doubt crossed his mind.

"The Whole Born." A ring of realization sounded in Cherille's reply. "What are you doing out here?"

"You know me?"

A thin disk widened on the surface of the water. The shape was a perfect circle for a brief moment, and then bent under the force of the current. "And now we are six days ahead of schedule. Nobody ever tells me anything," The ghost shouted. "We plan these things down to the letter and then we use them for couch cushions."

"Wha-"

"Listen Douglas,"

"Burroughs."

"I don't care. M'kay. There is a fellow walking the old foot path west of here and he is going to die if you don't find him. Take your stick and get out there."

"I'll just be going," Burroughs pointed over his shoulders, turned around, and walked away to collect his things from the dried creek bed."

"**Wait. Stop. No. No. No. No. No. No.**" The host blurted in rapid succession. It heard the clatter of the wanderer gathering his gear and added a tone of desperation to its voice. "**We really need your help with something. You're big, burly, and can brutalize things.**"

"Do you think I would get satisfaction from that?"

"**We were hoping so. Your father served in the army after all.**"

Burroughs snorted. In a short charge, he crested the hill and bound the distance between both shores of the creek. Chips of dark, rich soil skipped in all directions as he landed on the opposite side with a thud. The ... thing in the water kept talking, but Burroughs no longer listened. The ordeal was all too sudden, all too weird. He didn't believe any of it. So instead of giving into the demands of who most likely didn't exist, he left. He did feel a little thirsty, however.

After a short run the forest fell into its former silence, not a single noise save for the trampling of cones and branches under hoof.

As much as he wanted to, Burroughs could not stop thinking about the encounter, the lady-like voice, the short possession. And if he heard right, whatever-it-was knew him and planned something. The experience felt familiar somehow. He could almost place the voice to a face he remembered. Perhaps he ran into such creatures before when he was younger and simply could not remember. It certainly would explain how they knew of his mentor Andreas Viklund. Also, he knew the host could not escape the confines of the small stream, maybe just a good guess.

If circumstances were different, perhaps Burroughs would have accepted the request.

Cherille would have to find somebody else.

The sound of swarming flies gave pause to Burroughs' thoughts. A hint of decay wafted about the air. From a short distance away buzzed a hazy cloud. Burroughs approached and the cloud thinned into a roiling particulate swarm of insects. There on the ground rested a deer carcass. The large doe was torn open at the neck and nowhere else, as if the predator which killed the animal did so only for sport. If the red wolves had slain the doe the entrails would have been dug into, but the sides of the deer remained intact. The blood did not trail off, instead pooling in one place. Meaning, the doe either snapped at the neck at the first bite or had been pinned to the ground until it bled out; a cruel predator.

Looking again at the neck, Burroughs noticed the markings stretched far too long to be bite marks. No, the doe died from a set of claws. On the head, two smooth topped protrusions also revealed the deer had actually been a buck, but the antlers were sawed off, recently. An abnormally-large cat could have destroyed a full-grown buck in this fashion, possibly, and would have done it for sport as cats do. Harvesting the horns, on the other hand, no animal did such a thing. Except, maybe ... Abberants gathered deer antlers on the Western Continent, the dogs.

The hairs on the back of his mane bristled as Burroughs bent down to find the tracks. Mixed with the split hoof prints of the buck, he spotted the pad markings and heel prints made as the hunters planted their feet. Dog Abberants stalked the forest of Caiphon.

A sudden chill ran down Burroughs' spine he checked every nearby tree to make sure he truly was alone. Impossible, it had to be. All dogs weighing above thirty pounds were wiped out hundreds of years ago. The wolves introduced to the forest did not carry the aberration trait. The Mandross Imperative managed to ward off outbreaks for close to four hundred years.

Burroughs rubbed the two smooth, bony places at the top of the buck's head. A fine dust rubbed off on his fingers.

Of all the aberrations documented, Canid were feared the most. They were not the strongest of the demented creatures, or the fastest, or the most capable in magics. Birth defects occurred quite often, some to the point of being debilitating. In single combat a person could overtake a Canid easily, but dogs never gave anybody the chance. See one dog and there are certainly others. The pack tactics of canine Abberants were ruthless regardless if they ran in the hunts or roamed in feral packs.

The northern wind brushed the tops of the pine trees. A hiss rolled by as the wind shook the nettled branches. Burroughs wiped the bone dust on his breeches. He stood up and walked away. If he was not already hunted, he would be soon. There was no telling what the half animals would do if they found him, how they would react. If the buck carcass gave any hint, chances are these Canid were the worst Abberants to stumble upon; being human or otherwise.

Burroughs walked until the sound of the swarm of flies died to a dull murmur. He climbed hills gnarled by exposed pine roots. Heading deeper into the wood, a bright blue lichen began springing up on all the trees. The fungi reached outwardly with shapes resembling tattered cyan butterflies. The growths gave off a dull chalky smell. Dead trees on the forest floor blossomed with the lichen, completely covered.

He kept moving.

Petrified coral formations occasionally stood out of the forest floor. The porous rocks and hollow tubes starkly contrasted with the surrounding evergreen forest. Cones and needles clogged many of the exposed holes, as well as a few visible bird's nests on top. Dens of smaller creatures filed the openings along the sides, but Burroughs cared not to give a closer inspection. Freshly dug soil pulled up beside one coral rock told Burroughs all he needed to know, more than he wanted to know.

Moments later other footfalls crunched along the forest floor. Burroughs stopped and listened as a group meandered in his direction. He ducked into some brush as the noise drew closer. Some dark outlines weaved through the trees in the far distance then disappeared, taking the sounds of rustling, snapping, and thudding with them.

On average, Canids' eyesight and hearing were poor, but their sense of smell was astonishing. Journal entries from Andreas Viklund explained in great detail the dogs' use of smell. Once the dogs had a scent, they could follow it for miles. They could also tell things from scent such as size of the enemy force, weaponry, and perhaps more. How much a Canid may know from a whiff remained a great point of speculation among military strategists.

Generals tried tactics of scent masking scout parties. A few tried stink bombs and various smell decoys to throw off trails. Active assaults of smell in combat, trying to turn the tide of battle with stench, proved futile and often made casualties worse. Regardless of the ploy, nothing threw off the Canid's unshakable ability to track by smell.

To the Canid, Sargent Vick had a name. They called him "Bakirema," and they shouted the name in anger. In many cases he found himself singled out by enemies who had tracked him for days. At one point during his military tour, Andreas served in scouting missions thousands of miles from the Eastern Shore . Yet in encounters with Candid there the Abberants still howled the name "Bakirema" despite being far away from the initial packs who gave the name. This led him to believe Canid may share or communicate smell as if it were their primary way of defining the world. Their language defined smell most of all.

Burroughs knew if the dogs picked up the scent, if they were the least bit curious, they would find him. He immediately ran in the opposite direction. The noise of his foot falls were louder even though he tried aiming his feet at the softer places in the ground.

In the end, the Canid did not find him. He found the Canid.

## Dog and Pony Show

His pack rattled. The forest floor crunched under his solid feet as if a he almost intended to snap every twig in his path. Burroughs topped another hill, stepping on the pine roots, and when he looked up from watching his feet he came face to face with one of them.

The Canid stood nearly three heads shorter than Burroughs at roughly four and a half feet tall. It wasn't a feral Abberant, that became readily apparent. The dog wore green shorts which flared outward below the knee. It wore a green vest of the same dark color with a red tear drop shape stained into the front. The creature's face was clearly canine, albeit stretched slightly wider. A white downy fuzz covered most of the Canid's body.

For several moments they stared at one another, Burroughs' brown bestial eyes looking at the dog's yellow golden eyes. Both of their expressions showed visible surprise and their postures were both defensive, arms out.

The Canid looked Burroughs over. It snuffled samples of the air with its nose then spoke words which seemed impossible to pronounce through its long muzzle. "Huinie do."

Burroughs slowly edged away.

"Canay da fono tinst Mormo." The Canid pointed to itself. "Huinie do." It then pointed at Burroughs.

The Canid's name was Mormo, Burroughs could tell he was being introduced. "Burroughs," he pointed at himself and tried to shy away.

"Kam comalla tur mindar tinst. Canay da tar nimi stek barrenteger va poy. Jester da haquestovar ner. Tam tar tennis bal stek ner. Mo jester begamari tar poy. Bakirema da porropoy, charchini." Mormo kept speaking in a growling tone as Burroughs backed farther and farther away. Not a single word made any sense, and the words he did hear Mormo probably didn't intend. A sense of concern crept over the dog's features. "Oy huinie."

Burroughs stopped after being addressed, "Yes?"

Mormo gave his larger counterpart a measuring look. Lifting himself onto the ends of his elongated, digitigrade feet; Mormo shambled in close to Burroughs and smelled more thoroughly. When satisfied, he relented the space back and returned where he stood before. The Canid pointed down on his nose and rocked the finger back and forth. "Larkannistor ma."

"I'm sorry. I don't understand," Burroughs spoke politely.

Mormo's head popped back. The Canid's eyes widened for a second then squinted in concentration. "You. Arrive. Bad." Mormo croaked then pointed a clawed finger at Burroughs. "Stay. Brother. Take." The claw then pointed at the ground.

Burroughs nodded slowly, making and breaking eye contact several times.

With that, Mormo ambled away. Then it was the perfect time to leave; in a panic.

The Canid in the forest were part of the Hunt from the Western Continent. In the entire history of the Union of Fourteen Islands, never once had there been an invasion. Abberants never gave chase on the sea and kept no boats to do so. Many feared deep water, pitching crazed fits of fear if they fell off a dock or were taken asea as prisoners. For generations, the idea of an invasion of monsters was laughed off.

Yet they stalked the pine woods of Caiphon no doubt laying a trap or waiting to ambush someone. Mormo mentioned Andreas Viklund's name which set him further on edge. Burroughs worried the dog might have caught the scent on him, begin howling curses, and muster his pack.

The short time Burroughs shared with Mormo seemed to stretch forever. The shining predatory eyes stared at him from a nightmare a visage of jagged teeth. Mormo lacked the size, but put forth so much ferocity in his manner and speech to frighten Burroughs into a childish mania; and the wolf just stepped out to fetch his friends. Burroughs wasn't feeling very social.

Minutes later the wood filed with howls, a muster, a call to hunt. High tremulous replies range out in all directions, and as far away as Burroughs could hear. Their numbers were in the hundreds, easily. They were angry.

Heart pounding, Burroughs stopped dead as the ground trembled and hissed at the number of runners frantically coursing through the wood. The rumble grew more and more intense as it closed in. He heard their panting, their leathery pads striking the brittle nettles on the floor, and their growls.

Suddenly a half dozen Canid weaved through the trees thirty yards away. Their hands hovered over the curved knives swaying in cases belted to their pants or on their shoulders. Two more bolted by on all fours, kicking dead leaves and twigs into the air at each bound. A few members of a group running in tight formation broke rank and pointed at Burroughs yapping something in a guttural tongue. The whole troop stopped to look with curious expressions. Another howl rose out of the forest and they turned their attention away to answer the call.

The Canid Hunt wanted someone else. By the show of force, it looked like they would have whoever it was.

A runner spotted Burroughs, flipping into a human stance to break its speed by leaning back and catching the ground with the length of one foot. It cut a significant divet into the soil before turning around and stoop-walking to the horse Abberant. Unlike Mormo, this Canid had a tail which wagged behind it. Coming rudely close, the creature with gray streaked coat vigorously sniffed Burroughs down. After one last long inhale, it snorted and took off.

It was just a glimpse, but Burroughs could have sworn he saw the dog smile; the lip curving up one side of the head.

A few more teams ran by in dull brown outfits. A few had weapons of some manner ready, and each paid Burroughs little or no heed. In the stunned silence Burroughs remembered the plea of the voice in the creek, the fellow walking north on the path who would die without him. He was very glad he didn't take the offer. Still, his standing with the Canid death squad remained a point of speculation he cared not to explore. The grin from the runner could have been cruel or genuinely friendly.

While the unfortunate suffered, Burroughs trekked further on. He hoped to reach the central plains lands of Caiphon by sundown. From there he planned to stake out a claim in the sparsely-populated region and start his life over again. Granted, the wolves would have to allow it if they decided to track him down. While they were entertained, perhaps he could do something.

> Everybody stinks. Everyone. To make things worse, Canid know how to make you stink, be it browning your britches in fear or running you till you sweat like a Wellborn pig at Christmas time. When the dogs are biting at your heels, try moving your smell because dropping it never works.

Moving scent, Sargent Vick's journal explained as leaving a trail in such a way to throw off pursuit. Typical tactics involved scaling trees and walking from branch to branch as far as possible, a risky maneuver. A favorite, and more safe, way involved digging a short tunnel and concealing the entrance with soil. Once closed, the entry to the "Wipe Tunnel" blended in perfectly with the area; it had to for it to work. Most tactics involved water sources.

Burroughs neared another creek with some reluctance. He scooped at the waving surface, anticipating electrical burns to sting him. The stream did not hurt, and felt refreshing. He drank a few handfuls of the cool, sweet run.

A crash like a peal of thunder erupted to the south followed by a disordered chorus of howls.

Burroughs unslung his pack from his back. The pans, tools, and foodstuffs shifted about the bag as the horse Abberant tilted the pack up and held it over his head. He then waded into the stream and began walking the direction of the current. His hooves bounced off the soft creek bed's spongy surface. Just a few hundred yard would surely throw off the hunters. Memories of all the hot summer days when Burroughs played every day with the Portrams came to mind. The family kept a tank, a small pond on the farm with a gravel bottom. The watering hole was an oasis in the scorching heat.

**"There you are.**"

Numerous tugs assaulted Burroughs' legs, tripping his feet and threatening to pull him under. He splashed against an intangible attacker. The canvas bag slipped from his hands and vanished into the void stream. Cherille's pulls were weak, but her grip could not be broken. A vortex opened under Burroughs' footing, sinking him deeper and deeper. He starting pushing with his hands, and Cherille quickly took hold of the other limbs as well.

Water filled his flared nostrils as the phantom pulled him under. He tried holding his last breath in, but prying forces pushed open his lips. A rush of liquid filled his lungs, speeding his descent to the bottom of the stream.

**"That was very rude of you,"** Mrs. Greaves spoke coldly as the tingle of asphyxiation creeped about Burroughs' body to rob him of life. **"We were worried you might have sided with the mongrels for some reason, but since you're obviously trying to run away, how about a second chance, honey?"**

The shimmering surface of the creek blurred into a single point of light as Burroughs looked upward out of the water. Slowly, the spot shrank smaller and smaller. He found he couldn't move his legs, then his arms. The heart in his chest raced in a desperate attempt to stay alive. The chill of death set in. Then, suddenly bubbles streamed out of his mouth and nose. Streaks of bobbing, dancing beads flowing out and up.

**"Have some oxygen. We make it one hundred percent fresh from concentrate."**

In seconds the life flowed back into the drowning half man. His limbs coursed with vigor. His mind was fresh and alert. His whole body felt cool and refreshed, more so than if he'd been outside. Gradually, sight and senses returned.

The creek surface raced overhead, a glittering fall. Burroughs looked down to see the soft bottom of the stream running by. He had been captured, and Cherille was moving him away at an alarming pace. Dark shapes floated by, perhaps tree roots, rocks, or fish. The roar of the current beat on his ears, but Cherille's voice cut through with undisturbed clarity.

**"I don't expect you to understand how bad things are, how thin we're stretching ourselves on a hunch. You must think you don't owe us anything, and you'd be right. You're wholeborn, Douglas."**

"Blub blub blub" Burroughs launched several large bubbles from his mouth.

**"You're wholeborn. You don't carry the taint, and you can make decisions free of the Link. You're free. If**

you can save this man's life we will be forever in your debt."

Burroughs weighed the option of being torn to pieces by dogs against a life where he'd never take a drink of water in peace – let alone a bath.

"**Save him.**" the voice pleaded. "**If you can get him to me everything will be fine. Just grab the scrawny fellow and run, can you do that? I sent for help. We'll take care of everything. Mmmmkay?**"

With that, mud began rolling down his back. The soft gritty substance got down Burroughs' shirt and breeches, leaving a layer on both sides when he sat up. He beached. Rubbing his face and hands, he felt no moisture. The emergence happened so rapidly and so smoothly he hardly noticed. It was as if Cherille performed a traditional magic trick to fool his senses.

"**Got your stick. Your father would be proud to see you with it.**"

At the edge of the muddy embankment stood a peculiar tree. From the unmarked trunk and the shriveled branches it appeared to have once been a stout oak of some sort. A sharp concave pinched the sides of the growth just above the bottom. The body of the tree was compressed, darkened, and slightly twisted like a singed log in a fireplace. Char didn't coat the midsection, however. The black portion glistened slightly. The branches growing out of the marred section were puny and pathetic, shrunken from the lack of nutrients.

Burroughs grabbed the staff and the natural pieces to the tree fell away, leaving two rough, jagged ends to the weapon.

"**We don't know how Abberant things work, but we can jam sockets into things and make them dance. More predictable.**"

"What?"

"**Don't worry about it. They took our guy that**

**way.**" A series of wakes cut several arrow shapes into the creek pointing in the same direction. "**Grab him and run. Punish the dogs with the stick if they are bad.**"

Burroughs looked back at the void with a deadpan expression for a moment then followed the direction he'd been given. Wholeborn, able to choose his own decisions, still taking orders. The oxygen refreshed him, but he still felt tired. This was all too much.

What he did know was Cherille promised to end this drama and take him someplace safe. She'd done so once, and most likely would do it again. An exit looked very appealing. If he could get out, once again be uninvolved, putting his hand in it would be worth the trouble.

He rolled the oaken staff around in his palms. Was it oak? It felt as solid as hard wood, inflexible. The weapon fit to his hand perfectly. He flipped it over several times, catching the tumbling ends at the right intervals. A familiar feeling came to him, a reaction from inside the object, but he could not place the sensation. He struggled to recognize the staff substance, but in vain.

As fortune would make it, the Canid circled into a mob a little more than one hundred yards away. The crowd packed in dense at the edges, but the center of the formation looked almost vacant. A thin smoke trailed upward from the ring. The dogs, all of various body shapes, colorations, height, and clothing stood around. They all stared intently at the goings on in the middle and hardly paid Burroughs any mind on his approach.

A stench of burning flesh stung Burroughs' nose. At the base of a pine tree rested a line of dead Canid, all arranged side by side. The six bodies reeked a foul odor from dark singe marks at various points. One corpse was filled with a cratered hole reaching all the way through the chest. The blackened ribs froze like claws in the air. Another Canid had the top of its head removed by fire. The bottom jaw of the beast's muzzle jutted out like a morbidly obtuse under bite and a heat-shriveled tongue hung on by the slightest sliver of tissue.

Trying to block the fresh images from his mind, Burroughs joined the crowd. Most paid him no mind. A few dogs cocked a brow, muttered, "Huinie de," and pointed the first two half-clawed fingers of their five digits. Their friends would divert their attention a second, then turn back to the spectacle in the center.

In the middle stood Mormo and a few other Canid sharing his vestments. Kneeling before them was a fair-skinned man with golden blond hair. He wore some manner of dusty white robe or frock with baggy sleeves. In front of the human, Mormo and his fellows had placed a rough-hewn log beside a large jar.

On the other end of the circle two Canid tended a fire. One stoked the flames while another hovered a wicked-looking axe over the red coals. The blade of the instrument drew a wide crescent, and must have been exceptionally heavy as it appeared to measure an inch of thickness near the handle.

Three green-clad Canid stood around the prisoner. One of them, Mormo, turned over what appeared some type of bottle with a pistol grip at the bottom. The neck of the object looked to be a bottle top.

They planned an execution by chopping off the poor fellow's head with a blazing hot edge. It was quite obvious. The jar sharing the scene disturbed Burroughs greatly. He cared not to dwell on what things Abberants planned for severed heads.

This would not be one head for the collection, however.

## Blockheads Think in Block Quotes

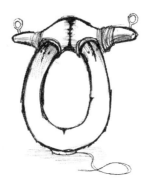

> Catching an enemy by surprise is the single greatest tactic choice, and being caught off guard is the single most frightening and humbling experiences a man can face. Confusion halts gun batteries, disarms opponents, starts a panic, and opens blocked roads. It is only effective as long as you can keep it going, which is always shorter than you think.

Burroughs mumbled to himself. He walked around the crowd and a few pine trees to the other side of the gathering. He leaned up to peek over the heads and check the goings-on inside. The axe was still heating up. An orange glow had taken to the front of the blade.

Burroughs backed up a few yards then launched into a barreling charge. The entire congress of onlookers fell into a hushed silence as one end of their gathering suddenly scattered. Then another part in the crowd opened up in a tumult of scuffling and grunting. The prisoner was gone.

"Whoa," the young man screamed he slid along the rough floor of the forest. His knees and ankles caught exposed roots and rock. The drape he wore did little to soften the blows. A vice-like grip threatened to tear his arm off at the shoulder. He kicked about, trying to stand. Try as he might, his feet could not match the pace of who pulled him.

By the time the captors realized what happened Burroughs was half way to his destination. The Canid howled out a chilling hunting cry, a primal roar; the kind which bellows out after bubbling up deep inside.

Burroughs reached the shore by the water and drug the unfortunate fool in along with him. A rapid undertow ran opposite to the flow of the stream's surface. The current twisted both bodies around mercilessly and sucked them away. Once again, the water forced its way down Burroughs' throat. The drowning sensation felt just as harsh as the first.

"**Nice job Douglas**"

"Blub blerb," Burroughs protested even though shouting liquid from his lungs hurt.

A light, masculine voice joined in. "**Did you have to be so rough Douglas? You nearly pulled me apart.**"

The gas bubbles finally coursed out of Burroughs mouth. The oxygen made him dizzy. His head spun as the dark scenery sped by.

"**He can't swim,**" Cherille explained.

"**Well, he can drag me over a bunch of Abbies and across half the woods without slowing down.**"

"**How many dogs are out there?**"

The fellow murmured for a second. "**Seven packs, minus six. Five Heartbloods. A handful of fleet mixed in. Not a small number. What's wrong with you guys? Why did you let them in?**"

"**We have no idea how they got in. We were hoping you could tell us.**"

"**What? No. I just ran my errand and half the binging wood filled with fuzzballs out to jar my head. They knock me down, take my gun, and sit me in front their Heartbloods. They came from nowhere as far as I** know."

"I see, well, My reach isn't as far as it used to be," Cherille lamented. "**And nobody is answering my call for support. I can get you two out of the woods. Once you're on the central plain, both of you are on your own reaching the mountains.**"

Burroughs bubbled out a startled, incomprehensible complaint. Nobody paid him any attention.

"**It's nice to meet you Douglas. My name is Shaw. We work for the Ministry, and I guess you too now. Is he all right Cherille?**"

"**He's very excited.**" She replied.

Burroughs thrashed violently at the dark envelope, shouting muffled screams.

"**Well, that's good because my first time was terrifying.**"

"**There is one thing you need to know about Douglas,**" Cherille added.

"**What's that?**"

"**He's a Wholeborn aberration we've been keeping our eye on.**"

"**Yes. I noticed when he dragged me like an unwanted sack of turnips.**"

The both of them lowered their voices for a few minutes to exchange private conversation. Gradually, the speeding tunnel glowed brighter and brighter as more sunshine poured in. Burroughs felt sick as the course became clearer. He saw the way twist and turn as he and Shaw seemed to fall horizontally through the narrow, watery passage. The roof sparkled and undulated in the sunlight. Through the refracting glaze, the trees appeared to be thinning away; opening up to a big blue sky.

At last the flying procession slowed. "**This is as far as I can take you,**" Cherille said.

Shaw caught his foot on the soft bank and walked

out upright. Burroughs beached like a log.

"**Wait here for your luggage to be unloaded. It had to be shipped separately. Some things don't change, right?**" the invisible lady chuckled at a bit of humor she only understood. A sopping wet bale of canvas launched from the creek. It smacked into the sandy shore with a moist slap. "**Yup. Luggage service just like when I was alive. At least I didn't lose it.**"

Burroughs rolled over his recovered pack to get at the straps. "Thank you?"

"**Don't mention it, honey. You two get along.**" With a streaking slosh Cherille Greaves disappeared.

Shaw walked up the embankment to top a nearby knoll of tall grass. They had arrived at the plains. The pine forest still obscured the horizon to the south, but the north stretched on seemingly forever. Green, grassy, stunted hills dotted the landscape. The grass rippled in the wind. Only a few yellowed tinges of fall colors marked the greenery. In the west loomed the ghost of Mount Mortimer and a few smaller mountains peaking up.

"We are a few days out from the mountains," Shaw bit his lip. "Are you carrying any food?"

Burroughs lifted the pack off the ground. Several individual rivulets ran onto the ground through loosened stitches. "Not anymore." The seeds he'd stored away most likely soaked, meaning the tiny things would germinate soon. He flipped up the bag to search around and see. All the paper envelopes sopped with moisture. Ink ran down the sides of his half-finished book. Every sack of dried food had been rehydrated, ruined. A few of the pots were trapping water. He poured those out, noticing some of the metal dented in transit.

"It's very empty out here in the plains, but the Crossroads town is still out here. We'll, um," Shaw swept his golden locks away from his face. He looked Burroughs up and down with his pale blue eyes. "I will stop in for some provisions, and we will hurry on our way."

Burroughs pointed a finger at the pale fellow on the high ground. "I am not going anywhere with you." He spoke flatly.

"Why not Douglas?"

"My name is not Douglas. My name is Burroughs, and I'm not part of your ..." Burroughs held out an arm over the running stream and shook a few rigid gestures.

Shaw's eyes rolled around in his head. He squinted. "Then why did you save my life?"

The black staff passed from one hand to another as Burroughs shouldered his pack. "Because I could."

"Well, thank you. Could you please follow me to the mountains?"

"Give me a reason."

"Over one hundred Abberants, and who knows what else, are on this island, and they want to kill me. Chances are they are thinking of killing you too. What are you doing?"

Burroughs kicked a few crescent shaped holes in the mud with a hoof. He poured out the wet seeds he'd carried and covered them up.

Shaw cocked a brow. "It's November you know."

The horse man grunted, nodding. "I won't get to use them."

"You are coming then?"

"Lead the way."

The fellow in white robes took off into a brisk walk. The grass sifted about under his feet and whipped against the sides of his long garment. A few paces behind, Burroughs followed as a bestial shadow. The huge burden on his back swayed left and right.

The two made eye contact a few times. Shaw's expression betrayed a short glimpse of panic before smoothing out to a smile. Burroughs remained empty in expression.

"I'm guessing you would like to know more about

the Ministry. Am I right Dou... uh ... Burroughs?"

"I've heard of Swimmers."

On the Western Continent, rare reports surfaced regarding people in tattered clothes suddenly appearing. These jittery, half crazed individuals received the name 'Swimmers,' as they were often sighted emerging from large bodies of water. When confronted, they would often gibber nonsense and run away into the awaiting dangers of the western lands or swim away until they disappeared – the strangest thing.

Tall tales sprang up about Swimmers showing up in towns delivering dark prophecies or healing the sick. Other rumors pointed to Swimmers as kidnappers and assassins secretly working for the barons, doing literal "wet" work. Still others considered these oddities a special form of aberration not yet documented, perhaps fish men.

"Yes that is us," Shaw admitted. "We try to be the best kept secret in the Union."

"Who in the Union do you work for?"

"Nobody. We've been waging our own war with the Abberants for several hundred years, all on our own."

"My father considered Swimmers a sign of good fortune."

Shaw spun around and walked backward. "I'm guessing by 'father' you mean somebody who raised you. Unless your actual father was a talking horse. I've seen some strange things mind you."

"Right. Yes." Burroughs sank his head to look at the ground.

"I was an orphan myself," Shaw turned forward again and pedaled to be shoulder to shoulder with the larger creature. "No parents. Hard life of getting into trouble, stealing just to eat, and sleeping under piers and bridges. All fun until I made the wrong guy mad and he tied a stone around my neck and threw me into the sea." The chatty fellow puckered his lips and glared fish-eyed into the distance for several moments. "So who raised you? A smuggling woodsman? Some breeder from New Kansas shipped in tainted wild horses illegally?"

"A retired army Sargent."

"So you were born in the west."

"No. I was born here on Caiphon"

"How?"

"Naturally ... Unnaturally."

"What? That's impossible," Shaw protested. "Aberration doesn't work like that. One parent has to be sick with the taint for a Wholeborn to come about. You said you were Wholeborn, right?"

"I am."

"You're sure?"

"I knew my mother."

"Who was a full horse? I'm sorry is this rude? I think what I'm asking is a little rude. It's typically an insult to call somebody's mother an animal of some sort."

Burroughs' brows furrowed. "Never thought of it that way. I suppose the truth can be offensive. In any case, I was born from a mare Andreas Viklund bought twenty three years ago."

"Sargent Vick?" Shaw inhaled sharply and exhaled a long Ohhhhhhh. "If that's how it is, then it's a real pleasure to be traveling with you. Vick is a big name even in the Ministry. We wanted him to join for such a long time, but he just would not die."

Burroughs shot the smooth faced talker a distraught look.

Shaw held up his hands defensively. "Not as if we're ghouls. The rules are we do not interfere with people's lives, and we only initiate people who've lost their lives; give them a second life after the first one is over. Borrow not steal."

"So Swimmers are actually dead people."

"Formerly deceased and repurposed, we like to say."

"Human beings."

"Yes."

"And what would that mean for me, since your Ministry's purpose is to fight Abberants?"

"I don't know Burroughs, but I'm thinking somebody in the Ministry planned this out. I'm thinking somebody high up. Whatever it is, this ordeal is big enough to have hounds nipping at our heels. No easy feat considering how we rule the seas. Those dogs should not have been able to shove off the Western Continent, let alone make it this far."

The walking pack beast rubbed his chin with fingers bigger than most thumbs. "I wish to be left alone. I will follow you to the mountains."

"Thanks big guy."

"Saving your life was a mistake."

# Impulse Spender

Two major roadways crossed Caiphon in its history; the Northern Road which connected Lagoona in the south to Leal's Harbor in the north and Lateral Way from the Baron's seat in Round Chamber in the east crossing the mountains to Maven in the west. Both Northern Road and Lateral Way criss-crossed slightly off of the center of Caiphon. In the crucial junction sprang the town of Crossroads.

The Crossroads had known better days. Empty, dilapidated buildings littered the shriveling village. The roads which fed the town had long since fallen to disrepair. Signs rusted on their posts. Vacant houses faced the streets with broken windows and flaking paint.

Motorized boats rendered traveling the old roads to reach the outer towns obsolete. Before long, the only industry remaining in Crossroads was the sale of grain from nearby farms. Even those farms struggled to compete with the mechanized crop productions in New Kansas.

Crossroads reflected the memory of exodus times, when the last pieces of humanity escaping the tilt fled the Abberant menace. In those old days much of the advanced technology was lost and had to be rediscovered, reinvented in some cases. Makeshift factories sprouted up all over the town, their roofs and smoke pipes jutting in many directions. Unsalvagable rusted heaps sat in the open. Red granules caked every inch of the ancient machines, sometimes floating away when a stiff breeze blew down from the north.

A massive vacant lot made up where the roads met. What once was the largest market square to be seen for all of Caiphon laid empty with stretches of weeds and dirt growing unchecked. Children and small dogs ran around the lot playing tag and throwing colored balls.

From the southern edge of the lot emerged an odd fellow shouldering a comically large backpack. The top of the bag lurched nearly two feet over his head, and the shoulder straps were actually wider than his shoulders. Regardless, he crabbed through the vacant field in a wide stance to the snickering delight of the children. The opening flap at the top of the bag lulled about like the jaws of some benign, toothless monster.

At the other end of the lot sat the last open store in Crossroads, The Fickle Finger. The brick and mortar building was the best kept in all the town. A sign of a finger pointing upward was nailed to the roof. The colors of the shop had not faded or chipped, unlike the neighbors. Also the front porch was swept clean.

Shaw eclipsed the store window of the Fickle Finger store for a few seconds, casting a long, moving shadow inside. Then the door opened and the young man entered, dragging a large clattering bag. He left it at the entrance.

"Welcome," spoke an old man behind a warped wooden counter. The shopkeep's face was lined and rugged with age. White hair accented the small shape of his skull by the way it was tied behind his head. His beard was trimmed and neat, his apron clean and straight.

"Hello, sir." Shaw almost waved.

The clerk nodded at the enormous pack leaning on the door sill. "Did you make that yourself young 'un?"

"No I am borrowing it from a friend." Shaw shuffled through the lanes of shelves scooping up jars and items as he went. He held out a piece of his robe to improvise a basket. Underneath his clothing the army issue boots on his feet became clearly visible.

"You mean to buy all that?"

"Yes," the shopper nodded eagerly and began unloading onto the store counter. "Start checking everything. I need a couple more runs." After finishing putting everything down, one of Shaw's hands disappeared into his baggy garment and began ferreting around. He looked up at the piered beams in the ceiling as the shop keep gave him an uncomfortable stare. "There," the odd fellow chirped, and slapped down a stack of notes beside his purchase.

The old man thumbed the side of the paper stack. His brows almost jumped high enough to reach his receded hair line. "Good grief, son. Where did you get all this?"

Shaw thought for a second. "Uhm." he pursed his lips, looked at the floor boards then back. "Donations."

The clerk squinted the shopper an incredulous look for several awkward moments.

"Yes," Shaw continued. "I am a clergyman on a pilgrimage into the mountains."

"Which Church?"

"Galilee."

The keep grunted. "I see. Well. I hope you have a nice trip. Watch your step out there. If you don't mind, tell your other monk friends about this place."

Half an hour later Shaw emerged from the shop grunting and heaving the full- loaded pack. The canvas sides scraped against the door frame as he pulled free and stumbled into the street. He tried lifting it. He tried wrapping his arms around in a hug. He tried tugging the mass upright with the pull straps, but the thing easily

82

weighed twice as much as him. So with great effort he dragged his belongings out of town. Citizens took the time to stop and stare, but nobody came to help.

Burroughs watched as Shaw tugged the pack past the last building and began grating it along the gravel path toward the west. The frail human's face glistened with perspiration and glowed red. He croaked and groaned under the weight.

Rather than expose himself to potential onlookers, Burroughs sat low in the tall grass as he'd been commanded. The crisp, cool winter wind from the north chilled the air to a brisk temperature. Earthy scents of the field stirred all around. He idly turned over the staff given to him in the forest, touching the bark-like texture on the ends. The pattern shrank away to a smooth surface a few inches closer to the center on either side. Thoughts of plants came to mind, how such a design matched something he'd seen in before. He could not recall the familiar texture, however. Perhaps it was only an interesting variation on oak bark.

At last the young fool pulled up beside his friend. "Oh wow, " Shaw gasped for breath. "I should have thought this through. You carry round a caravan on your back Burroughs." His jellied legs slid out from under him and he sat against the enormous canvas burrito.

Burroughs reached over and prodded the pack with the staff. "You loaded it too much. There is enough food for probably a month between us."

"Yes. Well. You did save my life. Consider it a gift."

Burroughs eyed the offering. The contents of his gear were half ruined by the creek bottom transit. The provisions looked to be fully restored and more. "Thank you."

Shaw nodded. Coughs and wheezes shook his frail frame as he tried to catch his second wind.

"Do you recognize this. What can you tell me about

it?"

Shaw watched Burroughs hold out the black staff. "That's the stick you've been carrying around. Why? Should I recognize it. Did Vick give it to you? Did you make it yourself?" He reached out a bleached white hand to take it.

Burroughs let go on his end. "Cherille took me someplace where this grew from an oak."

"One of the branches?"

"No, the trunk."

"So this pole is almost a whole tree?"

"I was hoping you would know something."

Shaw sighed and muttered, "Everybody thinks I have the answers." The staff fit better to Burroughs. In Shaw's hands the weapon was a good sized timber measuring wider than his palms. It weighed a great deal, but not enough to be crushing. "I can feel some sockets," he said as he ran some fingers over the smooth portions.

"Sockets?"

"Yes. It's some extra feelers that grow out of the skin when somebody joins the Ministry. They allow you to swim, talk to the host, and pass messages to other ministers through touch – handshakes mostly. We socket tools and weapons for added control and other things. My gun was socketed. Lets see what this thing does."

Shaw immediately began seizing. His legs curled up into his robe and his body shook fitfully. White, silvery tendrils flailed out of the staff ends; spinning, feeling, digging, reaching, twisting, twirling, curling, stretching. Each fiber moved in its own manner apart from the others and each measured roughly a foot in length. Shaw's face pulled tight to a rictus and his eyes showed evident pain and surprise. A sustained sucking hiss came from his toothy expression.

Burroughs wrenched the object free of the victim's forced grasp. A short crackling sound left both Shaw's palms as the staff peeled away. The smell of burning hair wafted out from somewhere on Shaw's person. Once the staff was freed, the tendrils vanished back into the ends.

Shaw blinked many times looking blankly out into the sky. Slowly, he came to terms with the fresh devastation visited upon him. He relaxed his posture and tried to breathe deeply.

"That was unique," he admitted. "It felt like a few hundred people dropped drinking straws in my head and everybody was very thirsty. You know ... I'm very thirsty." He crawled around to the pack opening and started rummaging through the goods.

"How did you do that?" The half man rolled the staff around in his palms. It appeared as it was before, bark-like ends and smooth center.

The magician seemed to ignore the question. His grasping hands produced a small plastic bottle from the gaping maw of the pack. The bottle let out a short puff as Shaw bit down and twisted on the cap with his teeth. As he chugged the beverage from its brightly packaged container with one hand, he held up his other hand palm out and fingers stretched straight. For a second it appeared he wanted to signal to stop, but bright red welts stood out on the bottoms of his fingers. Five points of irritation swelled up at the extremities of his palms just above the joints of each finger and the thumb.

The suction of Shaw's drinking crushed the bottle in its vacuum. Some of the shape returned as he pulled his lips free with a wet kissing sound. "Sockets." he said at last, then tore at the air with a rude belch.

In the distance a white, silent drift of snow fell down the jagged slopes of Mount Mortimer. The avalanche broke apart on its aerial descent until disappearing entirely. It flowed and scattered like smoke from a tobacco pipe, but climbing down instead of up. When the slide stopped, the needle of Mount Mortimer resumed its static looming over the scenery.

A red hue slowly darkened the sky as the sun sank

below the western mountains, pulling up the darkness of night up around the eastern edge of the horizon.

Burroughs gestured to Crossroads with his thumb. "Go back into town and rent a room. You'll be safer there."

"I can't. I spent everything stuffing your bag. Besides, I bought some interesting camping equipment I want to try out."

"Have you forgotten what is chasing us?"

Shaw blurted in a careless tone, "No."

Burroughs covered his eyes with one hand. "Let's move farther out in the field. At least so nobody will come to look at the camp fire."

"Fair enough," Shaw nodded. "Let's not be too long, yeah? I'm starving. How about you"

"I'm fine."

"Oh right. You ate the grass, didn't you? Must be nice to eat just about anything."

"You're misinformed." With a slight amount of strain, Burroughs heaved the pack off the ground. Items clattered about in the canvas cavern as the mass rotated perpendicular to the ground. The weight forced Burroughs into a slouch. He leaned on his staff like a walking stick. "We will camp just off the Lateral Way in an hour."

So they both walked the gravel path westward. A beautiful radial of colors bloomed behind the mountain destination as the sun set behind the ridges. Rings of color in the reversed order of the rainbow gradually shrank to smaller and smaller bands, chased by the expanding band of violet twilight. When, at last, the night stars came out Burroughs led the magician off the road and broke open the supplies.

The young fool must have spent a small fortune. There were jars of preserves, cans of meat and beans, a tinder box, a few wheels of cheese, bottled cola, a cast iron cooking set, soda crackers, empty canteens, half a dozen cured sausages, a fresh loaf of bread, a bale of rope wrapped together with twine, coffee, tea, tortillas, potatoes, a spade, and much more. Burroughs stopped digging half way through. Somewhere at the bottom sat all of the old things he'd packed.

To Shaw's displeasure, no wood could be found for a proper cook fire. It required a lengthy explanation as to why a grass fire was a bad idea. He, at last, gave in and ate a cold dinner of bread, cheese, and sausage. He ate until he had his fill then folded up the arms of his baggy robe into an improvised pillow and laid down with his arms inside the body of his outer garment.

Burroughs ate the same. He unrolled his hand stitched bedroll after packing back everything. "What is in the mountains," Burroughs asked as he stretched out at the opposite end of the camp site.

"I thought you'd never ask. Honestly was starting to think you don't care." Shaw sat up. "There is a important host in the Ministry called Maurius. I was sent out to find him. The Ministry hasn't heard from him in two weeks."

"Could he be dead?"

"No. No. Hosts don't die. They're already hundreds of years old as it is. Ministers like me can die, since we're flesh and blood. Host are ... They are something else, Burroughs. Something different."

"What are they?"

Shaw squinted up at the starry sky. He searched for the right words. "They're dead people; men, women, sometimes children. Swimmers like me are dead people too. I was brought back by a host. Hosts were brought back to the world by an angel, they tell me."

Burroughs said nothing. The void abyss between the stars kept his attention.

"And each one is four or five hundred years old. They remember things back before the Earth tilted, and even earlier when Abberants first showed up. Get them gabbing and they won't clam up."

"Do they understand why every Abberant turned and starting killing people?" From the corner of his eye

Burroughs caught the pensive expression on the human being's face.

"You want to know about The King of Beasts and The Mother? You must have heard all this before."

"I have. Is it any different with you?"

"The story is the same. A pretty lady sits on seven hills. She gives birth to The King of Beasts with six heads – his heads. She gets only one head. Anyway. On his six heads are five crowns. His servants are beasts who walk as men. Under his reign of terror the world will fall under darkness."

Burroughs sighed. "I see."

Shaw began tracing constellations out of the stars. "Sorry. We are the Ministry. Prophecy is popular with us," he said as it were an explanation, not an excuse.

The Abberant turned over in his bed roll. He no longer felt like talking.

Shaw, on the other hand, kept talking. "When the king sucks out your soul and forces you to kill me. I won't hold it against you Burroughs."

"Thanks ... Goodnight."

"And if you get the chance, tell him he can shove six thorns up his six bun-"

"I will. Good night Shaw."

# *Short Term Problems for the Long Term*

Morning dawned as the red sun rose above Lateral Way and lifted into the sky. The night chilled the grassland, leaving the ground sopping wet with dew. Burroughs woke up rested. He pulled his bedroll over his face during the night and escaped most of the cold. Shaw woke earlier, and busied himself wringing his white drape dry.

Out of his robe, Shaw wore the fatigues of an army private; gray pants and shirt with dappled pattern and solid black boots. He grumbled several angry remarks about camp fires as he thrashed the garment around. One last twist and squeeze and he put it back on. Muck and grass stains soiled most of the back and part of the front – if the robe had a front.

"Breakfast," the magician spoke with conviction then reached in the pack for jam and the remnants of bread left over. The young person's eyes lit up with joy as he opened the fresh jar of preserved fruit to see the flat, smooth surface inside. Suddenly a pallid mask of horror became his face. "We don't have any spoons," he drawled with somber lips.

"Use your fingers and let's get moving. We've wasted enough time as it is." Burroughs tied the bedroll back to the side of the supply bag.

Shaw grimaced in revulsion of the idea. From inside his robe, he produced a large combat knife. The weapon, sadly, measured much wider than the lip of the jam jar. He only managed to get a little on his bread before he surrendered everything to the pack master.

Low clouds obscured the top of Mount Mortimer. The fluffy bodies drifted lazily south despite the whipping breeze coming down from the north. They walked the path west. A few country roads branched off Lateral Way. Faded and worn signposts marked the junctions. A few names could be made out, and only because of a fresh application of paint. Besides the signs, Lateral Way was barren. Not a single farmhouse stood visible from the road, and no other travelers came from behind or up the road.

Gradually, the gravel road thinned out into a path of hard packed dirt.

"Do you see anything?" the pack mule creature almost whispered in his low voice.

"What?" Shaw turned around.

"Can you see anything coming from behind."

The human took a quick look past his friend. "Nothing."

They kept moving as a growing sense of unease sank in Burroughs' mind. He strained to hear over the incessant clatter coming from inside the pack. Disturbing noises broke the monotony of the blowing wind and hissing grass. The sounds were so short and so small, perhaps they weren't there at all. Some animal may have been snaking through the grass, shaking the reeds just barely out of rhythm from the others. A few baritone hoots and grunts seemed to come just behind a small nearby hillock, but nothing crested the rise to show itself.

"Take another good look."

Shaw walked behind Burroughs and returned. "A few dug up holes, but I don't see anything."

Burroughs immediately noticed. Holes had sprang up everywhere, along the side of the road and in a few hillsides. There were small animal burrows, scads of them, all roughly the width of a normal fist spread out here and there.

"Watch your step. A few are in the road. What do you think. Moles? Mice? Snakes?"

"Prairie dogs."

They walked farther along. Gradually the land became more porous.

"And not a single thing around to eat them. Look at them they're taking over." Shaw pointed at a hill ventilated with scores of holes.

"Feral cats run out here," Burroughs shrugged causing the giant pack to lurch. "But hardly anything can save crops from destruction. Lagoona worries the prairie dogs will one day plague the southern farmlands."

"I wonder what the Baron of New Kansas would do here," Shaw bit his thumb. "Poison. Most likely."

Ahead, the road sloped downward into a low flat plain. Unlike the higher grasslands, the lower plain sat slate flat. Purple and sickly green rock formations studded the surface in no particular order, dried sea coral. The alien stones jutted out of the green, placid skin of the plain like ticks feeding on the back of a shaggy animal.

Shaw pointed questioningly at a long stretch of rotting wood sitting directly on top of the path through. "Is that a bridge?"

"Was."

Jagged abutments, cracked and splintered at the tops, stood out of the ruin. Rotted and warped lumber littered the bottom around the shattered wooden columns. At the end of the wreck a red dirt road was barely visible.

"Why build a bridge?"

Burroughs pointed at the lowland. "The lake used to be here, but it moved north a hundred years ago."

Shaw slowly tilted his head upward, breathing a believing "Ahhhh."

Suddenly a tumult of wild barking rose out of the east. Howls mixed with jeering yaps in raucous, disjointed chatter.

Both travelers turned around. Several dark wisps of smoke lifted out of the earth where Crossroads once rested. No bodies appeared to be charging down the hills but the noise came menacingly close. Canid or no, both of them ran as fast as their legs could carry until the barking fell away behind.

"Stay on the north side," Burroughs half shouted through a frantic exhale.

"What?"

"Keep to the north side of the bridge and let the wind blow our scent into it."

"You seriously think that will throw them off?"

"No. Maybe it will slow them down."

"Sure until they look up at us."

"Just run it," Burroughs bellowed in anger. His hoof sank into a prairie dog hole. He fell forward onto the staff. In a split second the full weight of the fully-laden beast fell toward the earth. The white tendrils deep inside the weapon lashed out. The hand hold became much more firm as the fibers rooted firmly into the ground. Burroughs took the brief save with noticeable surprise. He pulled both his foot and the staff from their respective holes easily and continued running. The roots disappeared with a puff of dirt as fast as they had appeared.

Shaw kept running without turning around to notice. His lead on the race hardly increased at all.

To their dismay, the distant baying of the hounds dogged them the entire way across the empty lake bed. Shaw scaled the hill where the ruined bridge once joined the land. He collapsed to his knees, panting and wheezing. "Wait. I can't . Stop. Burroughs. Give me a minute."

On the opposite shore appeared a pack of small dogs and red wolves. Riotous yipping marked their arrival. The dogs scratched, sniffed the ground. They dug about for varmints.

Shaw sighed in relief. "Ha, see? We got ourselves worked up over that." He relaxed his posture and tried to catch his second wind.

The pack of wild hunters fossiked about on the opposite bank. They snarled. A few bit at each other. All snuffled the soil and occasionally dug up an unlucky prairie dog. One of the wolves pushed its front paws on the ground with enough force to tilt upright, but instead of falling back down it held vertical. The standing animal rolled back its shoulders to a broader position. The creature spoke to a few members of the pack, and soon five more flipped upwards and walked as people.

"Never mind we're in trouble," Shaw coughed. "Do you think you can fend off that many little Canid?"

The hunting Abberants belted out a fierce, combined howl and soon the hills came alive with replies. In surprise, the unaltered dogs in the pack ran off.

"No," Burroughs grimaced. "Get up. We need to keep running."

Shaw coughed, but he did not budge. "Go on ahead. Burroughs. You've helped enough."

"What?"

"Take everything and get out of here. We can't outrun fleet Canid. If you're lucky, they'll leave you alone after chopping my head off."

In the lake bed, the six pursuers had folded their stature back down and ran on all four limbs beside the broken bridge. Dozens of Canid poured over the distant hills at odd intervals, running upright. The packs merged larger and larger until they formed a stampeding mob. Their number swelled into the shallow basin

"Leave me. Just go." Shaw waved Burroughs away.

The horse-man did not move. "You will die."

"I've died a few times already. I'm getting good at it. Now go."

Burroughs stood in place as the inhuman army formed up on the opposite shore. The fleet stood a safe distance away in the low lands. They call the others to rush forward. So the armies all piled in.

"Go on. You don't belong here."

No response and no movement. Not even hesitation.

A spark flickered out of the approaching crowd. Clicking noises popped out from places near the magician and Burroughs, like tapping on the bottom of a full bottle with a single knuckle. Three taps and one sinister hiss.

Burroughs groaned a throaty, inhuman cry. The staff fell over and Burroughs soon with it. Contents inside the backpack crashed about as the horse hit the ground. His arm wrapped his abdomen. From the region lifted a small curl of smoke and the stench of burning hair. Burroughs' all-too-human teeth clenched in pain as he rolled over on the ground.

Shaw lost his composure. "No! Damn it. I told you to run."

A swarming clamor of beast men shambled through the lake bed. All who answered the call of the hunt filled the basin and their numbers were close to one hundred, possibly more. Shaw could almost see their eyes, and they all trained on him. At a guess, all of the pack would climb the opposite bank and shred their quarry to pieces in minutes.

For his final moments, Shaw pried the backpack off Burroughs and propped his friend against it.

"Do you know what stinks about dying? The nagging thought I could've done more. Even if I come back, I'm reminded of all the missed opportunity I left behind. Sometimes it's so much I wish I'd not come back at all."

The ground trembled, cutting Shaw's confession short. From the north raced a low, tumbling cloud of white. It devoured ground in a ravenous charge over the land. The rush appeared more dense on approach, a churning roil of liquid. It was a deluge of immense proportion, nearly taller than the lake bed itself. By some miracle Lake Caiphon returned to its former resting place.

For the first time in his life Burroughs heard a

Canid scream. Hysterical yodeling best described the act, and though the description does it no justice, it was the purest expression of terror and despair ever heard. It hurt to listen.

The unstoppable wall of water swallowed the entire throng, silencing them both instantly and cruelly. What remained of the old bridge dissolved under the wash as the waves plowed through. Burroughs watched the whole spectacle through watery eyes. Shaw stood dumbstruck.

Less than a minute later, the flow reversed, taking chunks of lumber with it as flotsam. The water level sank lower and lower until the flood subsided altogether. Every blade of grass pointed north and glistened with moisture. Hardly any piece of the bridge remained save for the thick abutments driven into the ground and sizable chunks of those fell were missing. Not a single Canid body littered the scene.

"Maurius," Shaw murmured.

A fresh jolt of pain wracked Burroughs. The hot welt throbbed on his side.

"They shot you with my own glass revolver, the bastards. Move your hands." Shaw curled the fingers of his right hand in front of his face. Twirls of a mysterious, sweet-smelling mist substantiated in his open palm. "I said move your hands."

The magician shoved his hand past Burroughs' defending arms and slapped down on the dark welt. The ruined flesh crackled under the pressure. Burroughs tried to roll away, but Shaw shuffled to stay on the wound. Instantly, Burroughs' body chilled as if he'd stepped out of his old home on the coldest day in winter.

Shaw pulled himself back, exhausted. "Not as good as the real thing," he lamented. "Can you move?"

Burroughs tried pulling one of his hooves under himself, but the hot pain rocketed back. He tried several times to stand to no avail. The jarring pain at the base of his spine halted any movement from where he sat.

"My patch won't last. You'll be as bad as before in a few hours. There has to be somebody out here. Stay still. I'm going to get help."

With that, the young fellow bolted west down the path. He kicked at the inside of his robe as he ran. Burroughs nursed his mortal injury as the pain slowly drove him to delirium.

## Skull and Crossbones

Alone, Burroughs sat dying in an open field.

Shaw's absence started hours ago, and the ruination in Burroughs' side almost finished creeping back. There was a hot nail. The wound felt like a long, red-hot pin attaching him to his bag. Try as he might, he could not move off the pin. Sweat soaked his clothes. He heart beat frantically. Soon, he knew, he would feel sleepy and it would all be over.

His dying thoughts bounced between Shaw and Joseph Portram. The way he denied the pleas from the father of Carver and Lana, the same plea from Shaw, echoed in his fevered mind. Both times he stood still, held his ground until disaster met him. Defiant? Stubborn? Indecisive? He struggled to remember, but he only recalled what happened; not what he thought. It was the same thought, Burroughs knew that much. The same thought led him to hesitate, kept him in place and blinded him to reality; a dangerous fantasy without a name.

A huge coal scar protruded out from the Abberant's burned shirt. The charred flesh reeked. Blood and salty fluid weeped out on occasion, further staining Burroughs' brown shirt and breeches. He couldn't eat anything. Shortly after Shaw wandered off, he had some food. After the pain came back, however, his stomach felt as dry and tough as a sailing knot.

Eventually Shaw would wander back after finding no one for miles. He would return to Burroughs' corpse, and all because Burroughs would not run away; refused to run away.

Though his heavy heart beat throbbed in his ears, Burroughs began hearing another thumping. The rhythm kept steady, but did not keep proper pace with his failing organs. The thumping grew louder. Something approached from behind.

"Hello?" shouted a feminine voice from the emptied lake bed.

With a painfully effort, Burroughs looked over his shoulder.

Tiptoeing up the bank emerged a peculiar creature. The slight figure wore a coat in a bright floral pattern and loose pants cut a few inches below the knees, which weren't very long at all. Her shins measured longer then her thighs, and her feet nearly matched the length of her long shins. A springy step bounced the girl about while walking. The tips of her feet ended in split hooves. Dew pads ended her ankles, and brown fur covered any exposed skin.

"It's a pony," Burroughs heard the visitor whisper excitedly.

Rather than answering, Burroughs turned his head around and leaned back into his pack. It had to be the fever.

"Hello? Anybody out here."

"Just me," Burroughs coughed.

The figure whispered again. "Magical talking pony."

"And I'm not magical!"

Silenced, the visitor rushed in to get a better look.

"Oh my," she gasped as her strange locomotion brought her before the injured aberration.

Burroughs looked up.

Aberration in deer rarely happened, but was not unheard of. The Mandross Imperative wrote off deer as a threat just from their rarity. If who stood before Burroughs was a wholeborn like him, she had beaten tremendous odds. First her biological mother must contract a disease which never appeared in Caiphon in its entire history. The mother had to possess the endurance to grow an Abberant child, which many did not. Once born, Abberant children faced the daily threat of being gored to death by courting males or even their own fathers. These reasons cast serious doubt on any deer Abberant reaching adulthood.

There she stood, regardless. The large ears on top of her head trained forward. Her large eyes half bulged from her sleek, hornless skull. The cleft lips on her mouth below the black triangular nose split into an ecstatic grin – bordering on insane euphoria.

Burroughs gave back a weary expression.

"Yee!" the creature screamed in joy. Her ponderous shins bent forward, planting her knees to the ground. She grasped Burroughs' shoulders with four digit hands and shook savagely.

Burroughs' let out a short grunt, winced, and fell over in intense pain.

"Oh my goodness. I'm sorry. What's the matter?" The visitor leaned in again. She felt about the head and the neck of the victim. "You burned yourself bad. Fever. High pulse." Her thumb ran down Burroughs' eye, spreading it open. "I see. Open up." She pried at his mouth with both hands.

Burroughs pushed the hands away and sat up. He felt the ichors in his guts run as he turned upright. His vitals gurgled.

"Oh no. How long have you been hemorrhaging?" the stranger asked.

"I don't know."

"What have I got," she asked herself. The scaffold legs folded out, raising her into the air again. She rummaged about in a satchel she'd hidden behind her back. Lanky arms and thin fingers dove into the open flap of the bag over and over. Her head bobbed about as she mouthed gibberish.

Burroughs rolled his head back. "What are you doing?"

"Getting you ready to move. Watch my hand." She curled the last two digits down on her hand and pointed at the sky with her index finger. The deer Abberant traced a few circles in the air to make sure Burroughs' eyes followed. She then pointed as high as could reach into the clouds.

Burroughs kept his eyes on the gesture. He squinted to see the pointing finger at its zenith. A few short moments of confusion passed by. Then a wet, stinging splash hit Burroughs' wound. The icy mixture soaked in, causing a fresh electric pain in the abdomen. Burroughs let out a yelp of surprise.

The girl put away an empty vial into her bag. "Okay. Easy enough. I need some cognitive tests before I feed you any medicine. Who is the baron of this island?"

"Baron Asher."

"Okay. How many fingers am I holding up?"

"Two."

"And now?"

"Seven."

"What is my name?"

"I don't know."

"Oh dear. You've suffered a concussion and can't remember your name!" The deer cupped a hand to her face.

The patient sighed. "My name is Burroughs. You were asking me your name."

"It's Viday. Nice to meet you. Eat this and wash it down with this." She broke off a length of a small wafer and held it out with one hand. In the other hand, Viday held a vial of dark fluid.

Burroughs took the small spongy tablet. The bitter,

oily morsel coated his mouth as he chewed and swallowed. The liquid in the vial tasted sweet and syrupy. When Burroughs looked up to hand back the empty bottle, Viday stared back in dismay.

"What?" Burroughs asked.

"You chewed the medicine."

"Is that bad?"

Viday shook her head, making her ears flap. "No. It's just gross. The treacle I handed you was supposed to help you swallow it because it tastes nasty. But, oh, never mind now." She socked away the vial. "I'm taking you to my house south of here. We've got stronger medicine there and a clinic of sorts."

Burroughs looked south. In the far distance stood a copse of trees, barely distinguishable from the green hills around. A passing traveler would hardly notice the darker green shade.

"Come on. Get up." Viday grabbed under Burroughs' shoulder with both arms. She hoisted both of them upward by using the force of her legs.

The pain had left, but the bubbling sensation in his innards implied something very wrong still threatened his life. Burroughs took the staff to lean on. Viday slung an arm over her shoulder and led him away from the path. They both left the pack behind.

Every step was a mile to itself. Swinging one foot before the other proved a risky prospect, as Burroughs could not feel his legs. He saw them working. He made them move, but the limbs became almost detached; alien. More than once his balance faltered onto Viday or the staff. The jelly of his organs sloshed around alarmingly. He feared he was killing himself just by moving.

All the same, he felt so light. No pressure pushed against his legs as he walked, giving the feeling of floating. His body became a marionette he controlled, but could not feel. What may happen if he lost hold of the strings?

The drug induced stumble carried on for its own

eternity.

"Come on. Giddy up. Almost there. You and I aren't too different from people. My mom should patch you up."

"Everything," Burroughs muttered.

"What?"

"Everything is blurring."

The edges of the small grove ahead, the grass underneath, and all the surrounding scenery became less distinct. Color ran together until two halves remained; green at the bottom, bright blue on top. Even those hues mixed until nothing but white remained, and the edges of his vision shrank slowly.

Then nothing became everything. There was no sound, no light, no sensation, no thought.

We have doomed ourselves to repeat our past failures. We've tried changing the playing field, bending the rules, and adding unpredictable elements to change the outcome. In the end, the only factor mattering was ourselves, which we refused to acknowledge or alter. We could have, but we fooled ourselves into believing our problems occurred by themselves; that it was not our fault. Therefore our suffering continues yet again.

A heavy weight sat on Burroughs' chest, shortening his breath. He couldn't move or open his eyes to see what it was. There came the sudden feeling of being watched. Whatever leered at him stood nearby, but he couldn't do anything.

A human being is not strictly flesh and blood. The physical doesn't matter at all.

"He's waking up."

"Another injection. He's lost too much skin. Stitching him up will last another hour."

It sat on his chest, choking out his breath.

Burroughs flew into a panic. He struggled to break whatever witchcraft sealed his eyes and deadened his whole body.

> Plant your feet Burroughs. If you are going to put your hands to anything, it's all moot if you can't stand straight.

It was no use. Whatever sat on his chest paralyzed the entire body.

> Fairness is a thing we decide for ourselves as a majority. If you aren't part of the majority, don't expect to be treated as an exception.
>
> Get up. Don't ever let them see you weak. Otherwise, they will never let up. Get up.

"Why is he moving? Didn't you sedate him?"
"I did! He must be hallucinating."
"You two. Hold him down until I'm done."

> *Get up.*

"Hold him down."
"We're trying."

> Let them know you have a right to live. If anybody tries to take that away from you, you show them you're just as nasty as they are. If they want it so bad, then show them the price of their murdering ways. Get up.

"Hurry up. I don't know what's going on, but he's really angry about it."
"Keep him down or he'll bust his stitches."
"He's almost foaming at the mouth up here. Oh cats-"
Burroughs swept away the two nuisances clinging to his arms and legs. In a fit, he fell off the surgical table.

His hooves hit the ground and no sooner he stood up. A blind rage filled his eyes. Screams of primal fury rattled the frames along the walls. Gulps of air filled his lungs and bellowed out, over and over again, until his head spun.

"Sit back down before you hurt yourself."

The nightmare ended.

"Hey fella," a short old woman stood under Burroughs. In her withered fingers she held a suture string running directly to the wound. She gave a few tugs. "I said sit down."

The patient climbed back onto the sturdy wooden table in the center of the room. The gray haired woman pushed her thick glasses back up her nose. She continued stitching without requesting any further pain killers.

Shaw lifted up from the brick floor where he'd been thrown. Across the room, Viday pushed herself against a wall to get back on her feet. Both of them appeared shaken up. They exchanged nervous expressions and kept a safe distance from the operating table.

With a final pull, the surgeon finished sewing the square flap in the shaved region on Burroughs' stomach. She snipped the string. "All right tough guy. You're free. Don't lift anything heavy for a few days." The gray bun on the back of the old woman's head bounced up and down as she scratched the back of her head.

Burroughs felt along the smooth portions of his stomach with his rough hands. Hundreds of tiny pimples stood out in the cold air. His skin, he saw, gleamed white; brighter than Shaw's pallor.

"Show our guests to a room, dear. I will get some supper started."

104

## Someone Gives a Fork

The ball peen hammer rapped into the tiny anvil. Under continual pounding, each utensil bent to Lana's blows to reach company specifications. The strips of metal curved into a slight S before joining the pile.

Take the flat fork from the left. Beat it into the cast iron bump in the work bench. Drop curved fork into the bin on the right. Repeat until the clock tower strikes five thirty.

This was her lottery, her place in the world. She made forks and sometimes spoons. It had not even been two weeks since Baron Asher landed in Lagoona with a short pile of envelopes. The greasy dignitary looked her up and down. He took a look at Lana's form, shuffled the pile a little, and handed out her destiny.

At one time, Baron Asher worked artifice himself. He fixed heels as a cobbler, a shoe smith. Asher spoke politics even at a young age. Back then he wrote letters to Round Chamber often. He organized parties of similar interests to petition the former Baron Giles. Before long, Asher shrugged off his artifice job to join the Baron as a counselor. Eventually Giles passed the title to Asher.

So Baron Asher began his life making shoes, to

later step on people.

Lana remembered back to previous visits from the baron. She expected the speech about how the lottery was not a judgment but a first step, a gentle push into the working world. Where the lottery took you need not be where you end, just where you began. She heard it many times over with each visit of Baron Asher, but this time he didn't say it. She wasn't sure if the state of Caiphon had changed, or if Asher just got tired of hearing himself talk – not likely.

Indents in the small anvil prevented most errors in hammering. So Lana sat there like a stuffed doll while her arms recited the hammer mantra into the workbench. It read, "Wham wham wham wham wham. Clink."

This weekend she planned to return home. The port master scheduled Lagoona ferries every other week. Lana wondered what she would do when she got back, maybe bring a present from Maven for everybody. She worried about the small family farm and how things were going now that the help comprised of Carver and her father. Burroughs came to mind and if Tracy Walsh still skulked about the vineyard. What would happen if Tracy caught sight of Burroughs? What a good bunch of help she would be hammering flatware hundreds of miles away.

"Wham wham wham wham wham. Clink."

Abandoning lots happened commonly among the young folk of the Union. Lana imagined the job she'd filled once belonged to somebody else before they ran off back home or wherever they wanted once they earned enough for the fare. There were no second lots, however. So running off meant you'd be on your own from that point forward. If Lana kept hammering forks, she stood a chance of promotion or getting shipped out to the academy for more advanced training if the job no longer needed work; or some other sod came along to fill her position.

"Wham wham wham wham wham. Clink."

Stay or go, Lana wondered. Would she stay in the

artifice lot or go home to stay closer to friends and family? As a child she sometimes dreamed of becoming a famous engineer. She imagined fixing up a piece of forgotten technology from the old world and wowing all her friends. Helicopters were a fixation of hers as a kid. If she abandoned the fork bench, well, she would never be get the education.

"Wham wham wham wham wham. Clink."

There had to be an end to the hammering job. Lana curved thousands of forks over the past two weeks alone. The Portram house used twelve forks for a family of four, and Lana considered this quite normal. A case of forks in the factory came out at two hundred per box. From what she saw in the warehouse out back, there must have been more than one hundred boxes stockpiled; forks alone. Lana did not have any census numbers handy, but she felt confident in assuming the factory housed enough utensils for the whole Union twice over. Future generations would not go without implements to shovel food into their faces. So they might as well slow down manufacture a little, because the production size bordered on ridiculous, blind-sighted madness.

"Wham wham wham wham wham. Clink."

In the workshop it always sounded as if someone knocked at the door. Which is why nobody bothered with courtesy and just walked in. A portly, balding man waddled into the middle of the floor. He cupped both hands to his mouth and shouted over the clangor, "Lunch break." Lana and the three other benders put down their hammers and followed the jovial man outdoors.

Another perk to the job was the factory based itself in Maven, The Crescent City. There was always something new in the big city, and Mr. Stinner kept a meticulous vigil for any restaurants coming or going. No doubt Carver glowed green with jealousy at the sheer amount of city life Lana absorbed on a daily basis.

"Any    suggestions?"    Stinner    addressed    his

employees.

Kyle from the spoon bench spoke up, "That Acostan place."

"Aaaagh," the boss waved a dismissive hand. "Twice is enough. Their barbecue may be the best in the world, but let's not eat it every day."

"Saporna," Linda from knife serration nominated.

"Yes, fried rice and chicken." Agreed Vera from the press machine.

Stinner pointed a thumb at the new employee. "Chinese food Lana?"

"Potatoes."

The unique food kiosk, Spud Loader, was a dock-side attraction and a favorite for all the flatware workers. Spud Loader sold baked potatoes exclusively on the menu, nothing else. The choice a patron made was between five different types of toppings to go on the spud. It was fast, simple, and surprisingly delicious.

Lana peeled back the foil on her lunch when Stinner pointed across the harbor.

"There they go," their boss uttered gravely.

Ranks of fully armed soldiers piled out of the naval barracks into awaiting shuttle boats at the dock. Commanding officers shouted over one another. The fighting men scrambled into positions on the tiny boats and held onto what they could for balance. Once full, an officer boarded and the shuttle cut out of the harbor at full throttle.

"Why don't they use the carrier? It's right over there." Lana pointed at the giant gray tub close to fuss. Its deck guns pointed out to sea.

"Too slow, and they may need to beach on Caiphon at any moment."

"Why would they do that? Do they do this all the time?"

Linda stopped her piece of potato just short of her mouth. "You haven't heard. Have you?"

"What?"

"The eastern half is being invaded. Abberants ran right past Lagoona and leveled Crossroads flat. Union is pulling every available squad of the army to scour Caiphon and put the Abbies down."

Kyle chipped in. "Yeah. Lock up tight at night. There is no telling when, or if, they'll come over the mountains."

"They probably carried the taint with them here. Soon our forests and fields will burn in a purge, and a ban on cattle will go up for Caiphon. Just you watch."

"No more cows for Caiphon," Vera mumbled to herself along with a few curses.

"Torch the pine forest, huh? They'd have to. Can't follow the taint."

"What about Mercer or Wellborn? They still have cattle there."

Stinner pointed a company fork at Kyle. "This is different. This is an invasion. For all we know, a second batch could be on its way. The Abbies want the to finish the job and wipe us off the globe. There may not be time for cleanup."

"How long to wipe out the first invaders? There can't be that many."

"Don't know."

"What of Lagoona?" Lana broke into the meandering chatter.

Linda answered. "Ran right by it. Marshals found a few dead bodies along Northern Road, split right open for one of their blood rituals. It's all we know about where they came in before they wrecked Crossroads."

"Rituals? As in Heartbloods? Oh-" Kyle covered his face in his hands.

The lurid conversation of Caiphon's fate continued without Lana's input. The story seemed unreal, like outrageous gossip. Could it be Burroughs? She wondered. If so, what about the Portram family back home? Could Burroughs really turn into a servant of The King of Beasts?

Maybe he turned over fifteen years ago after the accident, the day he stopped smiling.

It was hard to tell with Burroughs. Lana knew him all her life. He was always so quiet, detached, reserved. Perhaps he simply laid waiting all these years, to finally go on his murderous frenzy. Lana shook her head at the thought, surely not. He would never commit such gruesome acts, but no other creature she knew could have – Abberant blood rituals. Who else, what else, might have? Lana secretly wished one of the hunts actually landed on Caiphon rather than know her friend lost all sanity.

"Lana, you have family from Lagoona, don't you?" came the unavoidable question.

"Yes. I ride a shuttle to see them this weekend."

"Don't ride it. Safest stay here"

Linda slapped Kyle's shoulder. "Her family Kyle! She must be worried sick!"

A significant drift of snow dusted off the cap of Mount Mortimer. The tumble broke apart in the northern wind until it simply disappeared in the middle of falling. Mortimer loomed much closer to the crescent city than to the other side of Caiphon.

The red spire cast a shadow over the center of the great city every morning. Watching the sun climb up the eastern face and conquer Mortimer by about ten o'clock attracted many tourists to the area. They filled the central park on a daily basis. They oohed and aahed. Their children ran about unattended as the parents planted themselves in transfixed wonder. From so close, a spectator could see the blue-black flecks on the mountains surface revealing the solid iron core of Mortimer. For many Mortimer embodied the wonders on the new world.

"I should move the business to The Strand," Stinner rubbed one of his chins. "May be too late now. We'll just have to see."

"Things will be fine once the military steps in. We can hold out," Vera lobbed her empty potato skin at a nearby receptacle. The foil and contents sank into the awaiting hole without a sound.

In the short two weeks she'd been gone, Lana's home may have turned upside down. Everybody, even Burroughs, may be fine. She didn't know. She needed to know. She wanted to know right now, but there was no way. Caiphon never ran telecom system like the Strand, and all taxi services ran on the water rather than land. The weekend ferry would be the soonest she could get out.

"Will you be fine Lana? You hardly touched your lunch."

"Oh. Yes. I'll be okay."

# Where the Red Burn Grows

Two days of recovery passed by in the secluded coppice of alders and oaks. The painkillers wore off shortly after Burroughs witnessed the end of his surgery, the last few stitches. It was a small wonder he didn't kill himself during his earlier stunt, because the suture area stretched so tight and felt so tender he could barely move without the fear of spilling open. He spent two days looking outside a window from bed. The meals came to his room, and company was kept to a minimum.

Missus Harjones stymied her daughter's eagerness to visit Burroughs. The doctor insisted Burroughs needed rest. Therefore the patient was not to be disturbed. This order, however, did not stop the frequent glances through the door way.

After two days the pain of moving did not sting as badly. Burroughs toured the rooms.

The home was a surprisingly large cottage. From the outside the building appeared small and quaint. The floors in each room were cobbled stone and sometimes hard wood. Wainscoting paneled every wooden wall and the roofing beams hung exposed overhead. A few occasional odd implements hung from those rafters.

Beth Harjones and her 'daughter' Viday were alchemists and physicians. Their sundries and tinctures filled one side of the house with odd contraptions and odors. Long tables stretched the length of a few rooms. On them rested lengths of glass tubing, alembics, clamps, baffles, dishes, gaffes, burners, mortars, pestles, coils, copper cables, scalpels, hemostats, magnifying glasses, trays, and many more objects which defy definition. A stringent alcohol smell effused from the rooms, covering one half of the house.

The entire other half was much more habitable, with living areas and guest rooms.

All manner of odd plants grew out and around the tiny forest in individual gardens. Burroughs dared not venture too far outside for fear of straining himself too much. A simple vegetable garden, soon to meet a frost, grew behind the house. Many odd and unfamiliar growths were planted along the house and near the edge of the clearing. A few other planted clearings appeared in the woods beyond, but Burroughs could not get a better look from the windows. The cottage was nearly self-sufficient, but whatever they could not grow themselves, Viday fetched.

When Viday ran an errand for an herb or a fungus, Mrs. Harjones sent her to the mountains, or the bogs of Filster, or the alpine forest to the east; distances greater than one hundred miles in some cases. To which these tasks lasted only a few hours instead of days. Each time the deer Abberant returned, she would walk through the door without appearing the slightest bit tired or winded.

Viday, Burroughs was told, deserved the credit for saving his life. By a great effort on her part, she dragged his unconscious body the rest of the way. During the operation, Viday kept Burroughs' heart beating while her mother performed surgery.

At some point in the ordeal, she stepped out to

retrieve the pack left behind in the road. There she met Shaw. From there the details told to Burroughs became conflicting, because the meeting between Shaw and Viday turned unfriendly. Even two days later, they glared at each other.

Viday caught a peek of Burroughs walking the corridors. She closed in using a reserved, tiptoed walk. "You're out of bed."

"I'm feeling much better today."

"You shouldn't be out yet."

"Sorry, I will go back."

"Wait. Stop. Not yet."

Burroughs turned his long head back around. "Yes?"

Viday looked down at the floor. "Um. Do you like it here?"

"Hard to say. I've been confined to bed all this time," Burroughs looked up at a hanging set of tongs by the fireplace. There were four of them, more than enough to turn the coals over during winter time.

"I hope you like it here."

"It's very nice. Thank you."

"Where are you from?"

Burroughs paused for a second. He almost forgot he was not talking to a normal person. "Lagoona."

Viday recognized the name. "Are there more of you in Lagoona?"

"No."

"Oh. Well. All right. What do you do? I see you carry lots of traveling gear."

"I'm looking for another place to live at the moment."

"You can stay here." The corners of the eager creature's mouth curved upward. Her eyes shone like a puppy's briefly.

"I don't think that's a good idea."

"Why not?"

"I need to be off with Shaw soon. We've intruded on your hospitality long enough as it is."

A small sneer pulled up one of Viday's cleft lips. "Right. Him. Your friend."

As if summoned by the mere mention of his name, Shaw walked in through the front door of the house. He smiled at the sight of Burroughs. "Feeling better big guy?"

The patient nodded his elongated head.

"That's great. Hey girlie. I need to ask you about something I found."

Viday rolled her eyes. "Not now. You're interrupting."

"Can it wait a minute? I really want to know something."

The deer aberration waved the annoyance away. "Go bother Mom with your problems."

Shaw flustered. "Fine. I will." He left the living area.

Burroughs watched the magician leave. "I see we have already exhausted our welcome."

"No. No. No. That's not it," Viday protested.

"We need to be on our way as soon as possible."

The smaller Abberant fidgeted in place while thinking around her dilemma.

Shaw poked his head around a corner. "Dinner's ready."

The food in the Harjones house was undeniably the biggest attraction. Generous portions with overwhelming flavor poured out of the tiny kitchen when the house clock reached six-thirty. Then at seven Mrs. Harjones excused herself from the table and returned with dessert. Each dish was a masterstroke, a monument to the culinary arts.

It had been so long since Burroughs ate like a human being. For years he subsisted on five types of melon and the leaves from each of their vines. From time to time he would eat out of a can the Portrams bought, but it all tasted bland. There was no compare to what Mrs. Harjones could muster, meals fit for royalty.

"How are your stitches fella? We should check them this afternoon," old lady Beth eyed Burroughs across the table.

The large beast man at the end of the table swallowed his roll. "Much better. Thank you."

"Good. Good." The elder nodded. "I see you're moving about. That's good. Soon you and your young friend can take off to the mountains, but I must ask you to stay one more day before attempting to lift that campsite you carried all this way." She, no doubt, implied the backpack.

"You need to wear a girdle around your waist," Viday leaned in. "I'm almost done. You are going to love it when you see it."

"Kissy kissy," Shaw whispered privately on his friend's shoulder. He immediately saw the reaction on Viday's face as she hid her face away in embarrassment. Shaw buttoned his mouth and kept chewing. He should have guessed.

Missus Harjones looked her flustered daughter up and down, confused. "Yes. Well. We don't wish to pry any further into your business. Just know you're always welcome here. It is a rare occasion when the visitors we get are the visitors we want to see, if you catch my meaning. Seeing you again would be a welcome sight."

Burroughs nodded once in assent. "Thank you."

This, he thought. If he could live this life, he would never leave. Shaw still needed his journey into the mountains to meet Maurius. Burroughs agreed to make the journey with him. With the Canid swept away in the flood, the going must be much easier. After helping the magician, he could come back, and maybe everything would finally work out.

A hearty knock on the front door interrupted the pleasant supper.

"Urgent Union business. We need to speak to the

head of this household immediately." barked a harsh voice.

Viday's chair tipped onto the floor as she sprang across the dining room in a single long bound and closed the curtains. Moments later, everyone else heard footsteps circling around the house. The knock came again.

"Missus Harjones we have a few questions for you."

The lady of the house stood up from the table. "Please excuse me." She took one look at her daughter and pointed down. Viday nodded.

In a crouching walk, Viday motioned the others to follow. She led the travelers to one of the small hallways and threw back a rug revealing a trap door to a lower cellar. They clambered down the steps as softly as they could. Once the whole group hid away, Missus Harjones returned the throw rug over the hatch.

The rap at the door struck the home much louder.

"Coming," shouted the old lady. "Hold your horses." She unlatched the front door, glad in the fact someone locked up the house for the afternoon. "Hello?"

Outside stood half a dozen army officials. They each wore gray dappled suits and carried gas guns with the bottles in and the actions ready. A few turned their backs and eyed the grove suspiciously, expecting something.

"Missus Harjones. My name is Lieutenant Coles from the twelfth battalion. I need to have a few words with you about the type of establishment you are running."

"Yes?"

"As you may know, martial law is declared for the entire island of Caiphon.'

"Whatever for?"

"Ma'am. The Abberant hunt infiltrated the island and sacked Crossroads. We have confirmed two hundred dead citizens, and the pack of monsters is still on the lose."

"Good heavens this is horrible."

"I agree. We are part of a scouting party tasked with finding the Abbies running free. We happened on your nice little hermitage here and found something we need you to explain. Are you familiar with mandrakes Missus Harjones?"

Another suited figure stepped forward holding what looked to be a small toddler. Long, leafy, blades stood out on the head of the child in a shocking pattern. The skin of the mandrake matched that of a tuber. The growth mimicked a human being in both shape and proportion with the exception of extra lengths of root growing from its fingers and toes. Legend said mandrakes wear a happy expression while underground, but pulling them up contorts the face to an enraged visage; and the plant in the soldier's hands did not appear happy in the slightest.

"You know, Missus Harjones," the officer continued. "Mandrakes are one of the more severe forms of aberration. These fellows exude the taint as part of their life cycle, and any animals nearby stand a high chance of spawning babies who would serve the king. We don't need that, do we?"

"Lieutenant. This must be some mistake."

Coles crossed his arms. "You are under arrest and we will now conduct a seizure of your property. Please stand aside."

"No!" the old woman shrieked.

"As a citizen, you will stand a fair trial at the Inath Seat. Gomez, hold her. Bert, Felix, come with me."

Heavy boots tramped about the house as the soldiers scoured the rooms. Twice the solid boards over the hiding place rumbled as one of them passed by unaware.

Viday heard it all, as they clattered about the dispensary. The invaders knocked over jars, cans, and glass in the pantry. Drawers and cupboards clapped all throughout the home, in the living area, in her room, in her mothers, in the guest room. Someone played with the chimney flue. All the while, Viday heard her mother breathing heavily outside; nearly sobbing.

"What do you make of it, lieutenant?"

"Big stick. Big backpack. Big guy."

All three soldiers made for the front door of the house. "Where are they Missus Harjones?"

"Who? I am a lonely old woman, living alone."

"There are four places set at your table, Missus Harjones. I don't doubt you have eccentric hobbies, but I seriously doubt a little old lady could put away so much casserole."

"Nobody else lives in my house," Beth replied firmly.

The lieutenant paced the yard. He craned his head to maintain eye contact with the old lady as he moved back and forth. "You are putting me in a pinch ma'am. I want to do this like a marshal or a town militiaman – get you arrested and tried – but times have changed. We're in war, Missus Harjones. We have Abbies prowling about. Hundreds died a few days ago, and hundreds of thousands are terrified."

From his vest, the commander produced a short knife. "Do you know what is odd about all this? The army is flooding this island for the past few days. Entire regiments arrive daily. We barricade the towns and run scouts. My guys are the first out here. We followed the tracks out of Crossroads, and the tracks just dissapear for some reason. Five miles north of here, the Abbies just jump up and forget to hit the ground, gone. Odd, yes? Then we find you, some manner of chemist growing the dread king's carrots and hiding strangers in your house."

The interrogator stopped and ran a thumb along his blade. "Again, this is martial law. The army calls the shots until the situation is settled. I want to run this little show like a marshal, but if you refuse to cooperate, I may need to improvise."

Harjones bored a stare into the eyes of Lieutenant Coles. "No one else lives in this house. You are wasting your time."

"Obviously," the team captain put his knife away.

"You are not what we came for and we can't be bothered to haul you around as a prisoner at this moment. Know this, Missus Harjones. I must report your little project, regardless. You and your shy posse will stand in front of a judge. Given the current sentiment going around, you might find your necks tied to a sling."

Private Gomez let go of Beth Harjones's wrists and walked away to join his comrades.

"One last thing before we leave," Coles leveled a finger at the open door. "You look to be a veterinarian. You should consider putting some pets down. No need for them to have them suffer needlessly, yes?"

The old woman stood statue still.

"Make good use of the time you have left, ma'am. Someone will be along."

With that, the company filed down the gravel road out of the copse.

## Potato Salad and Melancholy

"You moron! You ruined everything!" Viday plowed into Shaw. Both of them fell to the ground from the forceful tackle. From there Viday pinned Shaw to the ground and hailed punches on his face.

"Help! Stop! I'm sorry okay?" The young magician held out his hands to block as many of the blows as he could.

Viday blew a low, bestial snort. Her ears flopped about as she shook her head and set her shoulders. She grabbed Shaw's collar through his robe and scooped him off the floor to hold her victim vertical. Thunder rumbled through the house as the deer Abberant slammed the white clad fellow into the far wall. Cupboards swung open from the quake. Framed pictures clattered to the ground, their glass shattering to join the debris left by the soldiers. A second great crash followed seconds later as an armoire on the opposite side of the wall fell to the ground. Chips of broken wood scattered everywhere.

"Burroughs help," Shaw called out in a hoarse groan.

The other Abberant in the room intervened. Burroughs grappled Viday's shoulders to slowly pull her away, but Viday would have none of it. In a few jabs of her elbow, she viscously ribbed Burroughs close to his surgical stitches. Gasping, Burroughs let go and shrank away. He pulled up his shirt to check if any sutures popped open.

For a brief instant, Viday showed fearful remorse. She quickly turned round to Shaw, more enraged than ever.

"Viday Persephone Harjones. You put that young man down. This is not how I taught you to behave." A steely voice froze the entire bedlam.

"Mom," Viday pleaded in a small, tamed tone. "It's his fault. He dug out the mandrakes."

"Will you gentlemen please excuse me and my daughter," Missus Harjones grabbed Viday's wrist and led her out of the room. "And, please, kindly return our plants to their garden."

Shaw wheezed heavily as he kneeled on the floor in a crawling position. He had a few fits of coughing, and eventually regained his breath. Welts stood out on his reddened face as he finally stood up. His legs felt like thin twigs, capable of breaking at any moment. Though Shaw saw many horrifying things, creatures, and circumstances in his several short lifetimes, he knew his encounter with infuriated Viday would be something he could never forget.

"Show me where to go," Burroughs' baritone lifted Shaw's gaze from the floor. The horse Abberant had fetched his black staff.

Slowly, leaning on the walls and stepping around all the mess, the magician led his friend outside. He pointed to an obscured clearing in the north of the grove. "I only pulled up three. They should be easy to spot.

The first mandrake lay flat on its back in the yard. Its face scowled a unique, vegetable wrath at all creation. The little plant man's stubby fingers and hands curled slightly toward its face. When the hands reached the mandrakes face, then an oily toxin would flow forth from the blighted eyes. Burroughs knew of this. The tears of the mandrake were a poison unlike any other.

Burroughs hovered an end of his staff over the small creature. With some concentration, He managed to will out several of the cilia and wrap the mandrake in an improvised hammock.

"When did you learn how to do that?" Shaw coughed.

Burroughs lifted the tuber off the ground and held it away. "I got some practice when I couldn't leave the bed."

"Nice work."

The beast man gave no reply. He turned and walked away with the vandalized plant held well away.

Yes, he knew about mandrakes, a plant so complex it qualified as a creature. The mouth served no purpose and was not an actual opening. Nutrients for the plant came from roots dangling from the chubby fingers and toes as well as the hair – which mimicked a pineapple. This was the most significant plant trait of the mandrake, because every other trait was human. A heart beat inside the mandrake plant. During the night, mandrakes used a tiny pair of lungs to breath. It had facsimiles of all the human organs, muscles, and even a simplified bone structure; all wrapped inside a potato-like skin.

Regarded as an abomination, mandrake were mostly benign when encountered on the western continent. They only wept after being pulled out and left to die. Shaw should have known better. The off-spring of mandrakes were plain tubers, no aberration at all. The children of mandrakes became as their parents only when a red lotus flowered atop an adult head and manufactured the taint. Then, and only then, would the child tubers metamorphose to be as their parents. Only then the perverted plants became a threat.

Burroughs found the two other things leaning against a tree near their garden plot, each of them equally unhappy. An enclosure of spongy loam made up the

123

mandrake garden. The tops of a few heads showed from the ground in no particular order. Long, shallow trenches in the ground trailed to the back of each mandrakes head, indicating they were alive and moving about slowly through the soil. A spiky top occasionally budged, ever so slightly.

Taking care not to hurt himself, Burroughs pulled open some soft soil by rooting the tendrils of his staff and tugging open a crevice. He lowered each mandrake in as gently as a baby without touching them. The three tiny faces seemed to round slightly. They smiled up at Burroughs as if they knew what was happening. Burroughs got one good look at them and quickly shoved the soil onto them, covering their eerie childish grins.

Mandrakes. A chill ran down Burroughs' spine. Harjones's medicine, no doubt, contained some of it. If so, how much he gotten? Worse still, what sort of witchcraft had Beth Harjones conjured using the root? It made her a 'daughter.' Perhaps they had other family they'd dare not mention, or simply lost track of. What if he belonged to the family?

He was neither amazed or dumbfounded by the thought. The swarming pit before him may well have been where his whole curious life began. A little bit of tainted pollen, a little bit of providence, and yes the impossibility of his conception became quite possible. This also meant he had a sister in Viday, in an odd fashion. There was no telling.

If he actually was family returned, then why did the Harjones treat him as a stranger and a guest? Burroughs pondered this circumstance as well. He had much to ask. Therefore, he turned about and made back for the house. Shaw stood beside the door frame, waiting.

"It's not my fault all of this is happening. You agree with me, right?" Shaw spoke in a tone as if the entire ordeal bored him.

Burroughs said nothing.

The magician's face grew more and more tired as the silence continued. At last he sighed, "So you're with the kangaroo. I see. Well, say your goodbyes because we are leaving." A small twirl of the healing mist twisted about in one of the magician's hands. He stepped over and dosed Burroughs with it. "I can't make miracles like those two, but I can at least seal you up."

A gasp left Burroughs as a tickling sensation sparked about the bare skin near his stitches. One by one, the threads loosened and fell away.

"Go in there and get your bag," the moody magician nodded.

Making his way through the ransacked house, Burroughs caught a glimpse of Viday and Beth. They both sat on the bed in Viday's room.

Though Viday reached the age of twenty-one, her fancies remained quite childish. Stuffed animals and dolls festoned the room in dioramas, sitting on furniture, and along the edges of the floor. The windows and bed were dressed in a lovely bright purple with lace at the edges. Pictures of the various Union houses of royalty hung framed on the walls. Many handicraft items and examples of artwork stood out in the room.

In the midst of this happy childhood sat two sorrowful figures wrapping each other in a close, silent embrace. It hurt. The scene of loss stung Burroughs' eyes. He had to turn away, but the image persisted in his mind. He quickly made for the guest room. Lifting the pack off the ground proved difficult, but once he fit it on his back it was no trouble. He took the longer way out, through the apothecary, just so he did not risk seeing the scene again.

When Burroughs reached the front door, Shaw eyed him from the doorway. The young human saw something displeasing in the Abberant's face. He jerked his head outside and waved over his shoulder to signal his pack beast to follow.

"Wait," spoke a soft, meek voice. Viday made her

unique, tiptoe walk into the center of the living area. She wore a type of duster instead of her typical floral coat. Two satchel bags hung at each of her hips. "I'm going with you."

"And your mother?" Burroughs asked.

The daughter's large ears sank low. Her body shrank slowly , and her glassy eyes stared profoundly at the floor. "She's staying here."

He wanted to say the right words, something he read in a Twin novel, but nothing came to mind except, "Are you ready?"

The unwanted creatures stood there for several minutes. They didn't try to make eye contact or communicate in any way. Shaw impatiently watched the two beast people from outside. He shrugged and turned about, waiting longer.

"Lets go," Viday nearly whispered.

Missus Harjones entered the room to give one final hug.

"I will be back." Viday promised

"I know." the old woman replied.

So they left Beth Harjones behind, and made their way out into the grasslands. A solemn silence hung over the procession westward. The sun sank down the western side of Mount Mortimer, skewering on the stony spine. The skies darkened to a blood red color as less and less of the sun rays reached around the mountain. Then, at last, night came out.

The travelers managed to make camp in a craggy alcove off the first mountain they encountered. Nearby wood and tinder made into a cozy campfire, but instead of sharing the warmth, all three sat as far apart as possible. They watched the flames in a stricken hush, occasionally passing glances at one another.

"Meant to give this to you." Viday held out a large brace at arm's length. Two long belts lined the top and bottom of nearly a yard of dense fabric. A leafy pattern was stenciled onto the girdle, all done by hand.

"You made this?" Burroughs reached for the gift.

Viday nodded somberly. "Yes. Some of your abdominal muscles are gone. You must wear this at all times or you risk injuring yourself while lifting. It will also stop your posture from warping."

"I can never thank you enough. You and your mother." The medical implement fit snugly around his waist as he wrapped it around and pulled the belt straps tight. He stood up straighter from the support. His lungs drew more breath, he noticed, and the little pangs he felt when reaching or leaning disappeared. It was a clever effect, and the work of the green pattern gave a bit of color to the otherwise spartan attire Burroughs wore.

"I was told to be polite," Viday told spoke cautiously. "Not ask too many questions, but who are you? How did you manage to cause such a stir so soldiers would start swarming the island and knock on my door?"

"It has to do with him," Burroughs jutted one of his thick thumbs in Shaw's direction.

"Figures. He ruins everybody's life doesn't he?"

The magician gave them a hurt expression for a second, then continues staring at the flames.

"He is hunted," Burroughs thought for a second. "We are hunted."

"By what?"

"A pack of aberrations, Canid."

"He's marked for death by the Dread King, Pantherian? The beast?"

"Maybe. What I do know, a large number of Canid followed him here and chased us down. They made the burn which nearly killed me, and he swept them away in a flood."

"The lake bed was wet, and the old bridge was busted up when I found it." Viday scratched the top of her head. "He's a wizard of some sort?"

"The water talks to him. I hardly understand it

myself."

Shaw piped up. "I wish I could be in this conversation about me." He caught a hateful glower from Viday. "Never mind."

"How can you stand this guy," the girl pointed accusingly. "He's rude, obnoxious, nosy, messy, and he treats you like dirt – making you carry around everything for him. Do you know what he was doing when I found him? Dragging your pack away without a care for where you went. I thought he was a robber and jumped him. Some friend, yeah?"

"Typical Abby. Assault somebody first and think it through later."

"I was right the first time. You are scum."

"And you're some overzealous science project from a foolish old woman who should have adopted."

In a blink, Viday bound over the fire and pounced Shaw into the stone floor. She pinned him to the ground. With one hand she grabbed his scrawny white neck, and with the other she balled a fist. "You walking sack of garbage! You don't even know. You don't even care. You use people, take advantage of their hospitality, and when you're done with them you look down on them like you're something better." She filled her lungs with an emotional gasp. "My mother found me near death, trampled like so many others. She saved my life. She raised me knowing full well what would happen if anybody found out. Now she's staying behind to save all our lives, and you look down on her."

Tears trickled down both sides of the animal muzzle Viday was cursed with. The fist she held up softened. "You monster. You don't know what love is, and you don't care. Burroughs may put up with you, but I can't stand it. Cross me one more time. One more time, I will pay the King of Beasts a favor. Can you at least understand that?"

Poom.

Viday tumbled backward off Shaw. The campfire

flickered wildly as a small wind buffeted the flames. A fine steam rose off the magician's fist as he stood up and held his hands out like a boxer. He backed away, expecting retaliation. However, the former assailant gave up any signs of aggression. She curled up on the floor, sobbing loudly.

"It's not fair," Viday babbled. "It's not fair."

## Human Resourcing

Viday woke up the next morning in the bed roll. The night before, Burroughs walked into her section of the camp and wordlessly offered his bag to her. She didn't turn it away, or give much as a reply. She took the large sack, rolled it out, and they returned as they were.

A nightmare came to Viday while she slept, a frequent one she had as a child. It started with her bouncing along empty grasslands like the ones back home. Then one of her landings opened into a sudden shallow pit filled with grasping hands, all grimy and frightening. She'd kick away, but always a few bounds later more pits cracked open and more hands seized at her feet. By the time she realized it was all a dream, it was already too late. She found herself face down on the rock floor with the bedroll rumpled around her legs. In the struggle, she managed to rip the fabric. Clumps of stuffing fell away as she slid the bedroll off.

Morning had yet to break and none of the other sleepers seemed to be up to see. The loathsome magician laid prone on the far side of the camp. Burroughs rested on his side with his back to the ordeal. One of his shaggy forearms was tucked under his head. They both breathed regularly.

This was not the first time. Viday often destroyed things in her sleep. Any month where she could wake up without a hoof through a nightstand or caught up in a drawer was a good month. She painted over scratches she cut into the wall so often that she kept a fresh can in her bedroom. At one point her mother put a kick board at the end of her bed, hoping to fix the problem. It only served to launch her out, as she did with sleeping bags apparently.

The explosive punch Shaw swung last night could not compare with how she jammed her chin on the ground. A few pebbles got in her mouth. She spat them out and rolled over, licking away the mineral taste. Her injuries didn't bleed. She felt her face and everything seemed to be in order, no breaks or fractures. It was only a sprain. Still, it hurt terribly, and a crimp in her neck made it to hard get up.

For a good few minutes, she laid out on her back in the chill night air. A perfect cloudless night covered the sky. All the stars twinkled down from their proper places in the heavens, and a half moon hung in the middle. As a child, she honestly believed she could make it to the moon; just climb to the top of Mount Mortimer and jump on.

With a few hours of sleep left over, Viday straightened the bedroll and crawled back in, head first this time. The new tear served as ventilation. Her legs ran out the opening of the roll. She slept well in the cloth cave for the rest of the night and woke up surprisingly refreshed, despite everything. The kicking continued during the night, because she crawled out of the bag several yards away from where she first laid down. She handed back the bedroll as a tattered, soiled mess. Burroughs, being who he was, didn't complain.

"Sorry."

"Hmmm."

The adventure continued with Shaw at the lead. They dared not set foot on Lateral Way to the south and kept well out of sight from anything remotely like a road. The going became much slower as the sloping grades intensified. At certain points the hills proved too steep to scale. So the travelers walked around through ravines filled with treacherous rocks.

Burroughs did not take so well to the terrain. His large, solid, inflexible feet tettered on many of the footholds. Several times he found it necessary to bring down his staff with a loud clack. The other two turned to see the source of the noise, and watch Burroughs negotiate a difficult step they had no trouble with.

The trek went on for hours with hardly any significant progress.

"Hey master," Viday bound forward over Shaw's head. She perched on a large boulder in the direction they traveled. The magician needed to look up to see the deer Abberant leer down on him like a fuzzy, chestnut owl. No small amount of vitriol went into the way she called him master. "Oh great and merciful master. Your horses and servants require rest, lest we succumb under the tribulation of our sacred quest."

Shaw squinted up and tilted his head. "So this is the way it's going to be?"

Viday gesticulated like a court jester. "Oh yes, master. Your servants dare not fain be as magnificent as thou. Your brilliance shines as a second sun in our weak, pathetic lives. A blessing to all who serve. We grovel for your tender mercies and quail at the rumble of your magical power. Please think no ill of my humblest request."

Shaw's face became a tired frown.

Burroughs stumbled into the scene.

Shaw turned about to the horse, "How are you holding up?"

The pack beast leaned forward slightly on his staff. "I will manage," he spoke in stoic tones.

"He's fine." The magician turned back about with the fullest intention of pressing the journey further. One glance at Viday's cool hating face changed his mind. "Yes." Shaw declared through a mask of fear. "We should take a break somewhere."

One of the rolling slopes leveled out at the top to make a suitable resting place. Brown, shrunken woodbine bushes, culled by the first frost, covered the hill. A few stunted pines stood out of the rusted brown mound.

Burroughs broke out a small camp and handed out some food.

Viday took some crackers and cheese. "Where, in the mountains, are we going?"

Burroughs replied. "We're looking for Maurius. Do you know of him?"

"No," her overly large ear flapped as she shook her head. "I've seen a few fortune hunting miners crawl around the mountains. Unless he's one of those, no. It's all rocks, ice, and broken houses."

"Broken houses?" Burroughs questioned.

"Yes. Abandoned mining camps. I scavenge them all the time. You probably saw some of the survey equipment back at my house. There are wooden shacks out here filled with things people left behind. I just find them and carry back what I can."

"And any active mining camps?"

"No. It's been years since I've seen anybody out here. It's just too dangerous all the time."

"So I've heard."

"So where is Maurius then?"

Burroughs nodded his head at Shaw.

Surprised he'd be allowed into the conversation, Shaw explained. "He's in a mountain meadow out here."

Viday spat a single word, "Where."

"I don't know. I will know it when I see it."

133

"So the plan from the start was to bust both of your backs wandering about the mountains for weeks?"

"Well, no. The plan was not to give up till we found it."

Viday jeered the young man in white. "So the plan was not to plan. I certainly see why Burroughs follows you around."

Shaw took a long, hateful drink instead of replying.

"In cases of treacherous terrain," Burroughs butted in. "It is best to be deliberate in how we move."

"Is this a Vick strategy, or are you improvising again?" Shaw crossed his arms.

"This is from the book," the horse aberration reassured. He swept a pointing finger all around. "Our visibility is bad. We can barely tell what is in the surrounding area. We can move faster if we knew where the better ground is, and we can avoid ambushes or stumbling onto trouble."

"I don't get it. What are you thinking."

"Viday scouts and leads us to Maurius."

The two other travelers breathed a sigh of recognition. The plan was to move Burroughs and Shaw from one safe place to the next. With her superior movement, Viday could run ahead or leap to better vantage positions they could not. Therefore, the responsibility to leading the journey fell to her. Viday agreed.

"One extra thing before you take off." Shaw dug around in the provisions bag for half a minute. "There it is." The magician held out a metal tube tied to a leather loop. "Take the whistle and blow it if you need help."

Suspicious, Viday accepted the thoughtful gift. The cord fit loosely around her neck. She blew a few short tweets to test out the whistle. It rang a high, shrill pitch. Viday knew if she put a full blast behind on the mouth piece it could very well deafen somebody.

"A meadow?" She questioned Shaw one last time.

"Yes, with a short waterfall in it."

Viday put her bags down next to the camp provisions. "Stay here." She excused herself with a tiptoed amble then launched away.

The slender aberration skipped from the top of one large boulder to the next. Each leap began with the whipping of Viday's duster, and ended with wooden knocks at each landing. Halfway down the ravine, she made a ten yard vertical jump onto an exposed ledge. Her hands found a solid hold and she pulled herself out of the ravine The magician and the horse gazed with admiration as the appointed scout climbed the rest of the imposing escarpment in a quick succession of hops; switching back and forth while scaling upward.

Looking out from a significant lip of rock, Viday waved to her friends and shouted.

"I can't hear her." Shaw cupped an ear.

Burroughs took a few steps. "Snow. She's warning us about snow."

"It's not even freezing out here. Are you sure?"

"I think so."

Suddenly, enough snow to fill a bath tub slapped down behind them.

"Holy cats!" Shaw spun about so fast he fell down.

On the ground a few feet away, sat a pile of soft ice appearing from nowhere. He looked up to see where the pile came from and saw a dust sliding off Mount Mortimer drifting toward their direction. The dust motes grew into pellets and the pellets grew into clumps. The clumps swelled to meteors. The volley of white spread wide. Other snow droppings fell down on the surrounding ridges, but none others landed near by. After a few minutes of anxiously watching the sky, the pelting storm ended. No more snow fell down the needle of Mount Mortimer and drifted their way.

Shaw grabbed a few soft handfuls. "That could have plowed somebody down. What sort of forsaken place is this? It's a bit of the western continent we can enjoy at home," the magician ranted. "If this much falls this far out, imagine how much more cakes up closer to the big mountain." He waggled a finger at the mound as the brows raised up on his head. "Oh, wait. This is pure water. Help me pack the canteens before it melts."

They both unpacked the canteens and scooped pure white slush into the open ends.

"Funny you bought three of these," Burroughs pointed out.

"Meant to have two to myself. I am always thirsty, if you haven't noticed."

What he said was true. Shaw drank several glasses of tea at every dinner with the Harjones, and often walked around during their stay with a glass in hand. Even at the moment, he kept a half empty bottle of soda nearby which he nursed over the past several hours.

"I see," Burroughs muttered slowly.

"A minister's soup never goes cold."

"What?"

Shaw held out two of the canteens. Shaking them, he revealed the contents as fully liquid. "Take these. I will melt the one you're holding." He stretched out his arms with both watering cans. Both of the flasks were warm to the touch.

The waiting travelers stocked away a full provision of water. Afterward, they rested on the ground facing Mount Mortimer – just in case more ice fell.

"Do you know what it is like when somebody makes up their mind to hate you, and they just look for any reason to hate you more? Anything. Most of the time, the reasons don't make any sense."

"I know about it." Burroughs droned laconically.

"I mean Viday. She thinks the world of you, worships you, almost. Thinks whatever you do is good and wholesome. Me though. I'm a villain. She got it in her mind I dug out those mandrakes and brought the soldiers to see them. I just yanked a few lads out to get a good look and carried one out to ask a few questions."

"Don't do that again. Mandrakes spoil quickly."

"I didn't know," Shaw shrugged. "I took it with me so I could ask about it, left it outside because dinner started, and Viday thinks I dropped it out there on purpose. She also won't believe I searched for help when you got shot either, only thinks I wanted to help myself."

Shaw threw a rock into the ravine. It ricocheted and spun away from a couple of jagged surfaces before disappearing. "Now I'm always of verge on the receiving a beating. What's a guy to do?"

"Be nice. You will be fine."

"No. You will be fine. I'm due for a few more thrashings before this is over."

"You did say some awful things."

"I guess so."

A small rock slide tumbled down a mountain nearby. The rolling group of stones crashed into the low ravine, adding to the detritus.

Shaw ducked low into some dead woodbine. Burroughs did the same.

Their scout ran out of sight more than thirty minutes ago. Though the whistle did not blow, it did not rule out the possibility of some hostile element wandering in on Burroughs and Shaw. At which point they would be forced to hide or stand their ground.

The horse aberration pulled his staff close. Shaw brought out his knife, and something else, a can of chili stew. Burroughs squinted in disbelief, to which Shaw nodded back seriously.

Another crack, a slew off of dust, and a figure approached. It wasn't human. The brief moment of apprehension, however, ended when Viday's outline became more distinct. She bounded down the cliff to meet them and share what she saw.

## Tomato Based

There was no mountain meadow for miles around, and no sight of an enemy. Viday managed to find a suitable campsite for the night, an old mining shack she knew. The shabby leanto rested on the wall of a mountain and had not seen inhabitants for years. The boards reeked of mold and seeping holes opened in the roof. Dust and sand coated most of the interior, especially the floor which was all sand.

Burroughs created a draw for campfire smoke by punching a hole in the ceiling. They cooked a few of the canned provisions and drank the last of the soda drinks. Shaw handed the drinks out, and when Viday and Burroughs took them they were ice cold.

"We're roughing it from this point, as far as I'm concerned."

After an hour the ventilation proved too poor. The air grew hot and stifling inside the shack from the small blaze. Rather than douse the flame, they buried the live coals into the floor. Yet, even with the heat gone, the leanto was till oppressively stuffy and claustrophobic.

Burroughs stepped outside for some cold air. Rather than share company with Shaw, Viday followed.

The pointed peaks of the mountains cut edges into the sky, closing up the sides. The night sky in the mountain was smaller in size, but no less deep and empty. Orion's Belt figured prominently, three bright stars binding the middle of an hourglass constellation. A strong northern wind gusted over the valleys, shaking the pines and stirring the air.

"Tell me about your father. He was a high ranking war hero?"

Burroughs shook his elongated head. "No. He never ranked past Sargent. He turned down every promotion handed to him or managed to lose it again. His career in the military made him very famous as the unkillable man. Invincible Vick."

"What was he like?"

"Tired."

"Tired? Tired of what?"

"Everything. I think. He spent the last years of his life trying to make sense of his tour of duty on the western continent, make sense of all the horrors he had seen." Burroughs stared off pondering. "It was the reason he didn't kill me outright, according to the memoirs he kept from me."

"So he trained you to be a soldier and sent you out," Viday sat down in some gravel.

Burroughs kept standing. "He died when I was seven."

The sad weight of the aberration's word somehow stifled Viday's speech. They both sat in stark silence as the breeze whipped by

"No amount of gunfire, explosions, or bloodletting can change the course of history. The world changes by thinking differently, when generations buried alive in the bodies of those who died before them crawl out into the hell their parents handed down and cry for a change, for the world to be different somehow."

Burroughs continued. " War is not the answer. It never was. War is a steaming pile of dung, foul, smelly, and no use to anybody except for fertilizer. Without anything to plant in the fertilizer, it's just shit. War is shit, and it's a soldier's job to spread it around."

"Let me guess," Viday flicked a few small rocks. "You're quoting your father."

"Technically, my real father can't talk at all. I was quoting Viklund's journal though. I've read more subtle authors."

"Do you have it, the book?"

"I burnt it before marshals invaded my home. It mostly contained ravings which would tarnish his reputation. Perhaps not the best idea, since I often think back to -"

"Shhh. Quiet." Viday raised off the ground, rattling pebbles. "Do you hear that?"

Burroughs trained his ears around. Something was out there. A low whooping sound traveled around the peaks, almost dangling. At each low beat were the flapping noises of leathery wings.

"Get inside and stay hidden. Do not make a noise," Burroughs murmured in a commanding whisper.

They rushed to the leanto, shut the door and blocked it with the massive pack. Shaw, who busied himself by drawing on the floor beside a lit lantern, gave a confused expression as Burroughs snuffed out his light and drug him to a corner of the shack.

Burroughs whispered one word. "Gargoyles."

The blood of Pantherian remembered. It remembered all the creatures who ever were, and knew all the animals which could ever be. At the blessing of a Heartblood, legends came to life. Canid metamorphosed into fleet, their shoulders and hips rolled freely between human shapes and four-legged dogs. Another metamorphosis shrank the arms short and stretched the hands wider and wider, until the skin between the fingers became wings. The Abberant dog then flew as a bat. Such was the nature of Pantherian's gifts, to bring the creatures of myth back to life.

Gargoyles circled the skies. Their wings beat against the night and fought the wind. Viday heard their rapid breath and the frantic flapping of their changed arms.

"One is coming this way," she hurriedly murmured.

The other two heard nothing until a distinct, heart-stopping, thud hit the ground outside.

It snuffled the air and seemed to waddle about, making spatulate slapping noises as it went. Labored grunts followed where ever if shuffled.

"Eeeee. Eeeee. Eeeee."

The thing tottered to a window, but the creature failed to see over the sill. A few gusts from the gargoyle's wing buffeted the side of the shack, but it was no use. At every attempt, the gargoyle fluttered backward when trying to hover up to the window."

"Eeeee. Eeeee. Eeeee."

Seemingly furious at its inability to master flight, the short creature waddled to the door and kicked angrily with its short legs.

"Bam bam bam Eeeee!"

The gargoyle had not given up yet. It hit the roof of the leanto after a few flaps of its leathery wings and found the campfire's vent hole.

Then, at last, the travelers came face to face with their hunter. The change into a flying Canid had not been kind. Many balded spots stood out on the gargoyle's head as it looked over the inhabitants. Once normal, pointed canine ears had warped larger with distinct ridges and spots of pink flesh exposed everywhere. The muzzle was pushed in as if with a clothes iron, and the two slits for nostrils pulsed and twitched.

Burroughs swing at the hideous face, but the gargoyle quickly pulled its head outside. A split second later it spread its wings to take off. Burroughs jabbed his staff through the ceiling vent and willed the fibers away to bind the gargoyle down. As fortune found it, the tangling end of the weapon put a strangling grip on the bat creature's neck. Burroughs felt through the strands. He felt the sensation of choking the gargoyle, and the contractions in its neck as it struggled to screech out into the night. There would be none of that.

Twisting the strands tightened a lynch. Burroughs squeezed with every effort he could give and pulled the gargoyle through the hole in the roof. Lumber creaked and cracked as the brute forced the bat creature through a hole it could not possibly fit. The gargoyle hit the sandy ground like a pile of dirty laundry, lifeless.

Burroughs relinquished his grip on the gargoyle's neck. The fibers retreated into the rough ends they emerged from.

"Did Shaw give you that magical weapon?" Viday pointed to the greased end of the staff.

"No. He's always had it." Shaw butted in.

Burroughs held up a hand, and gazed gravely into Viday's eyes. "Do you hear more?"

The deer aberration sampled the night with her turning ears. "Nothing. But there are more out there. I heard some more earlier."

"We can't leave this room until daybreak. Stay away from any windows or holes so they can't see us from the outside."

Shaw looked up at the hole the horse pulled open. It wasn't so large. The gargoyle crumpled up quite a bit on the way down. "What about the dog-bat?"

"It stays in here too."

Viday leaned over the corpse. "This thing is a dog?"

"Was," Shaw crossed his legs to sit down. "Canid sacrifice their body and mind to the King of Beasts for gifts like this. They gain power at the cost of their mind, and become feral beasts. Well, more feral. This is nothing compared to some of the other things they become."

"Why would they-" Viday sprang back from the heap she hung over. The gargoyle thrashed wildly at her, snapping its jaws and baring its teeth.

Burroughs brought down his heavy staff again. Spots of blood and juices spattered the floor and walls. The gargoyle shrugged off the trauma and kept fighting.

It lunged at Viday. Its shattered maw flapped open to bite down on the first thing it touched. She kicked the thing away, sending it fluttering across the room; where it found Shaw.

The magician coiled back from the flailing claws and teeth. He tried once to get a hand near, to try something, but retracted and shuffled away.

Burroughs leashed the animal again and dragged it into the center. He began crushing the vicious gargoyle with his hoof. Viday and Shaw joined in until the creature flattened into the most dreadful rug the world ever knew. All three of them felt unbearably filthy. Chunks of blood caked into the fur on Burroughs' and Viday's legs. Shaw soaked one of his socks, and fidgeted about from the tacky sensation.

They stared at the body for minutes on end, watching it twitch.

"Let's dig another hole, because none of us can sleep next to that."

Burroughs nodded.

The only place inside they could dig was where they buried the fire coals, and the coals were still smoldered.

"Let's be quick with it, or this will stink." Shaw enlisted Viday to help shove the dirt over the hole. "Drop it in big guy."

It was no use. They covered the cooking cadaver with lightning speed, but the reek effused out of the ground minutes later. It smelled of rancid bacon and burning hair, and lasted all night long.

When, at last, morning broke all three haggard travelers piled out of the grotesque smoke house into the sweet mountain air. Not a single one of them slept a wink in the shack that night. Bags hung under Shaw's eyes. Burroughs and Viday dragged their solid feet, their arms swayed back and forth.

"It got everywhere. I still taste it in my mouth. It's in my skin." The magician lamented.

"Please tell me we packed soap," Burroughs brushed some flakes off from his arms.

Shaw shook his head.

"I did." Viday dropped her bags. She turned about to go search for water but hesitated for a second. "There are more of those things out there. More weird things chasing you. What will I do when I see them – if they see me? Will they chase me down? What happens if they find you before I get back. What do I do?" She looked down at the ground and muttered, shuffling her elongated feet nervously.

Shaw waved for Burroughs to lean over and whispered something into the horse's ear, to which the large aberration sighed and nodded. Viday's exceptional hearing caught some of the transaction. She recoiled back in surprise. "No. I don't think thats..."

Burroughs put down his things and walked over to Viday. He towered over her with the way she curled down on legs. In a big scoop, Burroughs pulled Viday into a warm hug. "Everything will be all right," he spoke in a wooden tone.

If Viday showed any skin at all, it would have been glowing bright red. The embrace she found herself in was both strong and warm. But the way Burroughs droned his condolences sounded so phoney, so scripted, so absurdly forced – she could not help but laugh a little and found herself squeezing back.

When they broke apart, Shaw approached holding a full canteen in one hand and his sheathed knife in the other. "Feeling better?"

Viday cocked a brow and looked the magician up and down.

"Well, I'm not hugging you." Shaw wagged the knife in its leather case then shook the water can to show it was full. "Do you want either of these? Would they help?"

Viday looked over the offers and shook her head.

144

"No. I'll be fine."

"You're ready?"

"I'm ready"

"I can make him hug you again."

She bolted off, leaving puffs of dust behind her.

Shaw planted his full hands on his hips and let out pitiful exhale. He guessed Viday was spot on in her accusation. He really did use people to his own purposes.

## *Ruminating on Baked Goods*

A seemingly permanent grin spread across Viday's half human face as she sailed from one foothold to the next. She stopped to try straightening her expression, but it was no use. It wasn't even funny. It felt like one of the stupid jokes she annoyed her mother with until she got a scolding. She kept remembering Burroughs lumbering toward her, arms straight out. "Everything will be all right." The silly grin came back.

Wind roared in her ears through each jump. The brown cotton of her duster flapped around her. At last she reached a good vantage point, not far from her friends. Friends, wow, she never thought she would have any.

The mountains clustered more tightly to the north and south. She could hardly make out anything, save the white peaks. If she chose to take the journey toward or away from Mortimer it would require further scouting for danger.

There were dangers to watch for, nightmare reflections of herself; her own kind. Viday imagined stumbling upon another gargoyle. She imagined being chased down by one of those winged creatures then being bitten and scratched. Under the right circumstances, perhaps she could kick one to death. Then again, the creature from last night simply would not give up until it was flattened. The blood of Pantherian, blood is life.

Viday found herself staring off for a minute, daydreaming. She squinted, looking into all the craggy fissures. Nothing seemed to fly about the sky or weave among the peaks. A small, narrow valley meandered about to the west, which was where she decided to lead the party. Not before exploring every turn, however.

A low boom sounded a few miles north. Viday attempted to single out the source with the scoops of her ears, but it quickly proved unnecessary. Before her disbelieving eyes, a single mountain lifted a little taller than its neighbors and fractured. The snowy peak fell away first, then an entire section of rock slid off the side. For what must have been a titanic rockslide merely sounded like a low hum from so far away. What remained after less than a minute was a taller, slimmer peak than before.

This was a land for no man.

Watching the disaster gave Viday a sudden insecurity in her footing. She plotted her falls down the craggy cliff, drops ten to twenty yards downward. When she hit the ground of the grassy valley, she sped up the slant of a smoothed hill. At the top of the green mound, she stretched out to the tips of her toes. No sound. No enemy. She took off down the slope, crossed the green, and scaled another summit

Maybe this little bit of green field could be the meadow Shaw searched for. The magician claimed he would know it when he saw it, which didn't help much. As huge as the Caiphon cascade stretched, it could take weeks of hunting out in the mountains for Viday alone to find a singular meadow.

The gargoyles didn't appear in the day it seemed, but Viday guessed they would certainly fill the skies at night – just as bats do. If she and her friends slept outside, she could imagine the consequences. It was an extra thing to consider.

The boulder Viday balanced on rolled away. She hardly stepped off the heavy rock before it tumbled down a gravel slant. The boulder cracked open on a ledge below.

Another mining camp she knew came to mind. Hopefully not too far away.

Like a skier, Viday slid down the gravel coated side of the mountain she surveyed from. The rolling of all the small rocks sounded of a rain storm. She hit the green of the valley and sped back to where she left. When she returned she found Shaw and Burroughs brewing coffee.

"Have some," Shaw invited, but Burroughs held out the cup.

"Thank you."

"Sorry to run you off so quick," Shaw gave an empty apology. "You forgot breakfast."

"That's all right."

"Don't want you running around on an empty stomach."

"I have a rumin," Viday sipped the coffee.

"Oh. So you found something to eat."

Viday rolled her eyes around while finding the right reply. "Yes."

All three travelers sipped their drinks down. Then Shaw asked in an inquisitive tone, "What does a rumin taste like? I don't think I've heard of it."

Burroughs tried to explain. "You don't eat a rumin."

"Nonsense. She just said she had one." Shaw shrugged in Viday's direction.

"I have one," Viday snickered. "Do you want to see it work?"

Shaw's brows wrinkled in confusion.

Viday finished off the last of her coffee. "Watch," she said. Somewhere in her brown coat came a sloshing sound. Then Viday made a loud swallow, but instead of something going down, a lump traveled up her neck. Her

148

cheeks puffed out a little and she began chewing something. Mush. Mush. Mush.

Shaw's face became a mask of stunned astonishment. His mouth buttoned into a thin line as he stared rudely at the friendly creature. After rubbing his chin a few times, he asked another question. "Do you do that with normal people food too?"

"Cake," Viday swallowed her cud.

The green valley she lead them to was not the one Shaw looked for. She didn't find any water even though they quickly approached the network of streams which eventually became the mighty White Stag river farther south. Tomorrow, for sure, they would find a creek or spring to wash the filth away.

Hours later they happened on Lodestone.

Lodestone Quarry was a quarry in name only. Whoever named the site a "quarry" either didn't know how a rock quarry worked, or was firmly set on the name from the beginning. Perhaps they made the sign before ever building and never got around to changing the name. The abandoned mining site did not scrape away the sides of mountains as quarries do. Instead, the site opened a mine shaft near the back. Viday remembered the place well.

Lodestone Quarry looked the same as ever. Four perfectly straight long houses made up the compound, all spread evenly apart. A ruined water tower stood out front, bearing the name on its side. In the back were long, shallow pits filled with broken stone. The rocks in the pit varied widely in color. Some even sparkled. At the very end opened the mine itself, a dark and foreboding hole into the rupturing bowels of Caiphon itself.

"Looks deserted," Shaw appraised the place.

Burroughs put his pack down and held up his weapon. "We need to check all the buildings. Follow me and don't wander off." Viday followed Burroughs lead with her awkward tiptoe walk. Shaw trailed close behind.

The lumber on every building was gray and warped.

149

It gave off a dusty smell. Whistling noises came through the cracks as the wind blew by. The houses sat on wooden foundations with stairs leading up. Burroughs put a hoof down on one board and shifted his weight on the first step to see if it held. The stair creaked loudly, but did not break.

Instead of standing near the door, Burroughs took a low grip on his staff, reached out, and pulled the door free using the other end. The tendrils worked their way about the knob, slipping around the tarnished brass at first, then gripping tight. With a smart spin and a thrust, Burroughs managed to open the entrance from a few yards back.

The interior of the first house lay dark. Rows of cots lined the walls from one end to the other. A generous coating of dust covered everything, the bedding, the windows, the foot lockers, and the cabinets near the end.

"Two more exactly the same as this and a mess hall," Viday told the others.

"People just leave places like this behind?" Burroughs asked.

"You can't take it all with you," Shaw ruminated.

They inspected the identical second house with little adventure, but the third rest house lay host to a peculiar sight. A metal chair was jammed into the trusses of the rafters. The elevated seat stood over tight rows of beds, arranged just to be under the gaze of whomever sat in the chair. The words "Princess Vidé" were carved into the timbers all around.

"I forgot about this," Viday said in a shy tone. She twisted one of her split hooves into the floor boards.

Burroughs only gave a stoic, empty look around.

"Accented letters are fancy," Shaw nodded in agreement. He crouched down to a bed on the front row and carved the words "Master Shä" into the boards in front.

Shaw invited his larger friend. "Do you want a place before the princess too Burroughs? You can be a knight, you know, since you're a horse. Sir Burroughs."

Burroughs didn't share in the humor. "Do what you

want."

"Be a shame if I didn't. You have more vowels. And what's a princess without out some daring knight to sweep her off h-"

"Shut up!" Viday screeched.

The mess hall kitchen featured a gas stove and the cylinder outside still held a good amount of fuel to burn. The unlit pilot light sat deep in the belly of the cooker. Their campfire starters would not do for such a task. So the magician crawled down and reached into the dark recesses of the stove.

"Turn it." his voice muffled from inside the iron box.

Burroughs tried twisting the rusty valve by hand. It would not budge. He then used the staff as a wrench for greater leverage. The gas flowed into the kitchen.

A distinct poof came from within, followed by collective screams from Shaw and Viday. Burroughs peeked into the back door of the mess hall to see Shaw milling about the tables. The magician's robe caught fire. Viday chased him, swatting at the flames to put them out.

She got tired of following Shaw around, and kicked the magician to the floor. She rolled him about, patting him here and there. Eventually, all the flames were out, but the white robe was a charred and tattered mess. Shaw kept wearing it even though parts of his army uniform showed through the gaping holes in his garment.

Shaw was the only thing to catch fire that afternoon. The stove cooked up a good meal and shut off with significantly less fuss than starting it.

"We're getting close," Shaw shoveled beans from a bowl. They found spoons in the pantry, Stinner brand. "Maurius is one of the great old ones. I can feel his presence as we get closer."

"What happens then, when we find him?" Burroughs pushed away an empty dish.

Shaw shook his head. "I don't know. We'll be safe,

151

for sure. The ancients are powerful. Once we get to his domain, we can sort things out there. The Ministry takes care of its own. I can cut you both some favors. Find you someplace safe, even bust Missus Harjones from prison."

"You can do all these things for us?" Viday leaned in.

"We can. Our spirits embody the waters and oceans surrounding the fourteen Union islands. Our will forced back the Abberant legion for the past four hundred years. We're the secret guardians of the old world. As far as I'm concerned, you're one of us. So I must be able to swing something."

Viday eyed the young magician from across the lunch hall table. "Do you promise?"

Shaw thought it over for a second. "I will try to do everything right by you as best I can."

Viday silently mouthed back what the magician said. She went over the words a few times mentally before answering. "You can't very well say 'Yes,' can you?"

"Yes."

Burroughs rumbled a low hum, suspicious.

"So no gargoyles tonight?" Viday asked almost expectant.

"We barricade ourselves into one of the bunk houses. Keep the lights down, and block any way of them seeing us from the outside." Burroughs drew some lines on a dusty table. He made a rectangular outline for the house and two slashes to indicate the barricade walls.

"Use the beds and mattresses to block everything up?" the deer aberration's brow rose far enough to make one of her ears tilt to the side.

Shaw knocked on the table. "I like the big guy's plans so far." The magician paused for a second with his mouth open. "Except last night's barbecue."

Over the course of the day, they had forgotten the horrible scent reeking off them. The smell and recollection returned, as if the magician dispelled an enchantment protecting their noses. The newly self-aware aberrations sniffed themselves repugnantly with their animal nostrils.

"Well, master, can you make a room humid without a flame?" Viday began picking through the effects she'd packed in her courier bags. It sounded like several glass bottles clinking together.

Shaw looked at his hand. "My sockets can vent heat enough to boil water, yes. As long as I don't need to hold something boiling hot."

"Your what?"

"Here. I'll show you." Holding his palm out, five small jets of vapor spewed out just above the largest knuckle on each finger. Shaw closed and opened his hand over and over, sending puffs of steam through the air. "Not as awesome as having a rumin, but I use it for cake too."

That night they built their walls and blocked the doors with stacks of mattresses. Viday filled a tin cup with water from a canteen and handed it to Shaw, who heated the liquid after placing it on the floor. The boil rolled over the top many times, but Shaw managed to keep his hands back and away enough to be unharmed. The chemist's daughter then dropped some fragrance into the tiny cauldron. Clouds of aroma rolled out of the cup and filled the resting area with a most welcome scent.

"It smells like the Saporna lily gardens," Shaw whiffed the air.

"Pumpkin blossom," Burroughs guessed.

"It is pumpkin blossom," Viday put away the ampule and stowed her bags away. "I found a huge mound of vines growing one day and picked the flowers to make the perfume. Guess how large the flowers were."

Burroughs held his hands a foot apart. "Star shaped. Yellow. Out near Lagoona."

"Wow. Yes. Somebody you know?" Viday asked.

"I used to live there."

## High Beams and Low Blows

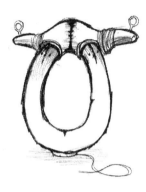

After catching no sleep from the previous night, all three of the travelers slept soundly behind the furniture barricade. They had no want for bedding, as they used as many of the bunk house mattresses and linens as they desired. It was like sleeping on a stack of pancakes: warm, fluffy, and sweet-smelling.

Nothing horrible visited them in the night. If anything did, it didn't make any noise or alert the prey animal instincts of the two sleepers who were less human.

Not a single shred of light penetrated the cozy rest area, throwing off any sense of time. So they slept in pitch dark after switching off the small oil lamp.

"Is anybody awake? I can't see anything." Came Viday's softened voice from the impenetrable blackness.

The magician whispered back. "Is it morning yet?"

"You tell me."

"Hold still. I can find the light."

A bloom of soft blue light glowed from the top of the magicians bed. Viday watched as Shaw's distinctive outline appeared in the luminous haze. As the magician sat up, she saw his eyes had become two blue glowing rings, the color of the sky. The way the shadows fell about his face in sharp lines gave Viday a noticeable tinge of fear. The eyes were judging, menacing. At the centers of the rings, Viday made out the faint red of Shaw's retinas.

"Yeah," Shaw said sadly. He caught Viday's distraught expression. The lantern rested across the room, he saw. Rolling off his stack of mattresses, Shaw softly stepped across the creaking floor and lit the light using a spark from his hand.

Burroughs kept sleeping. His giant lungs filled and emptied, creating a low hum over the room.

Shaw looked up after returning the light. The glow left the magician's face.

"What are you?" Viday pondered. "Do that again."

"Light the lantern?"

"No. No. The thing with your eyes."

Shaw found and drank from the canteen a few times before replying. "Sure." He said between sips. He put the lamp on the ground, and held his hands to his head as if were holding binoculars. From under the shade of his fingers glowed the rings of his eyes. He gave Viday a good leer before letting the lights die out.

"I used to have hazel eyes. You know," the young fellow waved his palm in a circular motion around his face. "Brown hair. The Ministry dried me out on the inside, like something left out in the sun too long." He picked up the canteen again and drank.

"Do you hate them?"

"Mmmm?" Shaw let a little dribble fall down his chin. He screwed the lid back on, sling the strap over his shoulder, and moved the lamp farther away from the larger aberration dozing away on the other side of the room. "No," he confided. "My life was over when they took me in. Now I'm just ... borrowed."

Viday turned one of her cleft lips up in a half grimace. "I don't understand."

"It's like you're playing a game with some people. The game is boring, drawn out, and you lose often for reasons you don't understand. These people are not friendly or helpful, and each time you lose they start over the same game. But, even though the game is impossible and the company is horrible, you're just happy to stay in because of the small winnings you make before you ultimately lose."

Shaw continued. "Each time I die. A little less of me makes it back. This keeps on going until the Ministry seals me up and tosses me out to wander the streets of some city with nothing but my tattered mind and the clothes on my back. I'll spout prophetic nonsense for a while and end up dead in some gutter. Dead for good."

"That's horrible," the brown creature gasped.

Shaw shrugged. "I guess. If you died and came back six times, you'd understand how disposable life really is."

"You're being used."

"Yes, but in the process of things, I've gone to fantastic places. I've seen the world in a whole different way, and done exciting things with the abilities the Ministry gave me. Even though everything I try doesn't work out, I'm happy to stay in the game; you see?"

Viday's eyes flickered in the light of the lantern like glass marbles. "Something big is coming this way."

The magician pulled out his large knife and pointed around the room, checking Viday's face for confirmation.

The large, long ears twisted about on Viday's head. She wordlessly pointed to the wall behind Burroughs.

Shaw crossed the room. He turned over a large padded mattress leaning on the wall, which slapped to the ground with a low thud. Jabbing his knife into the wall, Shaw carved a peeping hole. Whiter, brighter light beamed through the opening. It was the middle of the day outside. They had overslept for quite a while. The end of the neighboring house blocked the view of the entire outside.

Burroughs stirred from his torpor. "I hear drumming."

"Engines," Viday whispered. She nudged Shaw away from the opening to see for herself.

"It's the army," Shaw said. "We've got to run. Come on. Pick up your things. We've got to move."

"We can't. They're here."

Several score of motors thundered into the mining camp and suddenly died out. A rumbling rush of foot falls rolled about the compound.

A stentorian voice bellowed from nearby. "Box up people! We need this place buttoned down before we move the crew in. Gomez, I want your group holed back there. Shoot anything that crawls out. I want to see everything by the book. Is that clear?"

"Sir, solid copy." shouted soldiers from all over.

From the hole, Viday saw the silhouettes of fighting men coursing through the camp. Their hurried running thundered through the hall next door.

"What do we do?" the deer aberration looked up pleadingly at her larger companion.

"I," Burroughs hesitated. "I don't know." He knew if they stepped outside, they would be gunned down.

"Errrsh."

They both looked around to watch Shaw pull a rope knot tight around his wrists. He spat out the lose end from his mouth. On the ground crumpled his abandoned robe. He heaved a deep breath and closed his eyes shut as if he couldn't stand looking them in the face. "I'm sorry."

With that, he shoved through the barricade over the door. The exit flung open, drowning the room in light. Shaw stumbled through the opening. The magician abandoned his friends, betraying them.

"Help!" he screamed. "Abbies over here. Help me!"

Packs of soldier came running at the call. Stunned from Shaw's treachery, the two cornered Abberants hid away from the light.

"Where the hell did you come from, son?"

"My name is Private Belome," Shaw lied. "Research division working with the Academy. I'm out here doing survey work for the weapons development

157

laboratories. When those things jumped me, tied me up, and dragged me here."

"Stand back, son, we'll vent their hairy hides."

Shaw interrupted the soldiers as they drew back the actions on their gas guns. "No wait. Take them alive."

"Have you gone soft in the head boy?"

"They're spies, I tell you. They can speak, and they know what the Abbies are up to on this island."

"You've been sniffing your gun can, son?"

"I'm telling you they're worth more alive than dead," Shaw checked the shoulder of who was addressing. "Lieutenant. And if we play it nice and slow, they'll come quietly."

The commanding officer thought it over. At last he barked, "You bunch, back up from the door. Let fly if you see any funny business. You," the lieutenant pushed Shaw's shoulder. "Call them out."

Shaw tried to stifle a quiver in his voice. "Come out guys. Come out and kneel down. They won't shoot you if you just come out quietly and lay down."

Burroughs' large figure stepped slowly into the open as two dozen rifles immediately aimed at him. The monstrosity held up his empty, three-fingered hands over his shaggy, square head.

"Look at that big ugly bastard," he heard one of the soldiers mumble as he stepped out and prostrated himself at the mercy of his captors.

"One more. You. Get out here." Shaw cried.

Viday tiptoed out on her ponderous legs. She held out her slightly more human hands, of four digits each.

"What sort of dog is that, son?" the lieutenant asked the duplicitous magician.

"Look at the feet, sir. It's a deer. Jumps everywhere. Short temper. And it's a girl Abby, if you can believe it. Cut me loose and I'll tie them for you."

Viday didn't look Shaw in the face. She crouched next to Burroughs and put her hands on her head.

The army men held the Abberants pinned to the ground as Shaw fetched some rope from the interior of the bunk house. When he returned outside, more men flooded the camp and gathered to watch the show.

A high-ranking official galloped through the throng on the back of a white charger. Other horse riders followed behind. The official, a brigadier general, scanned the attraction. His white hair, mustache and beard twitched in the chill wind. He watched as Shaw secured the two creatures, then intervened.

"Lieutenant Coles. What have you found this time?" the general grumbled in a gravely voice.

"Sir, prisoners."

"More prisoners. I see you're doing better than old ladies this time. Explain to me why they are not dead."

"Spies, sir. Private Belome tells me they will talk if we interrogate them."

"By the fire," the general sighed. "Private Belome! I want the private up front right now."

Shaw pulled one last knot tight and scrambled to stand before the aged general.

"What kind of nonsense are you spreading about my ranks?"

The magician wet his lips, "Sir. I was captured by these scouts. They know everything about the hunt invasion, and they speak."

"Of course they talk, private, but who's going to interrogate them, " the officer pointed a thumb over his shoulder. "My horse?"

"No. No. We can talk to them and they have names like people. Watch. Burroughs! Viday! Look over here, please."

The two shaggy creatures raised their heads and regarded their betrayer.

"Every animal does that. Stand aside." the ranking officer pushed his way through the crowd to stand in front of captured Abberants He pointed at the larger one. "You.

Tell me your name."

"Burroughs Viklund," the half horse spoke low and softly.

Rows of wrinkles ridged the generals forehead as his eyebrows ascended. He pointed at the smaller, brown one. "And you."

"Viday Harjones."

"So you're both with the old woman we arrested, I take it? Missus Harjones."

Viday bit her lip.

The general rubbed his whiskered chin. "Well then. Since we have you two indisposed, there are many things we should talk about."

"Put these freaks in a tent to themselves," the officer shouted at his men. "I want men watching them at all hours. We still set up here. Move in the equipment."

Shaw turned his back and walked off into the mountains.

## Spoons and Super Heroes

"Wham wham wham wham wham. Clink."

Lana felt a tap on her shoulder. She turned her head to see Kyle from the spoon-shaping bench.

"Trade places?" he grinned sheepishly.

Lana took a look at her pile of finished flatware. In the space of time they both worked, she managed five boxes whereas Kyle only finished two. The problem with the imbalance lay in production demand. At the end of the day, everybody needed to stack out equal numbers of each piece of flatware. It was just how things were supposed to be packaged.

Kyle, who was as limpwristed and lazy as Lana's own brother, hardly kept up with his co-workers. Therefore they both forged an agreement to swap places whenever one table ever fell behind. So, once again, Lana faced life of constantly picking up someone else's slack.

The knife table never fell behind. Linda tapped a dull bladed to her carving apparatus, waiting. She kept her output always at the median between the other two dependant pieces of flatware, with lots of time in between for daydreaming.

Such were the inner workings of artifice career, a

simple routine of counting and negotiation; a numbers game.

Lana took her ball peen hammer with her as she traded places.

"Ping ping ping ping ping. Pop," was the sound of the spoon bench. A variation on the same theme.

Mister Stinner plowed through the workshop door. He let the door swing its full arch and jab the knob into the boarded wall. Everybody stopped to look at the commotion. It was not yet lunch time. Even so, no meal emergency ever gave cause for Mister Stinner to make such a dramatic entry.

"Everyone stop. We're locking down the shop."

"Why?"

The portly man held up a posted bill. "Evacuation orders for the whole city. Hundreds of them coming over the mountains, maybe thousands. All of you go home. Pack your things and meet me tomorrow."

"Where at?"

"The sweet shop on Coyle. The one selling jelly fish. We are all taking the first boat they give us," the boss instructed. He repeated the message a few times more, then pulled out his giant ring of keys. Two of the keys on the fob were useful, the rest were tokens of bygone days. Soon enough Stinner would add two more useless keys to the accumulation.

The workshop team formed a silent procession out the shop door. They passed through the warehouse floor filled with unsold flatware and into the street. Stinner pulled the shutter door down. The padlock over the latch secured tightly. From there, they all went their own way.

Outside, Maven changed. The people who once strolled carelessly through the streets now moved with a nervous purpose. Shops all over shut and barred their doors. Boards covered many windows.

A distinct military presence occupied the city. Groups of soldiers, holding guns more menacing than the marshals, crowded the street corners. Uniformed patrols walked the avenues night and day. They dug trenches into the green belt outside of the town. The dug-outs stretched daily.

The thought ran through everybody's mind, but would not pass their lips. The war followed them home, their home. What many believed impossible was simply an eventuality.

One figure stood out against the exodus, a haggard and dirty vagabond. The vagrant flailed in animated gesture. His filthy beard bobbed with his shouts. "Judgment is here," he shouted madly. "The beast who devoured God is coming. He raised up creatures in his own image to replace us. Woe and despair. His doom shrouds us all! Pantherian rises."

Lana made the mistake of contacting the drifter's eyes as he shouted the blasphemous message.

"Miss. Do you have any money? I'm so thirsty. Anything. Anything will do."

Against her better judgment, Lana pulled some gella notes and handed them out. No doubt the homeless man would waste it on booze and pass out in a gutter later.

"Oh. Bless you. Bless you," his gnarled hands snatched up the offering. He looked around at the passing crowd and edged uncomfortably close to Lana. "I was a wizard once. I done seen things, but no one believes me. I know. I done seen it. I know what's happening, but they don't listen."

"That's nice," Lana tried to walk away but the crazy person snatched her arm.

"It's you. You will escape the Dread King. I seen it. I seen you spit in his eye and run away. You're blessed. Old Harold knows the glow. The blessing is in you."

Lana broke the grip holding her and ran down the street. The panhandler shouted something over her head, but did not give chase.

## *Where to Find Quotes for Your Book Report*

The interrogator dismissed the guards from the tent and closed the flap behind them. An army profession entailed plenty of time in the sun, but apparently not for Sargent Setter. His pale skin, eyes, and lips gave him a ghostly face. Sharp cheekbones jutted out the sides of his head, and his slat nose ran a hard edge. He strutted about the room as he talked, flapping with this hands. Burroughs guessed he was being tormented by a crane Abberant.

"Ah, Mister Viklund, I hope you were not starting to think we forgot about you."

Burroughs made no reply, only looking up.

They secured him to a large steel feeding trough. Whenever feeding time came, they poured out a feed mixture into the bin, and water into the other end. Each time they did so they led a few horses in the tent to eat from the troth with him. Since Burroughs' hands were tied he ate exactly as an animal, snorting and chomping. He suffered the demeaning glances of his half relatives for the past two meals. Bits of food still clung to his face.

Viday was being kept somewhere else. Burroughs had not seen her for nearly a day.

"So we are told you are the pet of Sargent Viklund, the notorious Invincible Vick. Impressive. He was a little before my time, but I heard some of the stories. Mostly fantasy, I'm sure."

"A few of them," Burroughs replied flatly.

Setter stopped for a second. The interrogator's expression showed disgusted surprise, as if he couldn't believe what he was talking to. "Yes, well. Perhaps I should have questioned you first. You, no doubt, have respect for the military."

"Some," Burroughs answered laconically. He looked over to see Setter had brought in a gas gun with him. The weapon came from repurposed combustion driven machines, using petroleum fuel as a means of propelling slugs and pellets. The rifle in the tent was crafted recently. The cut steel of the truncated engine block glittered in the dim light, and a greasy coating had not taken to the propellant bottle yet. On the wooden shoulder stock showed the engine-maker logo, a tiny reminder of the old world.

Setter waved his hand in front of the object Burroughs stared at. He snapped his fingers a few times. "Focus, Mister Viklund. We don't have much time. Your willingness to cooperate with us comes as quite a surprise. There are not many people we question these days, and most of those people get to see a courtmarshal."

The interrogator put a thumb to his chin before carrying on. "Yes. You are an exception. Perhaps, if you help us, we can help you. Show a bit of loyalty to the army for your old man, huh?"

"I am listening."

"Hmm. Well. Let's start slow them. When did you meet the old lady, Missus Harjones?"

"Five days ago."

"Okay, and what was the nature of your visit."

"Medical treatment."

"Mmm. Yes, and how did you come to know you could find medical treatment there? Is there a network of Abberant hunt sympathizers among us? If so, I am prepared to make an offer for this information," Setter bent over, giving a conspiring grin.

"This is not the case."

The interrogator straightened his posture. "Perhaps. We have good people here in the Union, and sometimes they can be misguided. You were wounded then."

"Yes."

"By whom?"

"Canid hunt."

"Your own kind?"

"Canid. Dogs, technically."

Setter shrugged off the distinction. "And why would they do that?"

"I was aiding a person they pursued."

"Truly?"

"Yes, a swimmer named Shaw."

"A swimmer, you say? How odd.

"He's now named Private Belome."

Setter tilted his head back and cackled a few laughs. Pulling out a thin note pad, he put down something. "Oh my stars. We're back to Private Belome again. We caught that fool wandering off into he hills, and hauled him to camp kicking and screaming. He has since busied himself by pulling his survey equipment into the mine shaft to make some kind of hermitage. He won't follow orders, and we can't seem to coax him out. Last night, the guard caught him sneaking around. Do you know what he was doing?"

"No."

"We caught him strapping chili stew to the broken water tower, unopened cans."

Burroughs rolled his eyes and sighed.

"Let's skip ahead. What were you and Missus Viday Harjones doing here in the mountains before you captured Private Belome."

"Traveling to a mountain meadow to meet a magical being."

Setter put away his notes and pinched his eyebrows

together. "At the request of Private Belome, correct?"

"Yes."

"Do you know what I think?"

"Tell me."

The interrogator snarled a wicked rictus. "The King of Beasts has a sense of humor to send you all this way to bother me with such an outrageous ruse. What are the Abbies using to learn how to speak so well."

"School primers, and Alexander Twin novels."

"Oh, a fellow fan of literature. This makes what I have to do a little amusing. Excuse me while I fetch your friend." The thin man strutted through the tent flaps. Minutes later a dull scraping pulled up to the entrance, and Setter backed in dragging a chair. Tied firmly to the seat was Viday. She did not move.

With her duster off, Viday's narrow frame came short of filling the back of the chair. In nothing but her undershirt and breeches, she made a frail figure outside of her bigger, baggier clothes. Her overly large feet dangled out from the chair legs they were tied to. The flows of her chestnut fur were disrupted in places to indicate she'd received beatings. One of her eyes swelled shut. A blood welt stood out on her lip, and a dangle of drool trickled from her muzzle. Some weak coughs left Viday's mouth as she tried to say something, but her voice was too feeble.

"Have you heard this one scream. She makes quite a noise. Starts off normal enough, but gets throaty near the end. After a while, it's a honking sound. I'm not much one for animal cruelty, but I just need to remind you what kind of animals you are. I'm beginning to think you have forgotten."

"You animal."

Setter produced a small knife. "My my, look who is talking." Viday squirmed as the interrogator scraped the dull side of the blade against her nose.

"I wouldn't stoop to tormenting the helpless, if that

167

is what you're implying," it was a tone of voice Burroughs didn't know he had, rich and rumbling like a coming thunderstorm. "Otherwise. Listen carefully. It is true, I am half man and half beast. I may behave as an animal when needed, and carry myself as a person as I choose. You are no different. You're choosing to act like a depraved animal, even when you are fully human. Our bodies are not the issue, but the decisions we make."

"So I am the vicious animal now," Setter gave a nervous laugh. His eye moved to his gun a few times. "I bet if I untied you we would not be settling our differences in a civilized discussion."

"Care to find out?"

## *Animal Control*

"How long has it been standing there?"

"Five minutes or so."

"It must see us. Why isn't it running?"

"Shut up Gomez. I'm going to drop it before it runs off."

Pulling the trigger released a spray of petroleum into the breach of the rifle, then a spark. All of the soldiers in the camp sat up in their stations as the first gun fire sounded. Watching through his scope, Lieutenant Jones saw his target hit the ground and stop moving. He kept his eye on the Canid.

The general hurried to the perimeter, "Give me a status."

"Sir, Abby poking around down range. We requisitioned a sighted rifle from the armory and put it down."

"How many?"

"One sir."

Jones hissed and pulled back the action of the long

range gun. "It's getting back up." Another muzzle flash blinked from the rifle and the figure down range crumpled back over. The sniper adjusted where he rested the long barrel on the sand bag bunker and sighted his scope again.

The general pulled out a pair of binoculars to see the creature for himself. "Shoot all you want boys. That thing is not going down."

Down the field, the dog aberration stood back up, stumbling about for a second then holding itself erect.

"I'm calling all the patrols in. Make ready. It is going to be a long night." With that, the general ran to the communication tent.

Jones bit the inside of his mouth nervously. "So I'm supposed to watch this thing stare at us."

As if the aberration could hear his voice, the Canid made eye contact with the sniper through his scope. The golden eyes peered into Jones as if through a window, very close. "Agh, it's cursing me. I know it."

"Hit 'em again."

"Wait, wait, he's running off now."

"Finally, what was that thing?"

Shaw broke into the conversation. "Heartblood."

Startled by the sudden appearance, the guard whipped their heads over their shoulders. The two soldiers looked the magician up and down, taking in his burnt and tattered robe with curious speculation.

"Get ready. He will be back."

## This Stuff Will Kill Ya

Evening set in on the military camp when the sun lowered itself onto the needle point of Mount Mortimer. The ball of fire spread two imperfect halves. Minutes later the sun disappeared altogether, causing Mount Mortimer to make a crack in the glow of sundown, a pitch-dark nail scratching the sky.

The camp hustled with activity. Giving up on sandbag defenses, the fighting men pulled rocks from the trenches near the mine entrance and stacked them into makeshift walls. They heard the reports from earlier in the afternoon. Even though the patrols found nothing, they knew the monsters would set on them in the night.

Shaw knew it too. He hid away, inside the mine entrance. For many hours he sat there, dejected, defeated. He kept the timber Burroughs used as a staff next to him.

He traced along the bark pattern on the ends with his finger, and took special care not to touch and activate the magic within. The first shock made the message clear.

It had come to the part of the game where his unavoidable failure would come again. The dogs would come, overpower the soldiers, and get what they wanted. Shaw was about to fail at a mission, again. He found himself in hopeless situations before, but a weight of shame hung on this one.

The sensation of Viday pummeling him came back. He recalled in detail her animal snarl and the accusations. She was right. He did it again, used his friends for personal gain then dropped them when they became a problem. This time, like all the other times, he gained nothing for it. People suffered because of him, for his fickle ways.

"Hey Martha," Shaw began talking to seemingly nobody. "I botched it up again. It's pretty bad down here, if you haven't noticed, and some of it is my fault. So I'm about to do something stupid, just to give you a warning. I'm told you're the one keeping score. So I think you have a right to know. Let the rest of the guys know, at the end, I was playing to win."

Shouldering the ebony post, Shaw stood up and muttered, "At least I hate myself," as if it were a source of comfort.

The light dimmed, but Shaw could see the stone walls the other soldiers hid behind. The piles came to about a man's midsection in height. Most stacks were just a push away from falling one way or the other. Soldiers leaned against tiny, strategic mountains, groups of three to six. Every last eyes peered into the coming darkness. Rations of guns and ammunitions sat near the fighters. They had to share each small cache.

Two guards barred entry into the prisoner tent. Both of them saw Shaw from well away.

"Let me in."

"No one is allowed in unless they have permission

from Sargent Setter or General Clayborn."

"Well, I am with the general, I suppose."

One of the guards held up his gun and shoved it out without letting go. "Get back to your hole Belome, or pick up a gun and help out. Either way, move along."

Some murmuring seemed to die out in the tent. The callow face of Sargent Setter peeped out to see the goings-on. "Ah, Private Belome. I was about to go fetch you, but you've saved me the trip. Guards, restrain him. Bring him inside."

The guards set upon the magician, knocking the dark lumber from his grip. As they twisted Shaw's hands behind his back, the staff clattered on the stone ground. The sound it made was as if someone turned over a large xylophone, hitting many higher notes than it should have.

Then they came. Howling and clamorous barks filled the mountains from all directions. The cacophony grew slowly stronger, closer. All four men froze in horror at the howling darkness closing in. Quickly, the captors shoved Shaw inside the tent behind the interrogator.

Setter turned his back on Shaw for just a moment, but when he turned around both guards lay face down on the floor of the tent. The magician curled the fingers of his hands a few times, and felt along his wrists. Setter went for his gun. Shaw closed the distance before the barrel could face him and swatted the fuel bottle of the rifle to disable it.

The following exchange of blows went unnoticed from those outside. The melee swiftly became one-sided, as Shaw never received proper military training. The minister attempted to contact Setter with the palms of his hands, but the interrogator wore gloves. Each time the enemy dodged, or caught grabs at the wrist. Too often, Shaw caught on to a piece of clothing, which would not do.

Setter drove his assailant to the ground. He brought his boot down on Shaw several times until the magician stopped moving.

Panting for a second, Shaw got up and charged the

Sargent one last time. He managed to tackle the interrogator. They both fell down beside Burroughs.

Seizing the chance, the horse aberration brought up the entire metal feeding trough and sent it down on Setter. Setter's pale face folded around the steel foot of the trough. There was a splatter of blood mixed with saliva, and a crunch like biting into a carrot. Burroughs shifted more weight on his tormentor until the metal bin leveled with the floor. Shaw crawled away from the carnage.

Reaching around inside his robe, the magician found his combat knife. He looked at it for a second, wondering why he didn't use it earlier. It most likely wouldn't have mattered. He cut Burroughs free.

Burroughs looked fine, hardly touched except for obvious chafing around his arms and legs. Scrape marks marred the floor around the feeding trough they bound him to, and the heavy-duty stakes anchoring the trough were half pulled up.

"Viday, where is she?" the magician panted. Burroughs gave no reply, only looking at a chair.

The brown duster Viday wore covered a chair in the corner. It took a second for Shaw to notice her feet jutting underneath. Hurriedly, Shaw pulled back the coat and immediately winced.

So Setter tortured Viday and made Burroughs watch. Her condition was bad. Many open sores matted her fur with blood, Her breath was short and weak, barely at all. A few of her finger joints were dislocated. Worst of all, they cut gashes in her large ears, trying not to rupture arteries but not always succeeding.

Shaw cut her lose and her arms just dangled to the side. "We're leaving," he told her.

Viday's brows came together in a spiteful look.

Curling his fingers into claws, the magician glared at his palm. "Come on," he hissed. The vapor conjuration lifted from his hand, and he applied as much as he could to closing Viday's wounds. "I need to drink more water," he

174

explained. "Hold on."

Outside the tent, the rising tide of animal cries reached maddening levels. Soldiers fired at nothing, swearing and shaking their heads. Something bent over Burroughs' staff, trying to drag it away. Getting closer, Shaw saw it was a gargoyle. The beast flapped its wings to attempt a vertical takeoff and would have escaped with the weapon if Shaw had not intervened. Shrieking in rage, the giant bat felt the staff's end slip from its feet and hardly had time to retaliate before gunfire tore at its wings.

Shaw ran for the tent as the gargoyle crawled after him. A few final shots from a nearby fortification put the thing down.

Inside, Burroughs took his weapon. The horse aberration tapped an end to Shaw's shoulder. The white tendrils snaked under his shoulder and held tight. With that, Burroughs lifted the magician off the ground to look at him face to face. Shaw gave back a placid expression as Burroughs' brown, bestial eyes glared at him. Hot, angry breath jetted out of the horse's nostrils and into the magician's face. The big half man said nothing.

"If you want to," Shaw invited.

Burroughs dropped the fool on the ground, letting him go.

Shaw got up and tended to Viday, "Can you get up? We need to get out of here." She only wheezed back.

"Her legs are broken, Shaw." Burroughs explained in a dooming voice.

"I will carry her. Help me get her into her coat."

They both dressed Viday as she moaned softly in discomfort. Shaw pulled Viday onto his shoulders in a piggy back fashion.

"We're escaping through the mines, Burroughs. It's our only option. I moved our things in there."

"It's suicide. We'll be trapped even if we make it."

"Probably, but it's a big mine and we stand a better chance in there."

"Until you stab us in the back." Viday whispered in his ear.

Shaw bit on his upper lip. "It's straight out there. A dead run."

"We'll be shot down in an instant."

"I took care of that."

A hissing and crackling began around the water tower, followed by a chain of explosions. Blooms of zesty fire rained out shrapnel as well as cooked, greasy meat. Brown stains spattered all of the soldiers outside, and a spicy cloud of flavor lifted into the air as the rickety tower plummeted to the earth.

Burroughs ran ahead. A few soldiers stood in his way, and they quickly found themselves relieved of their weapons and swept off the ground. A group of five readied their guns upon seeing the approaching monster, but their volley only peppered the side of a bunkhouse. Shaw passed dangerously close to catching the gunfire.

The fighters left Shaw very much alone. No one seemed to notice Viday through her baggy duster. Besides that, Burroughs put on quite a show. The horse's powerful yet nimble pacing sidestepped bullets. His staff scooped up rocks from the ground, and Burroughs spun his weapon and flung projectiles with great leverage. Those he didn't beat senseless at close range found their legs pulled from underneath them and tossed away. The way the staff reached and grabbed instantly was wondrous and terrifying.

Burroughs finished carving his warpath and disappeared into the mine. While running deeper inside, Burroughs spotted the oil lantern Shaw left behind and latched it to the end of his weapon without slowing a step. The light swung fitfully at the end of the staff but did not die out.

"Keep going deeper. They're chasing us," Shaw gasped for breath as he tried to match the pace.

A clangor of boot steps echoed off the stone walls behind them, a score it sounded, maybe not so much. The

176

pursuit nearly caught up when Shaw had an idea. "Take Viday and hide. Give me the light."

Burroughs did so and disappeared into the darkness. The soldiers appeared seconds later.

"That was your light Belome? Give it to us. There is an Abby in here. The ones who captured you."

"You guys should know better than to run into a dark cave without bringing a light," Shaw snuffed out the lantern. The room fell into pitch darkness until two blue rings began glowing. A series of painful screams followed as the dim lights bobbed around the blackness.

Burroughs, in his hiding place, cradled Viday through the horrible shouting and wet noises. After less than a minute the screams stopped, leading to an eerie silence. Footsteps approached in the darkness. Something walked directly to Burroughs. He looked down to see Shaw's small face grinning with homicidal insanity. The magician's grin stretched oddly wide, and the blue, glowing stare was of an otherworldly predator. Burroughs nearly dropped Viday.

"I lost my knife," Shaw pouted. "Or broke it, rather." He lit the lantern with a snap. Streaks of blood lined his face and stained his white garment. "Come over here. I'll show you."

"No."

The dull chattering of the Abberant hunt abruptly roared outside. More voices joined the chorus. Guns fired off incessantly. All these sounds of battle echoed off the carved walls of the mine, distorting and amplifying.

"This is the last of the chili," Shaw took a deep breath and concentrated.

A huge crash riveted the mountain. Gales of dust buffeted all three refugees as the earth shifted not far away. The sound of raining rocks filled the dark passage, then nothing. No noise of battle could be heard. All three coughed for a minute.

"Is there a way out of this mine?" Burroughs asked.

"I'm not sure," Shaw replied. The magician dusted off the lantern and put it down with the handle up. He then held out his hands to take Viday back.

Burroughs looked at the blood and mud caking onto the magician. He hesitated for a second. "Best I carry." He pushed his staff into Shaw's hands. "Show us to our gear."

Grunting under the weight of the wooden post, Shaw picked up the lantern from the floor and soldiered on. They ventured deeper into the mines.

## Be the Light in the Darkness

The way was very deep and very dark. The single light of the small lantern kept them from complete darkness, but only barely. Frequently, the little flame flickered, giving brief moments of blackness where no one could see, except Shaw.

The magician kept the light of his eyes going, and only used the light as a means of guiding Burroughs through the passages as he carried Viday. "I bought the cheap one," he lamented along the way. "If I had known, I would have gone for the bigger one. It had a dish on it, little meshing on the sides. Fancy."

"Hold for a second," Burroughs asked. The procession stopped.

They listened to the craggy corridors for a second. He thought he heard a distant scratching along with a trickling noise. Nothing could be heard with them standing still. Perhaps it was only his hooves on the gravely floor playing back as a strange echo. When they moved, Burroughs made the most noise. His thick feet played off the ground with dull, wooden knocks.

"It's nothing."

Shaw was not convinced. "Viday."

She didn't even bother twisting her ruined ears. "Take me to my bags," she demanded.

They walked past a few overturned wheel barrows and broken beams, and in a large opening they found their bags. Burroughs put Viday down near her things and she quickly began pulling out items. The other two watched dumbly. She took out a few bandage rolls, and several bottles liquid and pills. From the corner of her eye she caught Shaw moving for a canteen. "I need water," she coughed.

The magician's hand quickly capped the water container. The ordeal outside left him parched, and this half full canteen of water was the last of it. If he went on too long without a drink, there would be trouble. He dawdled a little then handed the water over.

Sitting on the ground, Viday ran her fingers down her leg. She applied pressure, until she found the fracture. From a padded box, Viday produced a syringe. The needle drank for a bottle as she pulled the plunger back. "Hold the light closer," she demanded.

Burroughs secured the tiny light to the end of his staff and hovered it over Viday.

"Thank you," she held up the medical instrument to force out any air bubbles and then jabbed herself in both legs with the sharp needle, one and then the next. Bandages wrapped over one leg, which she treated with a stinging fluid and a chalky powder. Pouring water on the wrapping made a hiss and within seconds hardened into a cast. Viday probed her other leg and swore. "Help me set the bone."

"What?" Shaw looked up from the camping backpack. He searched for something to quench his thirst.

Viday looked at Burroughs. "Hold me down. You," she nodded at Shaw. "Pull on my leg until I tell you to stop."

"But it's broken," Shaw protested.

"It won't grow back straight unless I move it into

180

place. Now help me set my leg."

So the two men pulled on her damaged leg. Because of the injection, Viday felt very little of the pain. Her breath labored regardless as she spurred Shaw to pull harder and harder. On a few of the attempts, she let out a bleating groan.

"Again. Harder. They're not seating."

"I'm going to break it more at this rate."

"It's your fault my leg is shattered in the first place. Now again."

Shaw grabbed the foot again, but his tug softened noticeably.

"Harder you worthless bastard! If my leg rots off because of you and your weak wrists, I will tie you down and pull out your organs one at a time until you die. Believe me, it takes longer than you think."

The bones of her thigh came together with a neat pop. Viday screamed in agony as the other two dropped her and staggered away.

"Oh cats! I'm so sorry."

"No. You did it. We're fine." She finished up the second cast with the last of the water. Shaw licked his lips as the last drops hit the bandages. Viday flattened her back on the ground "You didn't pack any crutches, did you?"

Burroughs gave the magician an expectant look. Shaw caught it and shook his head.

The three of them devoured a large portion of the food. For nearly an entire day their bodies ran on hardly anything but the impulse of fear. With the threat gone they relaxed in the soundless underground, and the hunger set in. Nobody discussed rationing the food or if there were no ways out. Shaw slurped all of the syrup from a can of peaches and ate the contents. Viday choked down as much as she dared. Burroughs did his best to get the grainy feed flavor out of his mouth.

After the small feast, Shaw staked out a flat piece of floor and took his friends to it. Viday crawled into the bed roll. Shaw pulled his robe inside out to expose the cleaner side.

"Are you ready?" Shaw held up the oil lamp. They burned a good portion of the fuel, but there was an extra can in the bag. As least, he thought there was. He would check later. "Hear anything?"

Burroughs checked, "Nothing." Viday said the same.

Shaw put out the light and got a better look at the room. He saw the way they came. The square portal spilled gravel onto the smooth, flat stone of the floor they rested on. Two other exits continued farther into the cave. One sank downward and the other ramped up.

The presence of Maurius grew stronger. Shaw could make out the direction now. Unfortunately, the direction followed the downward path and not the upward. After a rest, he could lead them upward, but maybe he would need to double back. On the other hand, he could lead them down and chance into actually making it close enough to contact Maurius from underneath. Getting into the old one's sphere of influence would be enough. Up or down, he rolled the choices around in his head. He decided to sleep on it.

Hours later they stirred from slumber. Viday asked for some light. She swallowed some pills. Without any water to wash it down, she flushed some mush from her peculiar stomach and swallowed the medication with it.

"I wish I didn't see that," Shaw closed his eyes tight. He got a good look at the half digested slime.

"Well, don't look next time."

Burroughs attached the lantern to the top of his staff. He carried his backpack as well as the added burden of Viday's two bags. It was quite a sight, watching him move along with all the baggage; swinging the light to and fro as he stepped. Burroughs gave the look of a peddler, or maybe a gypsy, on a pilgrimage through dark and forbidding lands.

Shaw pulled Viday onto his back. The casts on her thighs made good hand holds. He lit his eyes and looked up at Burroughs with his ghostly face. "Follow me." He led them on the lower path.

The walls and ceiling became less defined. They shifted about, squeezing in and stretching out. Cracks gaped open in the floor, deep and treacherous. Little nubs began to appear on the ceiling.

All the while Viday smelled the blood under Shaw's collar and the sweat running down his neck. She felt sick all over again.

"What sort of mine is this?" Shaw thought out loud.

"The kind we die in," Viday gave Shaw a creepy whisper into his ear. "Trapped down here with good old Master Shaw. Underground in the most earthquake riddled land the new world knows. Hope we find our way out or the roof caves in on us. Because if we starve down here, someone will become food for the Abberants."

Burroughs guided the lantern down a crack, and ran the light along the walls. The enclosure was eroded, not picked. "We've reached a cavern," he concluded.

Shaw stopped the procession. "It that bad?" He turned about. "Do you hear anything."

"There is water down here," Viday spoke over the magician shoulder. "I can hear it when my ears aren't whistling."

"I don't understand, why?"

Burroughs held the light to the roof, illuminating a few stalagmites. "Not all rivers running from the mountains go above ground. Some can run underground and make caverns like this one."

"Then why aren't we flooded?"

"The water found a way out. It made a spring somewhere, above ground."

"Basic geology," Viday muttered.

"Then if we find the stream and follow it. We can get out," Shaw brightened.

"Maybe," Burroughs grunted.

Shaw didn't mind the pessimism. He turned about and confided with the deer aberration on his shoulder. "Point the way." She pointed to an oval opening a few yards away.

As the travelers continued, they found stalagmites jutting out of the floor in various lengths. Paired with the stalactites from the ceiling, the cave began to take on a jagged jaw of teeth; some white fangs, some gray. Then there came the dulcet dribbling of water. Shaw heard it and quickened his pace.

Viday beat on the magician's shoulder. "Slow down. Being carried hurts enough as it is."

"Shaw," Burroughs the pack master waved the light out. "Do you see that."

"It's glowing blue like your eyes," Viday whispered.

The magician's eyes dimmed. At first he saw nothing, but then a blue glow rounded the corner up ahead. "Soul source glow. Maurius? Why can't I hear him if I'm so close."

They followed the light and trickling sound to the source. A small subterranean lake pooled in the middle of a large room filled with spiny rock formations. The three weaved through the thick groupings of stalagmites to find the water's edge. One end of the lake cascaded down a stair into the darkness. Pores dribbled steady steams of water on the opposite end of the lake.

Somewhere under the surface gleamed a beacon of calming blue light. The moving water rippled the gleam about, making the shadows of the congregated stalagmites shift about the smooth cavern wall. The stone pillars seemed to form a somber crowd, milling about the edge of the lake but not making a noise.

"Maurius! Pontifex Maurius of the one hundred sixty-seven, blessed to know the face of Martha," Shaw gripped the top of a stalagmite and leaned on it. "What's wrong," he mumbled to himself. "That's him. I know it. Only the great old ones glow like that when they want. Stay here."

The young man let Viday down off his back. He took a knee by the edge of the lake and palmed the water. He cupped an elbow and rubbed his chin. In the blink of an eye, he vanished . A great shadow darkened the room for a second, then the light returned. With a splash, Shaw surfaced holding a magnificent stone in his hands.

The blue fire raged within the glassy rock. A smooth surface covered the stone, pock marked by a few pores. The holes on the skin of the gemlike object ran directly to the light in the center, becoming thin as pins. Overall, the shape of the rock was amorphous; a little flat in some areas, bulbous at other places.

Everybody gazed in wonder.

"He's" Shaw began. He tried to find the right word but he knit his brows and shook his head in disbelief. "Dead? They don't die."

"Wouldn't he be dead if the shine went out?" Burroughs put down some of the baggage.

"Maybe, but he's supposed to be diffused through the whole river system. Instead he hardened his whole body here and his mind is gone." Shaw licked his lips. "Gone. He's one hundred percent in this thing, but he's broken. This is how the Abberant legion landed on the island. Maurius died and nothing could stop them from crossing the water."

Shaw pushed the gem back into the water. The blue mote glided gracefully down the smooth walls of the pool to the point Shaw disturbed it from. "There is a good amount of power left. I can use some to fix your legs." He started to pick up Viday.

"What are you doing?"

"Don't hold your breath. I'll take care of it."

"I swear, I will actually kill you if throw me in there."

"Trust me. I'm a minister."

"I did. I remember what happened."

"Well trust me again," Shaw shoved the chestnut brown aberration into the lake. She shouted horrible threats as she thrashed around, failing to tread water. The magician knelt at the edge of the pool. The instant his hand enter the water, Viday was pulled under with a bloop. The sweet vapors Shaw conjured in his hand to close cuts began bubbling from the lake. Burroughs watched Viday kicking about near the bottom, next to the body of the departed old one. Streams of bubbles poured out of her mouth and trailed up to the surface.

"This is the real stuff. The real miracle." Shaw sighed whimsically.

The sweet gas formed a fog over the surface of the lake. It crept through the crowd of stalagmites and rolled past the magician and the horse. Beneath the cloud squirmed the form of Viday. Her shadow cast feral shapes along the roof of the cavern, trying to claw out.

"That should do it,"He willed the flailing puppet in his control back to the shore.

At the shallows, Viday felt the surface and instantly established a footing. She rocketed out of the water, leaving a trail of droplets falling away behind. Her feet hit the side of a thick pillar and she slid safely down the side. The bounce of her locomotion returned as she did her careful tiptoe walk around a few stalagmites. Her wet ears were bent down in anger. Her eyes gleamed with hate. Burroughs backed away.

In a flurry, Viday pounced Shaw to the ground. The renewed vigor in her arms helped scoop the magician off the floor. She snapped a tirade of sharp words into Shaw's distraught face. She shook her victim vigorously. Then she threw Shaw screaming into the lake with a great splash.

Viday rejoined Burroughs. "Help me break these casts off."

"Hmmm," Burroughs swung the light closer to

Viday. The coloration of the deer Abberant's fingers turned white. Also the healed portions of ears, eyes, and mouth bleached of color as well.

"What?"

"Nothing."

Breaking open the hard case around Viday's legs revealed more discoloration. White rings of silky hair wrapped her knees nearly half a foot above and below. The fractures healed, but she knew it already.

Shaw surfaced sopping wet.

# Someone's Funeral

The two aberrations spent hours waiting as the magician communed with the dying body of the old one. Shaw sat meditating, his hands held palms-down in the pool. Alien muttering passed from his lips as his eyed darted around the expansive room. The memories, he told them. He needed to find any recollection of Maurius before the old one's mind shattered and the body shriveled into a stone. The magician sat cross-legged before the glistening underground lake.

The old ones were the first and highest in the Ministry. They were people from the old world who escaped death. By some machination, the old ones boiled their minds out of their own bodies to become entities of fluid; surviving by the single necessity of water. In this simple form of life they planned on living forever, but instead they found themselves trapped in jarred prisons of their own design.

After years of suffering a false life, an angel came to them. In a single splendid night all one hundred sixty-seven minds came together as one, under the guidance of Martha. The angelic being transfigured the old ones. She revealed all mysteries on heaven and earth to those fortunate, and brought them together to form the makings of the Ministry. They also learned of the Beast's coming. So, in the one night, the trapped souls freed themselves. They shattered their glass prisons and drained into the rivers and oceans. It was then they took on a new purpose as saviors for mankind, indoctrinating people as lesser host and claiming the bodies of the drowned as servants.

It was all so fanciful to Shaw. He hardly believed it, despite the way evidence compounded before his eyes. He wouldn't believe the whole of it until Martha showed herself. With the opportunity to pick Maurius's brain, maybe he would finally see.

Shaw peeled away memories from the old one's shell; images, sounds, thought. He saw Maurius as he once was, an old man. Destroyed cities and their names took a portion of the search; crumbled towers, shattered houses, fallen bridges, great monuments of good will brought low. The fury of Pantherian rose out of the rubble, and his armies flooded the land. Some people fought, others fled the mainland to establish the new world. Brief glimpses of the Union's foundation rolled by. Shaw watched the founding of Acosta, Mercer, Wellborn, New Kansas, and the castles of Hope Standing. There was the unavoidable return to the main lands, and a war without end.

Laced all throughout were the dealing of the Ministry. Shaw saw firsthand as people took on the thirst; himself, Elizabeth, Hobson, Hotchkiss, Korman. He witnessed many of the magics he took for granted, all used in secret. Nothing new, all of these visions he either knew already or could have guessed.

"It's no good," Shaw stood up and shook the moisture from his pruned hands. "I can't find anything to help us."

"What do you mean?" Viday counted out her bottles and ampules in the blue cave light.

The magician mimed holding a box with both his

hands. "His mind is preserved, sort of, but none of it is helpful."

"Are you asking the same questions over and over again? I don't know. Maybe sit someplace else."

Shaw shook the imaginary box. "It's not like that. It's like reading a book."

Burroughs sat by the water stair watching hundreds of tiny waterfalls cascading into the abyss. "In that case," he commented. "Stop reading the same way."

"I don't," Shaw began. He puffed out his cheeks in mid-sentence, stopping what he was saying. His hands released the invisible box he'd held. The non-existent parcel vanished into the ether, and for some reason Shaw gained a profound sense of loss at the box's passing. Silently, he went back to divining by the pool side.

On the second try, the memories jumbled together with no regard to time or place; no context at all. Maurius' mind became broken puzzles. Some of the pieces were missing, and others were in the wrong place. Perhaps the old one decayed during Shaw's hiatus, or maybe the issue lay with Shaw.

The magician stopped thinking, a feat he found surprisingly easy. With his mind free, the recollections poured in in no order.

For a brief moment, a society came into view. Clean, paved streets ran between houses of varying sizes and construction. Among this happy community teemed anthropic creatures of all types, Abberant and human. They formed gatherings, conversed with one another, traded, and labored in the streets and buildings. It was by no means a utopia. Verbal and physical arguments erupted without notice. Many denizens used their physical advantages over other parties to both harm and good. All citizens stole, lied, fought, cheated, and even murdered; and all faced punishment. Yet the entire city kept thriving regardless as the collective majority continued to build, improve, and share their home.

Just as the sight intrigued Shaw, the vision fizzled away. He emptied his thoughts again.

Another vision of a great tree came into view, its boughs stretched as wide as continents and expanded into eternity. Its roots covered the entire world in a great tangled network. As the picture became clearer, the tree began to quiver and shrink. Animals of all walks formed groups of their own kind; flying, sprinting, clawing, biting, ramming, kicking, butting one another. Every creature living in the tree's branches fought for their neighbor's portion. Upon conquering a branch, the victor's former home shriveled away forcing the manic fighting ever onward.

The shrinking continued until hardly any creatures inhabited the world tree. So much girth left the tree that cosmic breeze began shaking the branches. Despite this, the struggle continued until the tree became the size of a city and only five creatures walked along the boughs.

At last, the contention stopped. The five wiser animals realized their situation and ceased their hostilities so they could preserve their holdings. The truce lasted for hundreds of years, yet the damage was not undone. The tree could not grow to its previous splendor.

Over time, each defeated creature emerged from under the roots of the giant tree. They prowled along the ground, looking jealously up at those above. Their numbers swelled in time, until their crowd stretched to all horizons. In their fury, they shook the tree at its base hoping to loose their triumphant enemies from the branches.

One after another the creatures fell, and the branches shrank away. At last, the final creature tumbled down. As the last one fell, the forever green leaves on the tree shriveled and blew away. The bark darkened and twisted on itself, shrinking smaller and smaller until a pathetic black shape remained.

The light died out.

When Shaw left his half dream, darkness covered the entire cave. He stood up and lit his eyes. A few paces away, Burroughs had a hand in the water. Near his frozen grasp floated a canteen the half horse attempted to fill. A bug eyes expression ruined Burroughs' usual calm. His square, protruding jaw quivered.

"Are you all right?" Shaw shouted. The magician's voice reverberated off the cavern walls. "Is everybody okay? Hold still. I'll get the light." He did so. Viday looked on as Shaw approached Burroughs holding the lantern up. "Hey big guy. You feeling okay?"

"I broke Maurius."

"He was on his way out," Shaw dismissed the blame. "I think I have an idea what is going on."

"For the true god to rule, the old gods must die. Maurius commanded me," Burroughs whispered reverently.

"Yeah," Shaw agreed. "Let's go back to camp. There is something I need to share."

They formed a small circle around the tiny light as Shaw began his story. The light played on their grim faces as they huddled together away from the creeping darkness drawing in.

"The Abberants flooding this island, they're not after me. They were never after me. They were hunting a tree stolen years ago. That." The magician pointed a finger at the staff Burroughs used as a weapon. "They want it back. They need it back, and Pantherian is willing to pay any cost to get it."

Burroughs turned the staff over in his thick hands.

Shaw continued. "Hundreds of years ago the Dread King foresaw his own demise. He envisioned a small tree planted in his chest, which grew until there would be nothing left of him. After searching the whole world he finally found the thing, a tiny white barked tree no larger than a sapling. Instead of burning the little thing, he kept it for years. The Ministry has been trying to get their hands on it so we could turn it against him, but he guarded the thing well. Thirty years ago, however, the tree went missing and the king went into a frenzy. We had to back off, but no one knew where the plant disappeared to."

"I remember a small white tree. We grew it in a terrarium by the window," Burroughs said.

"Nobody knew where it went. We suspected Andreas Viklund took it, but he did an excellent task of avoiding us. It was as if he knew about us."

"He had a good idea, but do you honestly think this is the same plant?"

"All I know is they want it, and it could be."

"The small tree I remember went missing for fifteen years. Somebody else must have it by now."

Shaw crossed his arms. "Then why is Maurius commanding you to kill Pantherian if this isn't the real tree?"

Burroughs tapped the end of the post into the stone floor, sending a knock echoing through the caves. His breath deepened and he tossed confused and questioning looks all about. "Then what?"

Without any hesitation, Shaw blurted. "We slay Pantherian."

"Lunacy."

"No, prophecy."

"Same thing."

Shaw put it flatly. "The choice is to hide and be hunted for the rest of your life, or plant the tree and end the war. With the power of the Beast gone, we can start making progress."

Viday scoffed, "As in killing or enslaving Abberants."

"No. I mean stop the war and actually change people's hearts for the better."

Burroughs put away the staff. "I had no idea you were so idyllic."

"Yes, well. I've led six ineffectual lives. I've stopped believing I can make a difference in the world, but somebody else might. It's like a cruel joke the universe

193

plays on me. Because I live many lives, I can barely do anything! But somebody who only lives only once can put all my efforts to shame. If I can keep you alive long enough, who knows? I'm starting to think. I know a fair bit of prophecy, mind you. It doesn't take a scholar to match up the clues."

"And you think we're chosen?" Viday arched a brow.

Shaw shrugged. "The choice is yours. I will help if you want to go west, or I can offer you refuge on another Union island if you want. Just like I told you. We just need to find and board a boat in Maven , and I can take care of the rest for you. Your choice not mine."

"And say we refuse," Viday put some venom in her talk.

The minister squinted into the darkness, calculating an answer. "You can try your luck living here as two armies comb every inch of Caiphon, or escape with me on a boat from the Crescent City."

"I'm saying, once we escape with you what's to keep you from forcing this quest to kill Pantherian."

Shaw gave Viday a short frightened appraisal. "You'd gore me."

Burroughs returned. "Arrange our safe escape with your host in Maven, and I may consider."

"Fair enough. With Maurius gone, the mountain rivers move on their own. I can't use them. There are two host in Maven, Nigel and Carraway. We just need to make it to the harbor and everything will be clean sailing. I prom-" Shaw clapped his mouth shut.

## Airing Grievances at Family Reunions

"We get out down here," Shaw pointed down the cascade fed by the subterranean pond. "It turns into a slide near the end and feeds into the meadow stream. Both of you share the light and watch your step."

They descended the stair. Viday took back the burden of her bags and led Burroughs' steps with the lantern light. At the bottom they found a rounded tunnel with the steady run of water cutting a stripe directly through the center of the floor. Following the flow, they wound about the roots of the mountain until daylight glowed at the end of a chute. Shading their eyes, all three shambled into the open air.

The beauty of the mountain meadow was breathtaking. Bright green clover covered the entire ground from one mountain to the next, forming a lush bed. Late flowers dotted the rolling scape at odd intervals. Spiny thistles and a few buttercups mixed in with the clover blossoms. Evergreens surviving the last harsh winter stood defiant over the scene, looming over the shattered logs of other former trees which cracked under the weight of ice. Spongy round fungus grew off the fallen logs.

"Hey look," Shaw pointed to grazing deer who paid them little attention. The gathering of deer ate away at the bountiful greenery. A flock of ducks waddled near the streams edge, pecking at the shallows. A dash of snow fell from the north. The sudden and isolated buffet of ice painted the side of a nearby cliff. The frosting disappeared within minutes.

"Oh man," the magician pointed at a buck. The antlers on the shaggy beast's head numbered at least twelve points. "Shame I don't own a mantle. Or a house for that matter. Can we eat him? Would that be bad?"

Burroughs spoke softly, "We have two ways of being cannibals, but you have only one. I am told we can get uncontrollable shakes, just like when people eat one another."

"The ducks then. We can grab one and," Shaw held out his hands and clapped them. "Hunting. Is anybody good at it?"

Viday descended on the troop of ducks like a brown grim reaper. They scattered about in a honking confusion. She scooped up two she forced to run along the ground and bounded back to her party. Holding both struggling birds by their necks, Viday applied pressure on the skulls with her thumbs to pop in the heads and kill her prey. All of this in plain sight of Shaw. The angry expression on her face made her position on the subject very clear.

"What if I get the jitters from eating duck," Shaw shrank away at the sight of the duck's lives draining away in front of his face.

"That's normal," Burroughs took the two fresh birds off Viday's hands. They plucked and boiled them for lunch using the camp pot. Enough left over for supper.

The meadow trailed south, and they followed it until they could find a descent footpath westward. From there, they grudgingly left the peaceful place behind and struggled once more with the rocky terrain. Slowly the sun's light dwindled without the obstruction of Mount Mortimer to cast a premature sunset.

"I've never been this far out. I don't know of any shelter we can take," the scout admitted.

"We're not far from the green belt. I know a house we can use," Shaw said.

"It's too late in the day. We should start hiding." Burroughs droned.

Viday stepped past them. "I knew it. Something is following us." She pointed an accusing finger at some rustling brush. The dried bramble shook all on its own several paces away.

"The same thing from the cave?" Burroughs inquired.

The scout nodded. "One set of feet and then it disappears. Hard to tell if I'm imagining it or not."

All three of them stared so intently in the distance they failed to notice a saturnine figure sitting up beside them. "Peace and stay a minute. I wish to talk," came a voice both sweet and aged. There, sitting on a rock as if she'd been waiting the whole day, appeared the Abberant Mother herself. Great curled horns mounted the top of her goatish head. Two giant yellow eyes with thin slits for pupils protruded from her face just above a muzzle not unlike Viday's. A swishing tail ran out the back of a blouse woven with flexible reeds. Her coat was so grayed with age, there was no way to tell what her original color of fur had been.

"Run," Shaw yelped.

"Stop," the ancient creature held out a fully fingered hand.

For a few moments the travelers fled, but a lethargy began to hold Viday. She quickly found herself walking then crawling as her friends left her behind. She reached for the whistle to signal trouble just as a shade covered her.

"My my, your are awfully far from home my little girl. Your kin must be worried sick."

Viday let out two sharp blows on the whistle before the Abberant Mother pulled it from her mouth and helped her to her feet. "Shush now. Don't worry. I'm here to help."

Burroughs and Shaw returned. Seeing Viday in the arms of the creature, Burroughs dropped the backpack with a thunderous clatter and readied his staff. The flowing cilia emerging from the ends of the weapon tantalized the eyes of the captor. The sight put a smile on her face.

"What was stolen from us is ours again. The Argol grows and walks. The tree and the son, what was half becomes one." The chimeric figure let Viday join her friends. "I come to tell you we are leaving."

"We?"

"She controls all of them," Shaw grit his teeth. "Every last Abby on the island knows where we are now. Look closely kids. This is your mom."

The aberration gave the magician a disgusted scowl. Viday did the same under the powerful thrall. "Only your kind knows me by that name, pond scum."

"Be glad. Old Goat hasn't stuck yet."

"Go back to your grave before we put you there ourselves."

"Aren't you a little overdue yourself?"

The two of them began flailing at one another as the two other aberrations looked on. Neither the mother nor Shaw displayed much physical prowess as they bounced off one another, slapping, kicking, and spewing horrible profanity. Shaw attempted a few tricks of his hands, but the sly creature spotted every move and stepped away before pressing the assault again. Burroughs receded the tendrils in his staff and broke the fight apart.

The hills came alive with the stampede of hurrying beasts converging on the scene. Viday turned from the scuffle to watch in disbelief as all the nightmare monsters she had only heard of scabbered in.

Dignified, the Abberant Mother straightened up and dusted herself off. "As I said. We are leaving, and I come in peace with a proposal."

Viday rubbed her temples. "Oh my head"

"I'm listening," Burroughs replied.

"Surrender the foul thing with you and come home with us."

"Give over Shaw?"

"The dead should remain buried, my son. When they walk among the living they bring pain and misfortune with them. They pox the living and stifle out new life. If you let them, they will coat the world in their staleness."

Shaw spat and crossed his arms, "And it is somehow better if you crush out free will? Make all the children hug their mommy whether they want to or not?"

"Silence!" the creature yowled. This time Viday snorted angrily.The deer Abberant shoved Shaw to the ground with a pounce. Just as she reached back to punch his smooth face, Viday's anger drifted away. A shocked dismay overcame her and Burroughs pulled her off.

The magician got up. His hopes sunk as almost human, earth colored shapes drew closer and closer in droves. A few ran along the ground on four limbs in packs all to their own. From the crest of the nearest ledge a flock of gargoyles leered down just as the stone versions did in the old world.

"What's happening Shaw?" Viday entreated the blond young man. "I can't stop it."

"It's not your fault," he sighed and rubbed Viday's shoulder.

"As I was saying," the saturnine creature threw her palms in the air. "We are leaving. You may want to come with us."

Burroughs' thick hand floated over the wound hidden beneath the band around his waist. "You are here to capture me."

"No, no,no." the salt-and-pepper-colored one half laughed. "You. You are precious to us. The fruit we labored to achieve has come to pass. The Argol chose one of our own when we feared it fell into the hands of our enemy. There will be jubilation at your arrival, feasts and revelry. Come with us and you will see the truth in my words."

"At the same time bring pain and death on him," Burroughs pointed a thumb at Shaw.

"Their evil is a sickness. Because they fail to name their sin, they perpetrate it willingly to their own benefit time and again. Grow in wisdom with us and you will learn not to mourn his passing." The she goat cast glances at Shaw expecting a rebuttal.

Canid aberrations circled the discussion. Their numbers swelled greater than one hundred. All of them held back as if commanded. They stood yards away, shaking their shaggy heads and muttering among themselves in their own language. Viday's head darted about as she caught pieces of conversations with her ears. Her mouth moved wordlessly. Shaw stooped his shoulders and stared at the ground waiting for the inevitable.

"Then if I refuse, you still intend on capturing me. Why even bother giving me a choice in the matter?" Burroughs keyed lowly. Shaw gave a small chuckle as if he sat in a peanut gallery.

"Do you honestly wish to take your chances here? You will be hunted and killed because of what you are. It would be a loss we cannot bear."

Burroughs brought down the Argol. Rocks scattered on the impact. The clear knock hushed the crowd. "And what if you risked damaging something precious? Would you reconsider?"

A stunned panic gripped the faces of the circling beasts all around followed by an unexpected sadness. Viday's ears drooped back as she caught the wave of command. The Canid's eyes and noses pointed downward as if scolded, and all the tails stopped wagging.

The Abberant Mother's eyelids slowly lowered over the slits of her eyes as she stared into the determined grimace on Burroughs' face. She traced the brown and white painted coloration on his head and arms for a second. "What alternative do you intend? You face certain death without our offer."

"I leave on my own. Without your help."

"You reject my offer? Wholeborn or not, all Hyuinin are stubborn it seems. You honestly wish to break yourself. If you do not come, then the tree is spoiled forever."

"What's wrong mom? Can't keep one of your kids under control?"

"You!" The old goat charged up to Shaw and stopped short of his face. "You have stolen our hope and

200

laugh in our face. You can't even begin to imagine how undeserving you are. But know this, wherever you go, you only live because I allow it. Wherever you go with these two, you are traveling with servants of the king. When they awaken to their folly, they will beg forgiveness and receive it. You will die."

Shaw did not seem at all concerned.

Mormo emerged from the crowd. In his white claws he held out a red wooden box with ornate scrollwork along the sides. He offered the gift up to Viday. Viday's hands clasped the sides of the container swiftly. The thrall controlling her arms willed her to take the gift.

"You are one of us, daughter, if you acknowledge us or not. Take our greatest blessing with you as you keep company with our enemy and use it when you have need. Protect the Argol from danger. Feel the might Pantherian bestows."

Mormo left and returned, holding what seemed to be a glass bottle with a pistol grip at the bottom. The speaking goat took it. "And you." She pointed the glass revolver skyward and pulled back the trigger six careful times. She then handed the weapon over. "Watch as our treasure returns to us. Guard him until then. When the time comes, we will pull this from your wretched hands again."

Shaw took his emptied revolver. He held it out in the light and counted down in his mind when he would be able to use it again. He doubted it would be enough to charge the chambers anyway, as the sun was not full in the sky.

"This is the best I can offer. Accept them in good faith," the Mother addressed Burroughs. To her surprise, Burroughs held out a roll of paper for her. She took the gift and unrolled it. Her body shook with laughter. Soon the entire gathering joined in; perhaps commanded, perhaps not. "What is this? Did you make it?"

"A human painted it."

A quizzical expression came to the goatish face. "A rare glimpse at their better nature. It is so easy to forget. Thank you."

"We may meet again."

The gray creature raised a hand, "We are leaving this land to continue its one thousand years. Your final trail awaits. I will prepare and hope for your arrival if you survive." With that the crowd burst in several directions and disappeared within minutes.

## *Someone's Birthday*

The campfire burned under the star speckled sky. They hardly believed any of what transpired earlier in the day. Shaw brushed and held his returned revolver over and over again. Occasionally he held the cylinder up to his face and spun the chamber around and around. He did not need to touch the side of the gun, as he managed to spin the mechanism using some magic impulse from the grip.

Viday hugged the box she received and rocked back and forth in front of the fire's warmth. She had yet to open the present. A few times, she turned it over to look at the swirling pattern artwork and guess what lay inside. Two polished hinges fastened to the back with a clasp on the other side. She also noticed the way Burroughs and Shaw eyed the prize suspiciously. They looked away when she caught them staring.

"Back there," the girl began. "Sometimes I could be myself and other times there was another telling me what to do. Another me in my mind, shoving me away and taking over. What can do such a thing?"

"She can," Shaw grumbled darkly.

"Why? How?"

204

"Both of your real parents are Abberant. They passed it on to you."

"No. I am wholeborn, here on Caiphon."

"You're not. You belonged to the legion from birth. Because of you, they knew exactly where we were. It's also why they want you following us."

Viday protested. "They're not bad. All they want is for Burroughs to come with them."

"Until something gets in their way," Burroughs tossed another dried piece of wood on the fire. "They willingly butchered people in Crossroads and soldiers back at the mine just to reach us, and they would have run over more. It is the link the Abberant mother imposes on you which can make you judge things differently than you would have on your own. If she wanted, she could force you to kill us all and feel no remorse."

Viday approached the fire holding the gifted box out. A look of consternation wrinkled her lips as she tried to throw away the present, but found something blocking her. "I need this," she told herself out loud. "We need this. It is important. It won't harm us. We'll be fine. This is a good thing." Viday hugged the ornate box again. "She loves us. They love us. When you love someone, you keep them safe."

Shaw edged closer to Burroughs. He saw Viday's ears aimed his direction and knew she would pick up every word. So he chose his words carefully. "She wants to keep it."

Burroughs rubbed his large calloused fingers together. "She's afraid of what is inside, and what she is. When she is ready she will accept the gift or throw it out."

"And you are fine with this? Do you remember who it came from?"

Burroughs brought his squared muzzle close to Shaw's ear. "I don't expect you to understand. Maybe you have always known who you were your whole life, and never came to a point like Viday faces right now. We can only give her our trust and see what happens."

The young magician held up his glass revolver one last time then put it away inside his tattered robe. "I can do that, for now, but it's driving me crazy. The hag wants Viday to have it. I wish I knew why, and what it is."

"I agree. The Abberant mother is frighteningly cunning. It only seems we are getting what we want by letting us free and giving back your gun."

Shaw gripped the sides of his head. Tufts of golden hair sprouted through his fingers as he rubbed his scalp and moaned with worry. "What's going on?"

"We continue on. You mentioned a house?"

The young man released his hair, leaving tangles trailing out the sides of his head. "Yes, it, yes. The Ministry keeps a house in the green belt outside of Maven. It is mostly a storehouse for ministers since we have two hosts in the bay. It has a fairly tricky design. The attic is connected to the basement through a hidden staircase. We hide lots of stuff in there. From there we can plan how to walk you two through the city. We get to the water, and we're free."

"I see," Burroughs watched Viday drum her fingers on the lid of her box. She stopped frequently to run a finger over the swirling patterns along the top or one of the sides.

Needless to say, Viday's thoughts fixed solely on what might lie within the present. When she received it, an overwhelming sense of reverence surrounded the gift. It was an honor, a blessing. She saw worshipful stares from the gathered aberrations as the white wolf gave it over. A sincere and glad smile filled the Abberant mother's face and all around for the brief moment. The warmth of the reception neared euphoria. This was the link, however, and not her own thoughts. She did not know if to trust them or not.

What if she was being used? Perhaps the gift was given sincerely. She belonged with them. They must not harm their own for gain. It may have well been only so she could help her friends better. Then again, she never had dealings with her own kind before. They could be just a treacherous as Shaw, or more so.

Whatever waited inside was for her, especially for her. Viday could not shake the idea they knew more about her than she knew herself. If so, the gift pointed to who she really was deep down. At this point it frightened her greatly. What rested within may warp her into a monster, a tool of destruction dancing to the Abberant mother's whim. It could also be the single most important thing in her life, making the difference between life and death.

Her head buzzed with so much confusion that she had not noticed her two friends were already asleep. She tried to get some rest, but found herself waking up often to check if the gift was still there – and maybe open it.

They made coffee in the morning. She wondered if swallowing a few scoops of grounds and storing them in her second stomach pouch would help make up for all the lost sleep, but decided against trying. When it came time for her to run ahead and scout, she took the box with her. She stuffed one end of the red container into one of her bags and took off with it peeking over the top.

Viday didn't turn around to check their gaze. She felt it. She heard their hushed breath.

The grades of the mountains decreased in intensity the farther she traveled until, at last, some greenery appeared in the distance and grass grew on the hills. A few miles out was the green belt, a lush stretch of land wrapping Caiphon Bay. The fertile farmland saw long growing seasons. Mountains covering the entire eastern edge of the belt fed the fertile hills with ample water and guarded the crops from harsh winds.

Viday took the last high vantage point she could find. All the farms she saw lay fallow for the coming of winter. Among the withering rows cut perpendicular lines for the farm roads. The dirt paths evenly spaced apart from north to south, all leading to the crescent city on the water.

Viday often dreamed of visiting Maven, but never took the risk of straying too far from home. The city was just as incredible as the pictures. Buildings packed tightly to the shore from the north to the south for many miles and farther out than she could see in either of those directions. Over the bay she could barely make out the twinkling lights from the other side of the city. Dark shadows of boats coasted over the sparkling waters. Scores of sea vessels sailed around in the bay, each one a distinctive size and shape.

The Church of Galilee rose proudly over the rabble of houses around it. Its blue stained glass relief glowed from the lights within. At the center of the crescent was the diamond-shaped park with the clock tower at the center. Lateral Way ran out of both east and west points of the diamond. One end terminated at a large harbor. The other portion ran straight into the mountains. The main road ran closer by than she previously thought. She had not seen it in days, but she felt sure they should have been farther south than they actually were.

A thought crossed her mind now that she was alone. She found a flat enough rock and brought out the red box. She sat down and gave another inspection of the blood red colored wood and the swirled pattern shaped into all the sides. Another good shake did not help. Whatever was packed inside did not rattle.

Pushing the lid down with a thumb, she flipped up the latch. Just a quick peek. If it was a trap, it would go off high up on a ridge. The idea stopped her for a second. She turned the box around so opening it would face the other direction. There could be scorpions inside, or snakes, or poison dust. She pulled back the lid and bounced away, nearly tumbling over the edge.

There was no boom or hiss. The lid swung all the way back and hit the rock with a wooden clunk. Viday stretched out on the tips of her toes to see rolls of cloth in the gift's interior. Nothing stirred about within. She reached over and pinched a free edge of the cloth and pulled it away to see what may be underneath. Nothing, save for the padded interior of the box.

Laughing nervously at all her anticipation up to this point, Viday looked over what seemed to be a garment. The colors kept shifting around on the cloak, if it was a cloak. The shapes of the mountains behind stood out on the surface. Making out the general shape of the clothing was difficult because the tones and patterns kept changing to blend in with the surrounding space. Pulling open the collar and front she noticed an interior of what might had black satin. She swung the thing around her shoulders the rest of her body disappeared. She kicked a foot from under the illusion to see the split hooves of her toes.

Best of all, she didn't feel any different. The stranger wasn't there to shove her away, take over.

When she rejoined her friends they hardly noticed her until she came very close. Shaw drew his gun at the floating head bobbing closer as if riding an invisible wave. He put his weapon away when he recognized the motion, and stared bug eyed for a minute. Burroughs appeared impassive as always.

"The box," Burroughs rubbed a portion of his face along a line between brown and white near his jaw.

"That's all?"

Viday held out the empty box. "Everything inside, yes."

"I've never heard of anything like this," Burroughs raised a quizzical brow. "What do you make of it?"

Shaw grinned a little. "The Ministry had a couple of these once. We lost them both. Does it have a hood?"

Viday reached behind her neck. She turned her ears down. Then a black void opened behind her head and swallowed the rest of her. A disembodied hand reached up and tugged the air to reveal a portion of Viday's fuzzy head.

"As long as no one looks down. You can hide in

209

plain sight," Burroughs pointed at the scout's exposed feet.

Shaw nodded. "Yes it's the same shroud. It could even be the same we lost."

"Don't look at me like that," Viday shoved Shaw away.

"Sorry. Are you feeling all right?"

A snarl curled on the white side of Viday's muzzle, "I'm fine." She caught Burroughs' reaction to the way she snapped. She softened her tone. "I'm fine."

"Did you find the house?"

Viday shook her floating head.

"Look for a short white house. There is a cellar door in the back and a flag pole with scratches running up only one side. Just run around in the green belt. Hardly anybody will notice you."

Viday dropped her bag and the empty box then took off. Puffs of dust were the only evidence she left.

"It's a trick. I know it. Did she really leave the island, or is she coming back to spring something? It's just a transparent shroud."

"Should she be using it?" Burroughs muttered.

'It's fine. Probably. She could walk through Maven with that thing on. Just what we need, but it's all too convenient. I don't like it."

"Hmmmm."

## *Violence of Many Types*

     Wearing both the cloak and the duster made it hot. Whatever cloth made the garment did not breathe in the slightest. Viday cut through the wind, barely rippling the first layer of clothing. She pulled the hood over her face a few times, but the air caught in the scoop and knocked back the covering every time she tried to move. It was pitch dark in the hood too, as black as the caves from yesterday. She imagined if she tried hiding with the cloak it would mean blinding herself as well.

     She sweltered in the cloak. A few times she stopped to pant, letting in the cool autumn air and exhaling heated breath. Due to the mysteries of aberration, she also sweated moisture. Before long she become unbearably thirsty and uncomfortably soaked.

     The fields of wheat and corn went on and on with a few rare roads to break the monotony. Sometimes she found irrigation ditches and got a few drinks. She hoped a cow pasture wasn't upstream.

The house she needed to find looked exactly like a schoolhouse from the front cover of the primers back home. On closer inspection the building truly was a schoolhouse. Several neat desks lined up in front of three blackboards and a lectern in the front. Empty shelves and closed cupboards lined the walls along the side and back. Just as Shaw said, a flagpole stood outside with distressing amounts of scratches struck to one side and the other absolutely unblemished.

She found the flat doors leading to the cellar in the back and threw them open. Several musty bookshelves lined the basement. Timbers holding up the schoolroom floor ran down into the cellar and planted in the earth. These strong, load-bearing hunks of wood served as the ends of all the bookshelves stored inside.

Regardless, she found the place. Done with the stifling garment, Viday pulled off cloak and ripped off her duster. A short, peculiar paralysis crept into her shoulders with the shroud off. Probably just the heat. Viday threw her regular coat into the book room before slamming the doors shut again. She took off with one layer of clothing subtracted.

"Found it," Viday reported upon returning to her friends. She pointed to one of the canteens Shaw started strapping to himself in a bandoleer fashion. Shaw gave one over.

"Which way is it" Burroughs blocked the sun with one of his thick hands and looked out.

Viday finished a few gulps. "It's, um," she stopped for a minute to find a familiar landmark but only saw uniform rows of dying stalks. She pointed in a general direction she thought was right.

They walked together through the maze of harvested fields. The stalks of corn were hand picked. Thus the tall, browning plants all stood up over everyone's head except Burroughs. Even Burroughs' advantage was not too grand. He only saw a few yards further. A few times, Viday jumped above the withered stalked to check their heading.

"One thing about the shroud, I remember." Shaw stepped around a corn stalk. "If you rub the sleeves together, the ends of them, the entire thing goes one color for several minutes. It should be green.You don't have to do it now."

"How long does it last?"

"I can't remember, but you can do it to keep people from having headaches while talking to you. It was a trick Hotchkiss found out when I knew him."

"Who's Hotchkiss?" Viday asked.

"Oh," Shaw began. "He's was a great guy. He was the few among the ministers who had a family. In fact, he died trying to rescue his son from drowning. You can't visit your family once the ministry lets you in, would cause a stir. I ran a lot of errands for him. Cute family, nice little girl and good wife. Me and Liz did favors for Hotch's family, helped them out; said we were Hotch's old friends here to lend a hand. Eventually the kid grew up and the wife remarried, but Hotchkiss was happy for them. He was a good guy, and it was nice to spend time with his folks for him."

"Where is he now?"

"No idea. It's been years."

Viday ran her forearms together and the entire cloak flooded with a rusted red color. Shaw gave a puzzled look and quickly set his composure back.

"Why is it so empty out here?" Burroughs wondered out loud. "Nobody seems to be at home in any of the houses, or on the roads." His observation seemed to carry some weight. The green belt was known for bustling farm activity, as every inch of the landscape fueled the nearby city with rich food nearly all year round. Each plot in the area was regarded as well-to-do and a lucrative venture. One would expect perhaps a couple of souls ambling around, but instead the surrounding area felt quite deserted.

"Those pens for cattle are empty and there aren't any in the pastures when I ran through. Not normal for whenever I see those wooden things." Viday noted.

"Byres," Burroughs found the word.

Shaw scoffed. "You're imagining things. This far out of town is always like this."

They crossed several roads and more farmland until they reached the schoolhouse. Shaw opened the way into the lower portion and descended the stairs first. He led them to a shelf near the back wall, which rested under the blackboards from the room above. He ran a shoulder against the sturdy timber used to hold the shelf slats to reveal the shelf was not fixed to the floor. Hidden hinges supported the book case. The tight stack of books swung out to reveal a door with a stair behind.

The attic at the end of the secret stair had a surprisingly high roof. Two separate rooms stood on either side of a short hallway with the hallway ending in its own room. All of the wood smelled old and musty. The air hung in each room, unmindful of the wind striking the slanted walls.

"What is that horrible thing?" Viday pointed at the very end of the hallway.

A stocky wooden chair was nailed to the floor. Extra support beams crossed underneath the seat and a few extra boards were also nailed to the outside. Atop the laddered back rested a metal dome with a spread of wires and metal protrusions littering the top. The underside of the wide helmet seemed to be filled with needles.

"That's the coronator. It's for," Shaw's voice sounded apologetic. "Therapy, I guess is the right word."

A stirring came from one of the rooms. Someone emerged from the left door, peeped around the door frame, and staggered back.

"Liz? You there Liz?" Shaw stepped forward.

A sort of staccato reply rang from the antechamber,

"Shaw? What's going on?"

Shaw thought for a second. "I've made some weird friends. Don't worry. Only one of them is violent."

Liz's head peered around the corner again with a very skeptical leer. Her skin was the color of chocolate. Like Shaw, her eyes shone a bright blue and her hair was blond to the point of almost being white. "It's not the big one is it?"

Shaw gave an introduction for everybody as Liz stepped out in a much cleaner robe than the one Shaw had. Viday gave a cordial wave. Burroughs slung off his pack and didn't seem interested in formalities.

The other magician held out her hand in greeting. Viday caught it first and gave it a friendly shake. Liz made a bemused smile. They made a firm shake, but the darting eyes on Liz's face made it clear this wasn't her intention.

Shaw reached out next. The handshake lasted uncomfortably long as the two creatures watched the magicians lock each other in a deadeye stare. It lasted for a few minutes as Burroughs and Viday shifted about, trying not to gawk themselves. After a while, Shaw tried tugging his hand free as Liz pursed her lips and held on tighter. A sense of urgency came over the young man's face as he tried to wretch lose. The other magician then pulled Shaw's arm back and kneed him in the stomach.

Liz spat angrily. "You're such a jerk, Shaw."

"He's trying to be better," Burroughs leaned on a wall. It creaked under his weight.

"Not if you could read what he's thinking," the dark skinned minister scratched an itch behind her blond ponytail.

Shaw held his midsection and wheezed.

"We need to get all three of you off the island. Losing Caiphon is something the Union cannot allow. Now with confirmed sighting, they are really in a panic. Come in here."

Liz led them into the left room. A simple wooden

215

table with chairs sat in the middle surrounded by locker styled cabinets with glass doors. Two simple candles on the table lit the entire room. Liz put fire to a few more candles and slid the lights to the farther ends of the table on their copper bottoms.

A crude map of Maven was scratched into the table cloth with charcoal.

"We are here," Liz put her smooth finger on a chunk of coal on her side of the map. "Army has blockaded every road into Maven, and they are busy cutting back the crops in the green belt as far back as they can from the city's edge." She traced the longest edge of the crescent city. "They have trenches dug out in most of the south and garrisoned roof tops for most of the north, lots of long range guns. We can't run straight for them. Especially not in the uptown district."

"Can we go under them," Shaw stumbled into the room. He spotted a fresh robe in a far locker and shambled over.

Liz picked up the crude writing implement. "Exactly the plan, Mister." She looked up to stare through Viday. Her brows twisted with consternation.

Viday caught the hint and darkened the shroud again. It felt hot and stuffy in the room, and the cloak added to the problem. Shaw watched the explanation play out.

Liz shook the confusion out of her head. "Right. I forgot about that thing. You could almost walk in if you wanted. The town is almost all evacuated . So once you're past the line, you're almost safe. About the line," she drew a triangle south of the schoolhouse and traced a pipe directly into town. "Douglas will have to take the covered cistern into town. It's not yucky. It's a stream the city uses for a fresh water supply. So they capped it off with concrete and buried it. You can come out at the vat station behind Mortimer Park. Just a small jump to get out of the way of all the machinery."

"Burroughs."

"No. More like a tunnel."

"My name is Burroughs."

Liz cocked a brow. "Is that a nickname?"

"We just introduced ourselves in the hallway," the deer Abberant pulled at her hot collar.

"You're still Viday, right?"

"Yes."

"Anyway. The pump station also runs the fountain in Mortimer Park. You could cut right across the park and down Lateral Way to dock sixteen where we will prepare the boat. Nigel and Carraway can shove you out into the sea. With a little luck nobody will see you at all."

"Are you sure the Esauphagus is the only one left?" Shaw pointed down at the dead center of the crescent.

"Yes. We can shake hands again if you want. The Esauphagus is all we have, and only because nobody can steal it. No motor, no sail, and we wedged the ugly thing under dock sixteen so tightly nobody can pull it out. We rule the waves. So no problem," Liz opened a storage locker along the wall and pulled out a dark green bundle with smaller red and yellow rolls sitting on top. "This leaves just one question for you two. Where are you going?"

"Through the canal and onto the boat," Burroughs ran his thick finger down the crude etching.

Shaw pulled up a chair while everyone else kept standing. "Which other Union island are you going to? We have stakes in all of them. Choose whichever one you want."

Viday's eyes swept along the floor for a moment. "What about my mother?"

"We're busting her out. Favors for friends. Your other two are fine, probably." The comment from Liz put some shock into Viday's face. The female magician went on. "Give it a name and we will set up your new lives."

Burroughs tapped the sides of his hooves with the Argol. "It can't be that easy."

Shaw rested his chin on the outline of southern Maven. "Living is easier than you think. If you want to obsess about the details, we can all meet in the Wellborn boathouse. The old lady can weigh in on it then."

Liz nodded. "Yes. Wellborn. We'll do that," she lopped the clothing over her shoulder. "Shaw can take care of things here. See you there," she left the room.

Books make the best liars. They don't hassle you into believing what they tell you, and they willingly trap themselves on the shelf for years. Best of all is fiction, where you know you're getting lied to. Fiction teaches you to sniff out the harmful lies people tell and teaches you important things you tried very hard to be ignorant of. Read all you can. You'll understand.

Shaw left for the city to prepare the Esauphagus boat for the voyage. He barely stood up when carrying the pack outside, but he insisted on relieving Burroughs of his burden in the chance they were discovered in their plot.

Before the young magician left, the large aberration took the lantern out. He used the light source to inspect the books in the basement. The Argol tangled its roots around the handle, and the lantern swung about as Burroughs walked among the volumes.

Most of the titles were the same for many stacks; Arithmetic, Citizenry, Grammar, History, Science, Geography, Technology. The shelves stored abandoned school books, it seemed. Some appeared to be older volumes of the ones Lana and Carver shared with him as children. The lending library was stored in the back. He could tell because the bindings became less uniform.

Why anybody would leave literature behind, Burroughs could not guess. Perhaps Maven held superior schools and this rural building became abandoned. Dust coated the spines of the books in layers so thick it made the titles unreadable. Burroughs let out a strong puff from this snout to unsettle the dust and immediately regretted his action. A cloud filled the corner of the basement. The haze held for many minutes before falling down.

The catalogs filled the shelves in no particular order. There were histories of warfare, ancient mythology, specific science studies, detective novels, children's rhymes, classics, how-to guides, art books, and young adult fiction. Burroughs guided the light hanging on the end of the staff from one spine to another.

"There you are," came a friendly voice. "What are you doing down her?"

"It's cooler down here."

Viday tested the air. "You should come upstairs and see what these guys are hiding."

"In a minute."

"They're sitting on old world technology. Lots of it is still working. There is this little box with buttons on it and it lets you play some sort of game on the other part of the box."

"How odd."

"And there are lots of things I bet they've fixed to react to their touch; torches, batons, guns, knives, and all sorts of things."

Burroughs lifted the light a little higher. "I see."

"They make disguises here too. They have army, marshals, dignitaries, beggars, merchants, doctors, and all sorts of other costumes. These people are spies I think."

"Probably."

"That chair Shaw called a coronator must be for torture. There is a nasty dark stain on it and a few all around. I think they kill people."

"Right."

Viday waved her hand in front of Burroughs' searching eyes. "Are you listening?"

"Of course," his thick fingers found a bound collection of Twain.

"Then why aren't you saying anything?"

Burroughs thumbed the book over and over, brushing the dust off its cover. He thought over what Viday asked him and what she may have meant. Turning to address her he said, "What would you like to know?"

Viday squinted skeptically at hearing the bored drone in Burroughs' voice. She immediately became angry. "I thought we could be having a talk now, with that creep gone."

"If you want."

"Well," Viday curled fingers in her direction and gave an expecting look.

"Oh," Burroughs didn't realize it was his responsibility. He swung the lantern close to the shelf. "Have you read any good books?"

"Not since I was a kid. All those stories were about princesses, dragons, and daring knights."

"Fairy tales. Did you have a favorite?"

"Cinderella."

"Not Beauty and the Beast?"

"No. No. That one is weird. Most of the ones with talking animals I don't like. I do a good evil wolf." Viday pulled her lips up enough to show her canine teeth. The smoothed down fangs were an obvious human imitation because of aberration. The effect appeared dog like, however.

Burroughs checked his own set of canine teeth, not as pointy as Viday's. "Hmmm."

"Yes. Frightening. Say, what do you want to do after we escape? You're going to follow me, aren't you?"

"I have not decided."

Viday's half smile fell down off her face and she tip toe walked away.

> Men play games with cards, dice and leather balls. Women play games with speech and subtle hints. Like in all games, you come across sore losers.

Burroughs tried recalling the past conversation but didn't seem to catch anything meaningful. He heard Viday step out of the basement and into the corn field nearby. Low crunching sounds came from the direction she went, the sound of chewing. After a while of angry mumbling and destruction of the local field, Viday took off. Burroughs wondered for a second if it was his cue to chase, but instead he sat in a cool corner of the basement to read.

He tried to read, tried to give the text on the pages sound. In the end, all his attempts at diversion failed. Thoughts of his life and recent events filled his mind with dark musings. For hours he simply stared at his hands, the Argol, and just the ground. He concentrated on who he might be, and where he should be going. It was the tree doing this. He knew. Ever since he pulled and carried the Argol, some sort of goading desire without a name or explanation took a space in his mind. Without an outlet to express itself, the desire raged in his thoughts, trying to take shape.

## Missing a Boat

The soldier spotted Shaw through the sights of his gun. "Got a mountain man walking our way. He's coming right down the road. Somebody get Corporal Lander out here to give him a hand. He's about to miss the last boat."

Shaw lost all his breath an hour ago. He had no idea what he ran on now to haul the giant pack, but it was costing him water. He remembered what happens when a minister runs dry. It frightened him. The canteen dwindled the whole time as he sweat like a pastor in a seaside pub. It was November, yet the heat beat down oppressively. A motorized wagon passed through the blockaded gates and rumbled up the road toward him.

The vehicle pulled up and a jolly, portly fellow rolled out. "Caught a bad time to play John the Baptist, son. The last boat is taking off."

Shaw's knees lowered slowly to the ground from the weight of Burroughs' pack. The giant pack did not feel as heavy as when he pulled it from Crossroads, but then he did not drag the burden so far. "What does this have to do with John the Baptist?" he panted.

Lander reached back into the driver's cabin and engaged the brake. "We'll you're not Moses or Jesus. You're missing the beard."

Looking down, the magician recalled he changed into a fresh white robe. He did look conspicuous. "Get me to dock sixteen?"

223

"Ferry moves out of dock seven. Headed to Acosta. Free of charge. Lets hurry it up. The Abbies are due to come down any day or any hour, and we're standing in the middle right now."

"How bad is it?"

"They are tearing us up out there, and we're having a hard time establishing forward posts from nightly hit and run attacks. We'll stop them here. Out in the open with no place to hide."

Shaw looked at a long, stretching black band marring the green belt. "I see that."

The pack fell into the wagon bay with a flop and they took off. The nice man left Shaw at dock eight. Shaw waved at the soldier until he disappeared then began traveling north to sixteen. He made it a few blocks before he gave up.

"Nigel, Carraway." Shaw leaned on a sea wall to speak to possibly nobody thirty feet below. Nobody or nothing responded. Moaning, Shaw kept dragging the cumbersome canvas bag. The dock stood too high over the water, and there were locked gates and high walls to keep people from falling in. A sound design, but it prevented Shaw from touching the bay and calling help.

Shaw absentmindedly reached inside his drape for the glass revolver when he spotted a padlock he could bypass. A band of soldiers loitered on a nearby corner. They did not eye him, but they certainly would if he pulled a rusty gate lose.

The fancier side of town kept a waterfront lower to the bay. It was where the yachts and personal water craft for dignitaries and merchants floated. All of it built on the other end of the city. Dock Sixteen emptied into the fisherman's market. Therefore, all the fishermen's boats moored there – or had. It appeared they had all left.

Shaw considered jumping the wall, but it would leave the provisions unguarded.

"Hey you!"

Shaw drank the one of the last mouthfuls of precious water from the canteen. Turning around, he saw a heavy-set girl stamping toward him. She seemed quite upset.

"Where did you get that pack?"

The young man eased the loathsome bag down to address the girl. His eyes darted about. "A friend of mine is letting me borrow it."

"Oh really? I know who that pack belongs to, and I doubt he's happy you have it."

"Do you, now? What's his name?"

"Burroughs."

Shaw curled one brow, "You know Burroughs?"

Lana planted both fists on her hips and spoke without hesitation. "As a matter of fact, I do."

Shaw stopped and sized up the rustic girl. No doubt she intended to rob him, and probably could. Her build was one forged in hard labor and toil, heavy shoulders, stocky arms, and bandy legs. A mean look came from her green eyes. "Well this is Douglas's pack. So I am afraid you are mistaken." Shaw began tugging the burden along the ground as fast as possible. The girl in overalls stepped up to grab his arm.

The magician snapped his other hand around Lana's wrist. His blue eyes glowed brightly for a second then dimmed. To his dismay, Lana kept standing. The determined look on her face said the conversation was not over.

Shaw took a few extra grabs at Lana's smooth arm holding him in place. "Doesn't this sting? Even a little?"

"Your grip is as weak as my brother's."

An irregular wooden knocking from a nearby alley gave both Shaw and Lana a pause. They saw nothing. "Tell me where you got the bag," Lana demanded.

Shaw looked a little confused. She was supposed to be punching him, he thought. "Burroughs," he answered and watched anxiously for the first signs of robbery.

225

She let the magician go. "He's here?"

Not one to waste an opportunity, Shaw began hauling the backpack. He tersely blurted. "He is." The farm girl didn't press her attack a second time. She followed Shaw many paces away along the dock street.

The sea wall still stood too tall. Shaw certainly could escape, but he would need to leave the pack behind.

If his stun trick didn't work on the robber tailing him, Shaw decided to burn her face off with the revolver – not in broad daylight. If a soldier happened along to see the murder, it would make things more difficult. He saw some warehouses at dock twelve where he could hide the bothersome girl's body. He'd plant two shots in the neck. Doing so would turn any screaming into sick gurgling.

"Why do I have to keep doing horrible things?" Shaw asked himself in a low mutter.

The warehouse bay stood wide open. All the things stored inside were taken in the evacuation. Shaw rounded a few broken crates in the back and drew his weapon.

The female robber introduced herself. "Burroughs. Are you in here? It's me, Lana." She began searching around the empty shelves and boxes in the back of the storage house, but did not round the corner Shaw pointed his gun at. Lana drew another breath to shout again, but a shimmering figure collided with her.

A scuffle broke out on the warehouse floor. When Shaw peeped to see who it was, he found Viday and Lana exchanging blows. Unlike Shaw, Lana held her own against Viday. The stocky farm girl caught the deer aberration's punches and kicks a few times and grappled her attacker to the ground. In the dust up, Viday's cloak stopped showing through and took its red color. Lana wrangled with Viday like with ornery livestock. Viday slipped away and resumed her assault.

Shaw took a good glance out the open door of the warehouse. Nobody seemed to be walking by to notice. He leveled his gun at Lana. "Stop it. Both of you. Viday. Back

226

off for a minute."

Lana shoved Viday back farther as the fight broke off. "What have you two done with Burroughs?" It took a moment for her to see the revolver and halt. She kept glowering at both of them.

The gun pointed directly at Lana's neck. Two smart pulls at the trigger, and the pesky rustic's head would roll off. Shaw caught a glimpse of Viday, and decided on a talk before committing murder. "He's not here. Who sent you?" Must have been the Abby mother, Shaw thought.

"Nobody sent me. I'm a friend of Burroughs, and I saw you had a pack exactly like his."

Viday stepped in. "What are you doing Shaw?"

Lana's eyes widened as she heard Viday talk.

"Shooting this nosy bumpkin. She'll ruin everything if we let her go."

Lana held up her hands. Viday shook her head. "No. Don't."

"Start talking. Who are you? How do you know Burroughs? Tell me why you wouldn't rat us out?" He caught a skeptical look at his gun. Shaw diverted the barrel to a broken wooden box and set it on fire. The recognition was immediate. The unwelcome tag-along began talking.

"My name is Lana Portram. I'm from Lagoona, where Burroughs and I grew up. We are best friends. If you doubt it, you can ask him yourself. I'm not going to tell the army on you because they would kill him."

Shaw thought for a second. "What is Burroughs, exactly?"

"Abberant. Horse. Big fellow at seven feet tall. Grows melon vines like nothing anybody ever seen. Brown and white blotchy color all over him. Raised by an old army Sargent."

"What else?" The magician bounced his concentration between the open door of the warehouse and his questioning. "Tell me about the tree. Where did it come from? How is he carrying it?"

Lana looked confused. "Tree?"

"The staff he's been carrying around, The Tree of Ages that opened the age of Aquarius. Why does he have it?"

"I swear, I don't know what you're talking about."

Shaw drew a bead on Lana's neck. "Shame. I'm sorry you had to see this Viday."

Two blinding flashes lit up the store room. The magician stumbled back, away from the brilliance. When his eyes adjusted again, Viday stood blocking any possible third shot at Lana. A shimmer took to her cloak. Tiny streaks of lightning sparkled on the dark red clothing. A few moments later the cloak resumed its invisibility.

The magician lined up another shot through the transparent shroud. "Move it, Viday. She knows too much."

A chestnut brown arm appeared suddenly and caught Shaw on the side of the head. The revolver fell away. Lana loomed from behind. The rustic grabbed at the approximate placement of Viday's shoulders and tossed the deer Abberant aside. She kicked the gun away, causing it to clatter along the concrete floor.

"Listen you psychopath. I'm just trying to look out for my friend. By the look of things I'd say he's in trouble. Now call off your kangaroo and take me to Burroughs."

"Let's take her with us," Viday pulled herself back onto her feet.

Beads of sweat hung on Shaw's face. Too much was happening too fast, and he couldn't figure how he got to where he was at. Some farm girl, immune to his magic, starts following him around. She asks all the right questions. Then Viday drops in to make matters worse.

Shaw pointed at Lana. "We're Burroughs' friends too. There are some nasty things chasing us. If you want to help him, take the boat out of here and act like you never saw us."

"You're taking me to Burroughs, pretty boy."

Shaw closed his mouth tightly. His unsure

expression looked at Lana, Viday's floating head, and the vacant street outside – which could not remain unoccupied forever. A spinning sensation filled his head. He began to feel dizzy.

"You win. Follow me, Viday. I don't know why you left the schoolhouse. Take my gun and keep hiding."

"I was bored," Viday said as an excuse. "I want to see the city." She hopped over to the revolver and tucked it away into thin air. The hood swallowed her head, including her ears. The bouncing knock of her hooves echoed off the cavernous walls of the warehouse as she made her exit.

As a gesture of good faith he didn't care to make, Shaw held open the palms of his hands to Lana to show he was unarmed. "Shall we go?" he droned in monotone. He tugged the pack along the ground with one of the leather straps. To his surprise, the farm girl took hold of the other end and helped out.

"Where is this going?"

"Dock sixteen."

Both of them hauled the luggage into the open street again and walked north. Shaw looked around the rooftops trying to spot Viday, hoping she was watching just in case the newcomer tried something. He had seen Abberant legion use people as traps. They scooped guts out and put different things in. They then sent the person walking mindlessly out. The empty shell clawed, bit, and belched poison clouds. In some cases, it took weeks for the trap to spring and the host behaved perfectly normal until then. Shaw leered at Lana's face, trying to spot any tar black tears on her face. She didn't seem too flattered by the attention.

"Tell me, Shaw, who are you. Who is your friend following us." Lana stepped around a crack in the pavement.

"Have you heard of swimmers?"

"No."

"How about phantoms or wisp men?"

229

"From the boogie man stories. They steal from barons, dignitaries, freight companies. Sometimes they burn to death anybody who crosses them. Ghosts, some say."

"We try to do that as little as possible, but that's who I work for."

Lana nodded up at a gutter. "So wisp men are also Abberant, I take it."

Shaw looked up to see Viday's feet resting on a shingled incline nearby. He sighed in relief a little, but quickly realized Lana saw right through the shroud. His face puckered a little. "No. No," he stammered. "She's coming with us." A picture came together in Shaw's head. He dropped his side of the pack.

"Sixteen is farther up," Lana raised a brow as Shaw held out a hand to shake.

The magician shook his head. "This isn't a trick. Well, it is, but I need to check something again. Shake my hand."

Lana's hands clamped down on Shaw's, and they shook vigorously for longer than necessary. Shaw grit his teeth in consternation then let go. A stinging smell billowed from his mouth as a series of coughs rattled his frame. Lana backed away and tried to wave the vapors away.

"A normal person would be in a coma now." The magician coughed a few more times. He held up his right hand to show his red, blistered palm.

Lana checked her own hand to see nothing was wrong. "What?"

"We call it Sane. You basically ignore magic and see things as they are. It's no wonder you were onto me from the start. Just please, try to play along. We're pushing our luck as it is."

## *Accuracy*

Shaw gave the padlock blocking entry into dock sixteen a few tugs. Both the thick lock and the metal chain held the bars firmly in place. He shook the canteen, but the thing was bone dry. Trying to kill Lana sapped his supply.

"You have a boat in here?" Lana said skeptically. Not a single vessel looked to be tied up behind the gate.

"Yes, a what-do-you-call-em schooner? It's jammed under the dock here."

"The Esauphagus? It's a ship wreck."

Shaw walked away from the thick lock. "It's a ship. Is Viday anywhere?"

"She's been watching us from the top of Parson's Seaside Restaurant."

The magician waved Lana to join him away from the gate. "I'm going to tell her to shoot the lock. She probably hears us right now."

"Maybe, but can she shoot a gun."

Shaw's face flushed. "Let's give her a little more space."

Lana followed the magician down the paved walkway. "Oh, so Viday is a she. I couldn't tell."

"I hope she didn't hear that, and yes. Otherwise

she'd have antlers, I think."

A smell of burning dust filled the air, musty and putrid. Sometimes Shaw found himself wishing his gun made more noise or a more apparent sign of firing. Just one click from the glass revolver's mechanism and things heat up instantly. He often found himself stepping on a hot patch he burnt into the ground himself, or firing wildly after he lost count of how many shots he used. It was a tricky business managing the gun. With it in Viday's hands, he imagined horrible things happening by accident. Two of his six deaths were by his own gun, and not in enemy hands, either. They were completely his fault.

The iron gate leaned off one of its hinges then fell down. The padlock remained unscathed. Dark spots marked the wooden dock in Viday's line of fire. Shaw sighed in relief. "That works."

The pack lifted up and over the freed gate. Lana pulled the bars back into place to make it appear the way was undamaged. They carried the pack to the middle of the dock and sat it down near the middle of the boarded walkway.

"Watch this." Shaw dove off the edge of the dock and into the bay eight feet below. Lana waited for the young fool to surface, but saw nothing. It was a trick she'd seen hundreds of times before. Shaw would come out on the other side quietly and try to surprise her. She looked around to guess where he would come up. Two minutes rolled by without any sign of the magician.

A sleek white hull slid out from under the boards of the dock and stopped still at an access ladder. The boat's mast had long since snapped and rotted away. No motor powered the vessel either. A tiny cabin and ship deck was all there was to the Esauphagus. The unimpressive boat froze in place at the ladder up to the dock, undisturbed by the waves lapping the sides. The boat did not even rock as it should naturally.

Shaw stood on the gliding platform. His hands

rested idly by his sides and this face looked dead ahead as if he were bored. Not a drop of moisture dripped from his head or his robe.

"Try to drop it gently," Shaw beckoned from the deck of the enchanted ship.

Lana shook her head in disbelief. "What?"

"Drop the bag down. We're storing it here."

"Right," Lana lifted the heavy pack off the dock and managed to slowly lower the canvas campsite a few feet over the edge all by herself. Shaw tried to slow the crash as best he could, but nearly crushed himself in the process. Shaw stowed the bag away into the boat's cabin and slammed the door shut.

"This dock yes," Shaw leaned overboard and held a conversation with no one. "We're going to bust the gate and make a straight run out of here before anybody sees us. Shove us out to sea someplace and we'll decide what next from there."

"Who are you talking to?" Lana asked.

"Nigel. Oh right, you can't hear him. He says hello. He likes your pony tail." Shaw looked back down at the bay. "Yes. She's sane. I guess so. Hold on. I'll ask." Shaw addressed Lana again. "Do you want to stay on the boat while I go get Burroughs? You can come with me to the schoolhouse, if you want, but waiting here will be safest."

"I'm staying up here," Lana eyed Shaw suspiciously.

The magician shrugged and apologized to the bay. "I tried." He scaled the ladder and left his imaginary friend behind.

"Hey, the boat."

"Don't worry. Nigel will move it back for us."

Lana saw the Esauphagus turn on its own and head out to sea. It moved like a giant bath toy being forced by an invisible, giant toddler. Not a single wave rolled off the side of the boat, and not even the smallest wake trailed behind.

233

Shaw mouthed off some unintelligible speech as the farm girl gawked. He nodded to something he thought then spoke plainly. "All right then. Let's go see the big guy and get this out of the way. Things aren't so bad. Just a little change in the plan here and there."

There came the sound like a gust of wind followed by two wooden knocks on the dock boards. Viday's head emerged from a hole in reality, ears first. "You're letting the boat float off, moron."

"It's fine," Shaw said. "Nigel has it now."

"There's nobody on it."

"He's under it."

Lana shrugged, giving up. "Something has that boat."

Shaw held out his blistered hand to Viday. The chemist's daughter looked at the scalded red flesh and backed away. "The gun needs five minutes of sun."

Viday held the revolver out of her cloak."I used all the bullets."

"Hold it out for a while and it recharges. Hand it here."

"No."

Shaw thought of asking why, but knew the answer. Lana presented a bothersome addition he was eager to get rid of. Viday knew it. She knew his games, and guessed the machinations in his head. For reasons confusing to Shaw, Viday had taken up the protection of Lana. If Lana ended up conveniently dead, there would be no excuse he could give to assuage Viday's accusations of murder.

Shaw licked his lips and tried thinking up some crafty way to convince Viday to hand back his gun without alerting Lana to his intention of scorching her meddling face to ashes. Nothing came to mind. "Okay," he chirped in false cheer. He had fun while it lasted, but once again his gun was lost. Viday disappeared in a few jumps.

Feeling empty and helpless, Shaw led Lana out of dock sixteen. They crossed the street onto Lateral Way.

The diamond park in the middle of the crescent city looked beautiful as they walked by on a side street. Every soul evacuated the city, but the fountain kept running. The clock tower at the center showed half past two.

Shaw took a quick glance at the pump house Burroughs would charge out of. It was a simple concrete building buried into a grassy hill in the park. A gray stone stair led down into the guts of the facility. A bolted door barred entry, but Burroughs would easily bust through it from the other side. On second thought, he could just turn the locks from inside. Either way, it was no problem.

Seven city blocks down Lateral Way the army erected a blockade. Improvised palisades were nailed to the sides of buildings using scrap lumber. Soldiers stood on the raised platforms facing out to the east. Equally tacky barricades blocked the road out of the city with men stationed behind them. The soldiers turned around as they heard the two approaching.

"Orders are, no civilians in the no man's land. Please turn around," said the nearest soldier.

Shaw looked at his robe as if he were embarrassed by it. He pulled it over his head and addressed himself to the guard. "Private Belome. Orders are to escort this civilian to the old farm school and hightail it back."

The soldier eyed Shaw suspiciously, as did Lana. "What's with the cover private?"

"It's for dust and mud. We wear it to keep our suits clean for inspection."

The soldier sighed and pinched the bridge of his nose. "Afraid of a little dirt newbie? Is that all you learned from basic? Where is your gun? Who is your commanding officer?"

The magician flung his robe over his shoulder. He crossed his arms and said testily, "Cut me some slack. Are you going to bust my chops all day or let me through before the Abbies come charging down the hill?"

"You watch your smart mouth, new guy."

Shaw held his ground.

"Let this idiot through." A few other suited figures moved the wooden barricade a few inches to allow the two to squeeze through and walk on the road. At about a mile out, Shaw pulled his white cover back over himself.

"Are you actually army? I mean, wisp men are army?" Lana questioned. She looked back at the distant city buildings.

"When we need to be," a few tugs on the shoulder and the drape fit correctly again. Shaw stopped to view the lay of the land. It lay very much the same in all directions, with the exception of the scorched field leading back into Maven – lots of corn. His mind tricked him into thinking he'd only need to walk as far as he had from dock eight to dock sixteen. In reality the farther he got out from the city the longer the radials stretched. It was the way circle-like shapes worked. Shaw squinted at the distant flagpole of the schoolhouse in disbelief until his shoddy knowledge of geometry caught up to him. They deviated from the road and trudged through the field.

"Is Viday with us?" Shaw asked.

Lana stomped along the ground in her workman's boots. "Your deer sweetheart? She hung back at Mortimer park and didn't follow us up to the road block. Haven't seen her yet."

"I'm not in a relationship with anybody, especially Abberants. She actually hates my rotten guts, and takes many occasions to tell me so. She's thrashed me four times already. Number five isn't too far away."

"Yup," Lana chuckled. "You sweeten up when she's around. She's your little pudding pie."

Shaw shook his head and rolled his eyes. "You're wrong."

"You told me yourself. I see things as they actually are," the rustic rebutted.

The magician bit on his lower lip. After a few minutes of thought he managed to retort, "I hate you."

After half an hour of rambling through yellowing fields, the schoolhouse came into view. Visitors settled into the classroom. Close to twenty fighters stationed themselves at the windows. Their gun barrels pointed out into the open fields, shaking and moving to show someone held the other end. The desks were strewn about the yard in no particular order. Vehicles and horses littered the schoolyard as well.

"Cats," the magician hissed.

The smiles caught her eye. The ruby red lips of the pictured ladies on the storefront welcomed Viday. In the posted signs and adverts the ladies wore luxurious jackets with frilled collars, cute ear muffs, sometimes caps, mittens, and huge padded boots. So happy, they were. They threw snowballs at the boys then sat around a huge fire pit and drank hot drinks from pretty mugs. A few brushed back their locks of hair, brown, black, blond. Some held up bottles of perfume in their hands. Their buttery-smooth skin stretched over their cheeks, their hands, and arms.

Unlike some of the other baser shops facing Mortimer Park, the clothing outlet had color. Alabaster trim borders lined the glass windows. Lavender satin curtains flowed to the floor beside the mannequins. Black granite slabs made the shop facing walls, lustrous, dignified. A folded metal mail drop box was nailed beside the door with flowery shapes pressed into the smooth portions. Most of all, the models in the pictures wore bright and stylish jeans, belts, hats, shoes, and purses.

Their powdered and painted faces glowed with

feminine beauty, grace, wealth. They were the women of the new world, the civilized ideal, the future.

Viday wanted to see more. She had to see the rest. She had to see it all.

All six shots from the revolver could not burn the bolt off the door. The gun was not nearly recharged. Instead of waiting the requisite five minutes to heat the bullets, Viday unslung one of her bags and broke a window. She reached around the broken glass to unbar the door and let herself in. She put the gun and her belongings in the sun beaming through the shop window.

Inside was dark. Pale human dolls in clothing posed over empty bins and leaned on empty shelves. There were abandoned stacks of clothing, but not as much as Viday expected. She held up a pair of cotton denim jeans and tried to imagine where her knees would bend in such a thing. A small chuckle passed her mouth as she put the garment back down.

A few neglected sweaters caught her eye. They looked to be baggy and comfortable, the way Viday liked it. She threw them at the her pile of belongings and moved on. A scarf, she thought. If she could wear one, the thing would float behind her like a ribbon. There didn't appear to be a scarf. The pictured people had them

The corner of the store for shoes was completely barren. Empty cubbies yawned back at Viday. The circumstances did not feel like a lost opportunity.

Some earrings were left behind at a counter in the back; simple brass, not even worth the effort to take with the evacuation. Viday picked out a couple and rolled the baubles in her hand. The little spines meant to go through the ear lobes pricked her fingers. Of course, she didn't have the flabby tissue to hold earrings, but she still looked around for a mirror. There was a full length on the wall.

"Ah?" Viday walked closer to her reflection. The floating dark mote in the mirror startled her for a second. Then she ran her forearms together to disable her shroud.

There was still something not quite right. The white marks of her scars caught her attention. Snow white flesh and hair spotted her usual chestnut ears. A bleached streak trailed away from the once-swollen eye, another from her lip on the left side. Viday felt along the fingers they had broken. The agony remained fresh on her mind. The way they whispered threats into her ears after scraping away at the insides with a knife. Careful girly, if you twitch I might cut something important.

Viday backed away from her reflection and looked around at all the gaily colored faces. The ladies made demure smiles as they walked their groomed dogs through pristine parks and clean sidewalks. They courted with well-dressed gentlemen at extravagant balls, arriving in shining gas powered sedans to the undivided attention of all less fashionable. The men took them sailing on private boats to luxurious getaways. All of them were friends or lovers, every beautiful one of them.

"Ah haha," a feeble grin curled the side of Viday's dog face. "I got. Haha." She gave the big bad wolf act she gave Burroughs to the mirror. She hung her long tongue out for extra effect. "Haha. Yes. Yes. I know."

The printed people on the walls inherited the glorious lives of fairy tales. Viday was meant for something different. The human race painted their faces in color, but they painted Viday's face in scar tissue.

Viday did not cry or kick or shout. She stood in stricken contemplation.

## Half Life

Burroughs ducked into his corner of the dusty book cellar. Dust sprinkled to the floor from the boards above as the soldiers threw out the desks and fortified the school. The cracks of light between the warped boards flashed with passing shadows. The soldiers shouted from their guts. One of them carried a command radio. Burroughs heard the buzz of magnetic speakers.

Holding the Argol close, Burroughs calmly waited for an opportunity. If he made for the secret passage the hidden door may creak too loudly, he thought. Also the wooden stairs would give away the sound of his hooved feet. His best option was to stay on the soft dirt floor of the basement. Even so, only a few minutes would pass before they found the way down.

"Captain," somebody from the yard shouted. "Some stairs on the outside. Looks like a cellar."

"You two check it out. Block up the door when you're done."

The falling specks of dust swerved in their descent as the doors flung open and two figures stepped down into the musty room across from Burroughs. The horse aberration stepped carefully to avoid being seen as they scanned the room. They split from the door and walked in opposite directions. So Burroughs gently moved along the back wall.

"Somebody's down here," The closest intruder reported and rapidly stepped toward the lantern Burroughs left on the floor. The soldier in gray attire eyed the cracks in the bookshelves suspiciously and made eye contact with a creature peering through the top and second highest shelf. A gun shot fired into the thick volumes separating them, and the startled fighter cried "Abby!"

Books shot out at the soldier as Burroughs speared his staff through the shelf and ensnared the gas gun. He tore the weapon away and brought the soldier staggering into the books. Burroughs them plunged his fist into the gaping face causing the one who gave the alert to fall over on the dirt floor.

The other investigator rounded the distant corner and opened fire from yards away, but the two-legged horse fell back behind a row of shelves before the gun's barrel aimed down the lane. Charging down the line, Burroughs caught the second soldier before he could side step into view. The tendrils of the Argol took hold of the hapless soldier's shin. In an upward swing the human lifted off the ground and slammed into the floor boards of the school above. Many of those in the classroom swore and shuffled away. After a second crash into the boards, Burroughs let his victim's limp body free.

"Confirmed Abby in the basement of the school," the radio operator clicked a button on his apparatus. "Two men down. There is an Abberant in the bottom of the schoolhouse, command."

The fizzing box garbled back a reply.

"Repeat command."

No intelligible response came.

"Piece of junk."

"Drop your weapons and run for your lives."

"Who is this?' demanded the captain.

"We are the servants of old times, Wisp men. You trespass on our domain. Remove your presence or suffer our wrath." The distorted voice sounded like Shaw.

"Somebody get this clown off the box."

"Prepare for our wispy fury. When you see us, put your hands over your face if you want your loved ones to recognize you at your funeral. Meaning, we will kill you. I will hurt you because you angered us. The hurt is coming for you. Drop your useless guns and flee." Shaw continued transmitting his threatening nonsense to the soldiers in the schoolhouse.

The captain threw away his radio. "Group up. We're pulling Wellington and Markson out of there, if we can, and taking off for town. Shoot the Abby on sight."

As they clamored out to circle around the building, Burroughs pulled open the secret passage and held the entry tightly closed from the inside. More than a dozen soldiers stomped around the sodden floor of the cellar. They found their friends and pulled them safely out.

One of the soldiers spoke up, "We can't find him captain."

"Good. Everybody dump your cans on the books and head out. We're torching this place."

A few of them snapped the fuel bottles from their guns and drenched the shelves with acrid smelling liquid. When the whole group left, the last to leave lit the fire and slammed the basement door closed. The building was old and very dry. Burroughs knew he would not last long where he stood. He quickly thundered up the stairs to the secret attic.

Thick smoke already began rising from below and a red glow lit the dark corridors. No windows opened to the outside from the rooms. So Burroughs ran for the executioner's chair at the end of the hall. He jabbed the staff at the roof to clear a hole then stepped on the sturdy seat and pulled himself through the opening.

"Up top," a soldier pointed at the escapee from the

243

school yard. The other twenty in the company aimed their rifles at the Abberant on the roof and peppered the building with shot.

Burroughs rolled onto the opposite slant of the roof to get out of sight. He checked himself for holes. They seemed to all miss him. He then slid down to the ground and made a run for the fields before the army could possibly draw another shot.

The yellowed corn stalks closed up around him as he escaped. A familiar voice called from close by: "Hey." Burroughs swayed in his course to find Shaw. A look of surprise came to him as he approached Lana as well.

"This way," the magician blurted urgently. The withering plant stalks whipped Shaw's robe as he glided south through the rows. The Portram girl broke her stare at her old friend to follow and Burroughs quickly caught up. The riled army soldiers swarmed behind them as they left the scene.

Shaw looked over his shoulder at the two following him. "The call for help they made on the radio still made it to whoever they were calling. We need to drop down the city water line fast."

Bullets fired from behind. "It's going this way. Hurry."

The three escapees jumped an open irrigation ditch and crashed into the awaiting corn field beyond. A few seconds later, their pursuers did the same. At last an empty row appeared ahead with a simple stone well. A wooden cover laid over the top of the gaping hole, which Shaw threw away immediately.

"Drop in. Now." He became angry as the other two hesitated. "Now."

Burroughs took one look at the little rivulet running at the bottom of the hole and stepped over the edge to land on it. All of his body splashed into the underground current. It was very dark and his feet did not touch bottom as he swam up to get air. When he surfaced, his muzzle rubbed into the concrete roof. There was barely any room for his head. He looked for something to grab, but the cistern walls were smooth to the touch.

Holding the Argol up, Burroughs attempted rooting the tree into the concrete. Each time his head submerged under water, and the current pulled him farther and farther out. Another splash echoed down the waterway, then another. The two humans sounded so far away. Their chatter and gasps were distant whispers.

The horse Abberant tread water as best he could. He was never very good at swimming. With his hands full, it was especially difficult. The current moved faster and faster, it seemed. From far behind, Shaw shouted something Burroughs did not catch. The ceiling suddenly leaped ten yards higher to become a dim room. At the other end, Burroughs noticed the walls begin to move. A succession of panels dipped into the current. It was a water wheel.

Before he could move away or negotiate his way through, Burroughs smacked into a few of the wheel's paddles. The spinning motion pulled him deep under. The underside of the mechanism barely held enough room for his large frame to squeeze through. The staff scrapped the concrete as it ran by, and Burroughs nearly left it behind as he struggled to surface for air.

The room beyond the wheel held the interior of the pump station. No doubt the complex fed the homes and wells for the entire city. Huge vats filled with shimmering pools packed close to one another, three by three. A spillway for the excess ran down the side through several small gutters in the back.

Burroughs flipped over as he fell from the feeding cistern into the first vat. He splashed and surfaced again in the first pool. A ladder worn with green rust ran down the far side, and Burroughs immediately made for it. The flimsy thing crackled under his weight. Halfway to the top he felt sure the holding would fall to pieces and send him back down. The ladder held, however, and he pulled his sopping wet body on to a metal platform overlooking the plant.

A rumble rolled through the complex as a great whirlpool formed in the tank Burroughs just escaped from. The mighty churning current swirled all the way down to an ominous drain at the bottom. Half a minute longer in the water, and Burroughs knew he'd have been pulled under and torn apart on the rusty grate of the drain.

A realization hit the horse Abberant. The next person down the falls would certainly tumble to their death. They would hit the shallow water after plummeting forty yards and break on the concrete bottom.

"Lana!" the baritone of the large beast's smooth voice crackled with panic. He paced about on the steel catwalk . The pool at the bottom of the primary vat filled, but not nearly fast enough to break such a fall. "Lana. Hold onto something." It was no use. The roar tumbling out of the cistern above was too loud.

A full minute of agonizing anticipation passed, then another. They had disappeared. Otherwise they would have made the fall. Burroughs shouted to let go when the tank reached a good height, but nobody responded and a second flush cycle ran. The waterwheel mechanism, he decided. The suspended walkway over the processing facility shook as Burroughs searched frantically for a door or a way down. A type of overseeing room jutted out of the wall on the opposite side. Its glass panels leaned out over the edge.

The door held shut, barred from the opposite side. A second later the hinges flew off the walls and the door fell down. Burroughs stepped into the room. Two other doors stood on the walls of the control room; one in the back and another on the side. A tacky sign reminding employees to lock the door behind them was nailed to the back door. "Exit to Mortimer Park." it read. An outline of locks and keys made the picture of the warning sign.

A light began flashing on the switchboard. The bulb

246

blinking on and off indicated a problem in the electrical sector.

It was electric. He had never seen the like, only heard of it from stories of fancy cities and talk about the old world. The lights in the pump station used the old great technology, and so did the console.

"Burroughs!" rang a familiar voice from the facility behind the glass booth. To his relief, Burroughs brushed aside part of his soaked mane away to see Shaw and Lana on the catwalk. He punched a severe dent into the broken door in the floor as he ran out to meet them.

"Where did you go? We couldn't find you." Lana looked straight into her friend's large, brown, bestial eyes.

"There," Burroughs pointed at the cycling first vat.

Shaw elbowed past them on the way to the exit. "You smell awful when you're wet," the magician cited in observation. "You two can catch up when we float out to sea. Let's keep running."

The three rattled the walkway as they ran for the exit. Shaw spotted the exit at the back of the command booth immediately and hurried to turn the locks open. When the door cracked open, shouts and the stomping of boots came from the park outside.

"Cats," Shaw hissed. The magician held up a hand to signal his friends to stop. They did. Then slowly Shaw slipped through the crack outside and skulked up the stair to peek out. Two or three dozen soldiers swarmed the park in packs of four or five each. Some ducked behind trees. Others lay prone under bushes. Rifle barrels rested on the back of park benches with men crouched behind. Every one of them watched the plant exit.

Poking his head up provoked a volley of shots. Shaw stumbled back down the hard stairs as chips of rock scattered around him. The farm girl and the horse gasped. The dust settled, Shaw caught his breath. His golden hair lay distressed on his head, and he panted heavily as he clung to a wall. The surprise on the magician's face shifted away to disappointment. He swore and slammed his fist on the wall he leaned on.

Footsteps started creeping up to the ledge. Burroughs led Lana away from the exit. Her eyes widened as the tiny vines crawled out of the staff's ends. Burroughs then watched around a corner and waited to attack anything else which might shamble in. Shaw stood in the way, muttering.

At that moment a specter fell down from above and landed next to the magician. Viday's face seemed to pour out of the opposite wall. She looked Shaw in the face. The young fool felt something being shoved into his hands. Looking down, he saw his revolver returned. Without saying another word, Viday leapt straight upward. A rumble of gunfire quickly followed.

Shaw unslung his canteen and quaffed as much as he could before running up the stairs. Those soldiers not distracted from the bouncing shimmer caught a glimpse of a man in white emerging from the pump station. The robe spun around and four explosions bloomed in the park. Men on fire milled about the greenery as they tried to put themselves out. They threw down their ruined guns.

Those not caught in the initial set of blazes unloaded their weapons on Shaw. The white wrap around the magician quivered violently as its wearer stumbled around. Shaw tripped around but did not fall over. As he walked he blasted two more fuel canisters. He then ran straight into the last group of men who stood their ground. Holes perforated the magician's chest as the remaining four soldiers shot at close range. They pulled their rifles back to protect themselves, but Shaw reached out and ignited the closest fuel bottle with his free hand.

Half a minute later, Shaw descended into the pump station. Black spots and holes pocked his robe. The smell of charred flesh rolled off his person. Shaw pointed outside. "**Run for it.**" Shaw's voice rasped with the sound of a water host. Burroughs stared at the weeping wounds in

248

Shaw's chest. Some of Shaw's flesh had scraped or burned off his skull. Despite all the grievous injury, the magician did not bleed. Instead trickles of moisture wept from his openings. "**Go. I will be ... I will be behind.**" A trickle of spit dangled from Shaw's mouth as he leaned weakly on the exit door.

Burroughs grabbed Lana by one arm and led her outside. Blackened bodies littered the park. Soldiers moaning in agony and clutching huge burns lay prone on the grounds farther out. Those who lived sucked frightened breath as they stared fish-eyed at the shaggy beast stepping through them.

"Sixteen," Lana pointed at the large road to the west. She turned around to see Shaw dragging his feet behind them.

They ran down the cobbled road until the dock appeared in sight. Lana pulled away the broken gate and Burroughs lopped over. When Shaw pulled up, she helped him over the bars. "**Ah ahaa,**" the moist cadaver groaned as it strained to take the longer steps. He handed the revolver over to Lana then dove straight into the bay. Splashes riddled the dock and splinters of wood sprang up around their feet. Gunfire sprang up all around the crescent city. Both Lana and Burroughs danced around the boarded walkway as bullets spun by.

The slender white body of the Esauphaus darted in. A thick Mercer accent shouted from the bay's surface. "**Get in lads, hurry. Carraway tells me gas gunners headed this way and they're loading up the big shooters up north.**" Burroughs obeyed the voice. Lana followed. "**Get your noggins down, mates 'for they shoot them off.**"

They both ducked low.

"Where is the guy and the jumper," Lana asked her friend. As far as she knew, it was just him and her alone.

A white hand reached over the port side and grabbed on. Shaw pulled himself up, panting and wheezing.

Unlike the two others, his clothes were clean and dry. He rolled onto his back and counted those boarded on the vessel. "Viday," he yelled.

"**Hang on lads.**"

An explosion shattered the dock, scattering lumber down into the lower numbered ports. The giant splash of heavy artillery fire fell several yards further up the dock.

"**We're taking off boss.**" The Esauphagus sped out of the floating debris. Cannon fire trailed behind them. One shot hit close enough to spray the boat.

"Turn around," Shaw commanded.

Nigel replied, "**No way. They'd tear you to pieces boss.**"

"We're not leaving her behind."

The shrill tweet of the whistle sounded between shots of heavy ordinance.

"Where is she?" Shaw brought his head over the side to see the city shrinking away. "I told you to stop Nigel. Turn around and pick up Viday."

"Nineteen," Lana shouted from the other side of the deck.

In a maneuver which nearly threw the occupants overboard, the boat spun in place and sped back. The white spade ripped the open water. The alerted battle ship drew closer and closer. As their deck gun leaned down to aim at the water craft, their facing began to turn. Sailors and deck hands shouted and staggered about as their great steel ships pulled against their ropes on the docks and turned completely around.

Burroughs and Lana gazed as the titanic bodies made a slow dance in the harbor. They bucked and twisted. Many cursed sailors stumbled over the edge and swam to safety. Pier nineteen ran up to meet them and a body jumped high from the docks to try and hit the moving platform.

Viday missed and splashed down into the bay

behind the boat. The Esauphagus turned around again in a fashion actual vessels cannot and sided up to the Abberant thrashing in the water. Shaw reached in and pulled Viday onto the deck.

**"Not turning 'round again boss. Carraway is tuckered out."**

The gun crews on the row of battleships righted their aims and pressed the barrage again against the escapees. On the second escape, they got away without any fire landing near them. Maven, the crescent city, shrank smaller and smaller behind them. They raced out of the bay, right between the two lighthouses. The open ocean stretched in all directions before them.

Shaw rapped his knuckles on the floor of the boat. "Slow down. I'll take it from here."

## Dropping Off

The four sailed westward until the sun set and a lovely half-moon rose into the night. Mount Mortimer sharpened into a needle and sank beneath the waves. Shaw guided the boat with powers none of them had seen. His voice returned to normal and he whispered nonsense at the ocean with his hands out. When he shoved out his palms the sea gently pushed the vessel.

"Ah," the magician sighed. He breathed in the salty air. Turning around, the three others sat beside the deck house opening. The door was cracked open. The pack inside had the flap pulled back with a few things placed on the floor. "We're safe," Shaw told them.

"Are you sure?" Burroughs opened the camp kettle. His thick hand pulled out the remnants of the ducks. He threw the waste out.

Viday poured some jam on crackers. "Won't they chase us with their warships?"

"Ha," Shaw scoffed. "They're welcome to try. This is our domain. The most anybody can do is see us on the horizon before the Mindless shove them back."

"Mindless?"

The magician swung a wide scooping motion out to

252

sea. Immediately a huge wave reared out of the placid ocean. The huge wall crashed down with force enough to sink or shove away a ship. The crest measured nearly half a mile high. Both the sheer size and violent speed of the swell instilled awe in the other passengers.

"As ancient as the old ones themselves. I'm told as Pantherian salted the sea with the bodies of people, the Ministry saved as many as they could. Most were beyond help, but they still joined the water. Hundred of thousands of people's broken memories. Millions, eventually. The Mindless are an eternal fuel source for us. They all bend to our whim and give us supremacy on the ocean."

Lana spun the cylinder of the revolver Shaw handed her. "Who's this Ministry? Never heard of them."

"Aaaah, cats," Shaw slapped his forehead. "Nobody. We don't exist, but, oh. I'm in so much trouble."

Lana cocked a brow. Viday chewed on her dinner. Burroughs looked through the cans of vegetables.

"We're tossing you out at Lagoona. Say your goodbyes, because you're not seeing us again. These two are getting set up with homes elsewhere. No visitors. So, where do you want to live the rest of your life?"

Burroughs made his plan clear. "The western continent. Send me there."

"What?" Lana stammered. "Burroughs, you don't belong ..."

"Your father wants it this way, Lana. I am not living near any human settlements anymore."

Shaw's eyes widened as the girl pointed the glass revolver at Burroughs shoulder. He stepped in to gently pull it away without causing an incident. Lana let the weapon go and substituted pointing her finger instead.

"My father has nothing to do with this. You're just afraid of being hurt again. I know you. You run away and hide."

Burroughs shook his long head. "It's best you do not follow me."

253

Shaw butted in. "Expect me to follow, big guy. I'll drop these two off somewhere and take you right to the beast himself."

Viday threw her unfinished cracker into the ocean. "Put my mother in a nice place with lots of people. I'm following you two."

"No," the magician shook his head. "No. You can't come Viday."

"Why not? You need me, and I also belong out west."

"Because," Shaw emptied three shots into the deer Abberant's rust-red cloak. The garment shimmered brightly. "The Mother gave you that so she could kill me at any time. She will just give you the command and you would lose your mind and maul me. My gun would do nothing. Also, you are a natural Abberant. When we get close to Pantherian, you will be his."

"You," the deer-faced one stuttered. "But. No."

"I'm sorry. Viday, I am. We'll set you up a happy home in New Kansas. There is a store house we can give you which will work just fine."

"To die all alone. Never get to see Burroughs again." A quiver took to Viday's voice.

Lana crossed her arms. "Is this how you treat your friends? Shoving them away like this?"

"Better than watching her degenerate into an animal and wake to find herself covered in my giblets."

Sheeplike bleats punctuated the end of Viday's sobbing.

"Take her with us, Shaw." Burroughs' face set in an expression telling the magician he was not asking.

"Have you been listening big guy?"

"I have. She's right. We need her."

Shaw gestured wildly. "They'll turn her into a tool. A trap for us. Do you honestly want that for Viday?"

Lana broke in: "This coming from somebody who is already a tool for mysterious interests."

"You're getting off first, you burly she-yokel."

"That so? What if I wanted in on this adventure too? What do you say Burroughs?" Her shaggy friend nodded in assent. "See? As far we're concerned this is our business and you're trying to horn in."

The magician sat down on the railing of the Esauphagus, stunned. His brow twitched in anger as he chewed a lip. "I really hate you," Shaw exhaled in a tired voice. "I really do."

"Drive us west, pretty boy, and if you want to follow us that's fine."

- - -

The prison guard looked the marshal up and down before turning the key and rolling the door open to the cells. "The new look coming out of Acosta?"

Liz shrugged. "Wouldn't know. I'm from New Kansas."

"How do you get your eyes and hair like that?" The guard lead the chocolate-skinned lady through.

Liz rolled the can of chili stew to her other hand. "Bleach. Believe me, it hurts. Which way to the old lady?"

"D block. We're keeping her in a wing all to herself until a judge can sort it out." The man pulled a singular key from his ring. "Turn right there and you can't miss it. Hand it back when you're done."

Liz took the key. "Thanks. This won't be long."

Beth Harjones heard a visitor approaching through the hallway of empty cells.

"Missus Harjones? Where are you?"

"Back here," the old woman swung her feet over the edge of the prison cot and stood up. To her surprise the marshal paying her a visit was unlike any she ever met.

"There you are," the female minister greeted the prisoner warmly.

"I keep telling you folk, there are no Abberants in

255

my house, and the mandrakes are sterile."

The key unlatched the cell door smoothly. "Interesting." Liz stepped through and left the exit wide open. "I was wondering about that on my way over. Anyway, I'm here to tell you your daughter has made many friends recently. I'm here to repay a favor. You raised a good daughter. She is a deer friend of ours."

The pun was not lost on the old woman. "Who are you?"

"Can't tell you, but we have a nice life lined up for you in the Strand. A Room is ready for you. Certainly better than having your head jerked off by a sling. Honestly, what are they thinking?"

"I don't understand. What are you here for?"

Liz held up the can of chili stew. "You're a chemist, right? This thing is loaded with fat. Lots and lots of energy pent up inside. With the right reaction, it turns into an explosive."

"You're in league with that Shaw fellow, aren't you?"

"Not telling." Liz shook the can vigorously and placed it down between the bars of the window. She then led the elderly lady out into the hall. When they stood far enough away, Liz snapped her fingers. A huge chunk of wall plummeted into the sea below. The two of them scooted close and peered over the edge.

"The fall would kill us," Beth Harjones gasped. She measured the drop off the Delphinium Sea Bridge to be at least two hundred feet. The choppy water at the bottom churned.

Liz took a good look at the fall, a straight drop. In one smooth nudge, the magician pushed the old woman into the open air. A shriek trailed away on the sea wind as the prisoner fell and hit the water. Liz jumped after her.

Made in the USA
Charleston, SC
06 July 2013